Chet
To a great friend,
Best wishes always.
Jack

THE IRISH CORSICANS

Sequel to Loyalty

By

John A. Curry

This book is a work of fiction. Places, events, and situations in this story are purely fictional. Any resemblance to actual persons, living or dead, is coincidental.

ISBN: 1-4033-8379-0 (e-book)
ISBN: 1-4033-8380-4 (Paperback)

Library of Congress Control Number: 2002095120

This book is printed on acid free paper.

Printed in the United States of America
Bloomington, IN

1stBooks - rev. 11/15/02

Acknowledgments

First thanks to my daughter-in-law, Susan Curry, for her technical assistance with the manuscript and to my daughter, Susan Brown, for her time, advice, and faith in this project.

This book is dedicated to my aunt Alice Meade, a special lady who is always there for all her relatives.

Special thanks to my wife Marcia for her love and encouragement.

1

For the two weeks prior to Christmas, 1982, it had snowed intermittently virtually everyday, mostly white fluff of little accumulation mixing into the soot and creating dirty puddles everywhere, making the streets of Lynn appear dirtier than normal. As Ray Horan eased the Toyota Camry through Wyoma Square, he took care not to splash water on the few pedestrians heading to and from the small shops ringing the area.

He adjusted the rearview mirror and studied his own profile. He was getting older, no question about it. Still tall, still broad through the shoulders, but the cowlick was almost totally gray now above full brows speckled with silver. Weary lines appeared everywhere, and the thick scar coursed his lips under a hooked nose. Aging was a bitch, he sighed.

He focused his attention on the two young men sitting in the back. Jack's son and Jack's nephew. The two of them the spitting image of him. The Irish Corsicans Jack had often called them.

As they turned into St. Joseph's Cemetery, Marty, the nephew, sat straight as a ramrod staring out at the winter light and at the bare maple trees riffling in the breeze. His face was smooth-grained and handsome, the jet-black hair neatly parted. He was as tall as Ray but more patrician in his bearing. The nephew was decidedly more like Jack himself, Ray mused.

Aside of Marty, also in his mid-to-late twenties, sat Timmy, Jack's son, his cheeks as red as a doll's, his thin mouth belying the athletic build, the blocky frame reminding Ray of Jack's brother Tommy, now deceased.

Both brothers, his compatriots, were in fact now deceased. Jack and Tommy Kelly, the leaders to whom he had given a lifetime allegiance. As he eased the car to a stop along the line of graves, he felt old and yet not ready to be put out to pasture. He knew it was because there was something in the nephew that inspired confidence, much in the same way that Jack had. The posture, the élan, the movie star looks, the coolness under fire, the don't-fuck-with-me smile at once sinister and seducing, the eyes as intense as a butane burner.

The nephew and the son stepped from the car onto partially frozen ground, the sky above now weeping just a bit, the grayness fighting the perennial December battle with the light and winning.

Marty approached the driver's side and signaled Ray to join them. The older man shook his head. "Not this time, Marty. I'll come by on my own later if you don't mind."

The nephew touched his arm and nodded in full understanding. What made a lieutenant like Ray Horan special was his ability to know the right thing to do.

Marty and Timmy Kelly approached the three workmen busy placing the headstone above Jack's recently dug grave. It was sized exactly like the other two, the one dedicated to Jack's parents and the one in memory of his murdered brother Tommy.

Carved into the granite in grand lettering the inscription covered the entire stone, framed by a square line at its edges.

"John Anthony Kelly

1936-1982

Father to Us All"

"Is it what you wanted?" one of the workmen asked.

Timmy brushed the wet hair back from his brow and nodded. "It is fine, very well done, Dan. What do you think, Marty?"

The nephew dropped to a knee, made the Sign of the Cross, and prayed silently for a moment. He then stood and stared at the stone. "I think he would be very pleased."

"Leave us alone now would you, Dan?" Timmy directed more than asked.

The three workmen gathered their tools and trudged toward the circumferential roadway ringing the different sectors of the cemetery. In the east the sun suddenly gained the upper hand, slanting through the barren trees, bathing them in a faint shimmering light.

"Let's pray for one last time," Tim said, kneeling. Marty joined him, each of them lost in his own thoughts, remembering the father and the uncle who for over twenty years had coalesced Irish crime families across the Boston area, and in the process had built a legendary reputation.

They stood almost simultaneously like Dumas' Corsican Brothers, cousins more like twins, together since their childhood years, inseparable, fiercely loyal to one another, their youthful irrational tendencies now subdued, checkered by the need to care for those dependent on them, especially now that Jack was gone.

Thanks to Jack, they were at peace with the Italians. And they had regained the territories lost to the Mafia in the late 70's through the deal he had cut with the New York families just prior to his death. There was time now to run their interests in relative calm.

They walked to the roadway separating the long rows of graves, the slush crunching under their feet.

"Bobby's coming in from California tomorrow night," Timmy said. "Can you stop by my mother's for dinner?"

"What time?" Marty asked.

"About six. We'll have a couple of drinks with him before dinner. Okay?"

"I'll be there," Marty replied. "One other thing," he continued. "Arrange a meet over in Charlestown for tomorrow morning at nine. Be sure all our guys are there. Chris Kiley says we have some troubles he needs to air."

"Fine," Timmy replied.

As they entered the Camry, Ray adjusted the rearview mirror. "Where to?" he asked.

"Drop me at my mother's up on Copeland Road, Ray," Marty replied.

"How's she doing?" Timmy asked.

"Not good. Drinking too much according to Dad."

They drove the short distance from Wyoma Square to Copeland Road in silence, the lush homes along Lynnfield Street leading to the even newer developments in the hills surrounding the main thoroughfare. As they approached a red split-level at the top of an incline, Ray slowed and pulled over to the curb.

—

She responded to the first ring, opening the door widely. Sheila Kelly embraced her only son and began her nervous chatter as soon as the door closed behind him.

"Marty! What a pleasant surprise in the middle of the afternoon! Do you know Bobby's in town to see his mother tomorrow? Can you make it?"

He stepped back, holding her at arm's length, smiling in his attempt to relax her, to unwind her. "Hey, Mom, slow down! I was just in the neighborhood. Timmy and I stopped at St. Joseph's to see the new headstone at Uncle Jack's gravesite. We..."

Sheila flinched and stepped away as if a cloud had passed over the sun. She raised a shaking hand toward her hair and played with its strands. She put her teeth on her lower lip. "It's been a month since his death, hasn't it?" she said, not really meaning anything, not really asking a question, her mind instead centered on the evil now touching her life.

Marty watched her move into the kitchen and around the island in the center to the cabinets above the counter. She still walked like a Radcliffe graduate, the posture erect, the bearing noticeable. At fifty she was still slender with dark eyelashes and brown eyes, but the eyes had lost their luster and the scared rabbit look seemed to be causing lines to form above her lip and under her chin. Worry lines, she called them.

"Would you rather have a drink?" she asked, turning toward the coffee pot.

"Coffee's fine, Mom," he replied. "Where's Dad?"

"Over in Wakefield at the office. He says he's got a good chance to pick up the account at Polaroid."

She poured his coffee and set the pot back in its place. "How about some apple pie?"

"No thanks. So the food services contracts are keeping him busy, huh?"

She moved toward the small portable television and lowered its volume just as the announcer offered a pop-culture challenge. "Who shot J.R.?" he asked. "Tune in tonight."

"You don't come by much these days, Marty," she said softly, reaching for the whiskey bottle in the cabinet above her.

"Mom, do you really need that at three o'clock in the afternoon?"

She ignored the question, reached for a tumbler, and poured what looked like a double shot.

"Mom?"

"Marty, if I want a drink, I'll have one," she answered abruptly as she sat down, the bottle in hand. "You're as much of a thorn as your father. So why haven't you been by?"

Marty sipped the coffee and let a beat pass before responding. "I'm not sure Dad wants me around much," he said evenly.

Sheila swallowed some of the straight whisky, almost gulping, rather than sipping the amber. "He loves you, Marty. Jerry loves you. He's just having trouble with..." She stopped in mid-sentence.

"With the same thing you're having trouble with."

Sheila shook her head slowly, avoiding his eyes. "Not exactly, Marty. Events have come on him too fast. Your father lost his brother Tommy—murdered. Then Jack passes away prematurely. And then his son—you—assume leadership of the Irish Mafia. All in a very short period of time. He got hit hard, Marty. What do you expect? Just give him time."

"And what about you, Mom?" he asked, pointing to the drink.

"What this? I'm usually not much of a drinker."

"You could have fooled me," he replied.

"I'd like you to show your mother a little respect," she said haughtily. "Is that too much to ask?"

Marty stood and walked to the window. The storm had passed and the snow had stopped altogether. In the distance, iron-grey clouds now completely sealed the sky.

"You're drinking too much, Mom. I don't like to see that."

Sheila responded by pouring another shot into the tumbler. "And there's a lot I don't like, either, Marty. But I hold my tongue. Your Uncle Jack used to tell me he was watching over you, making sure you were protected. And I was happy to hear that because otherwise you would have been into a life of crime anyway. You know?

"And then later I hear my son, my only son, isn't really just involved in murder, extortion, drugs, and God knows what else. In fact, he's now the leader of the tribe. And you wonder why I need a drink, Marty? You just hold your tongue."

He braced his arms against the kitchen sink and watched two grey squirrels scamper with their booty up a bare oak tree. "I have to go now," he said.

She rose to meet him as he turned toward the island. "Give your mother a hug will you?"

He pulled her into his embrace and placed her head on his shoulder. “I’ll see you tomorrow night at Aunt Marjorie’s,” he said.

“You’re not mad at me are you? I couldn’t stand it if you were mad,” she said, her voice quivering.

“I could never be mad at you, Mom. Ever,” he replied, stroking her hair.

2

The director studied the shot through his camera and then stepped away and looked at the set once again. In front of him the ensemble clustered around the kitchen table ready for the call to action.

"Glenn, move in closer to Bobby," the director spoke calmly. "Okay, all, we're just about ready for the scene. Let's quiet down to a mild uproar, huh? Quiet! And on my count—five, four, three, two, one and action!"

Glenn Close stood up and began speaking, weaving her way around the table, talking about their life together back at college, the camera focusing on her, panning now to the other men and women wistfully recalling a better time back when they were all much younger.

"Cut! Perfect!" Lawrence Kasdan, the director, shouted. "Print it!"

Bobby Kelly, Timmy's brother and Marty's cousin, laughed along with the other members of the cast of "The Big Chill" as the director once again called for quiet.

"We did it, people. On schedule, and if I don't miss a guess, we may have a big hit here. Wrap-up party starts at 7 P.M. I hope you can all be here. We've rented a room at the Century Plaza."

Bobby Kelly, better known to them by his screen name Sean Kielty, stood up between Tom Berenger and William Hurt. At twenty-seven he was more beautiful than he was handsome. You noticed his beauty right away. Dark black hair was combed straight back, his eyes a deep blue, his nose perfect, the mouth sensuous.

"Larry, I've got the flight tonight, remember?" he shouted above the din.

"You're excused, Sean. Mother's birthday, right?" The director yelled across the set.

"You got it!" Bobby replied.

"When you get back, we'll show you the rushes," the director said.

Bobby Kelly clasped the hands of his fellow male actors and hugged and kissed the females. From the heights the electricians and the cameramen broke out in applause, joined on the floor by the welter of aides, production assistants, and technicians. They all smelled a hit in the story about baby boomers coming to middle age.

To Bobby the end of production signified the finish of a grueling schedule and the chance to rest, relax, unwind. To do something for himself. But then with it came anxiety, the loss of a job, with no surety yet regarding the future. Granted, he was only a step or two away from real stardom. In this his second film he had a reasonably substantive role, but not a breakthrough part. Not yet. He had hopes to audition for "Risky Business" which was coming up, and that might do it. The end of production for an independent actor in this age—so different from the old studio system and its contracts for even marginal performers—was a cause for exhilaration only if you knew exactly what lay in the future.

He could always go back to the soaps or audition for a new Broadway play, but his aspiration was to become a major movie star and there was still a measure of road to be crossed before he was there.

He shook the last hand, kissed the last lips and proceeded to the exit. He wandered out into one of the three days a year that Los Angeles wasn't shrouded in smog. He searched the lot for his red Miata and found it approximately where the attendant said it would be.

Glancing at his watch, he noted he had four hours before the flight to Boston. He aimed the Miata toward Pico Boulevard, just outside the Fox studios and headed back toward Century City. Jason would be waiting in their small apartment off Wilshire, another frantic day at his public relations firm behind him, stirring the martinis, ready to enjoy their last hours together for the next week or so.

—

"Phone-in talk show? It's fuckin' phone sex is all it is," Chris Kiley was saying. "Dr. Ruth Westheimer, my ass. They ought to throw a bag over her face so she won't scare people. Those German women have faces like bulldogs."

"My friend says all women look the same upside down," Joey Dunn, the numbers coordinator, replied.

"If they look anything like that kraut, they all ought to walk through life upside down," Stevie Guptill said.

"The Russians look as bad as the Germans. Their women look like they fought on the undercard at the Garden," Freddie Quinlan contributed.

The six men sat on wooden boxes and kegs in the warehouse on Medford Street in Charlestown, not far from Monument Square. The cavernous space was strewn with junk of all kinds—car parts, old kitchen appliances, discarded cartons. Above, weakened pipes weeped incessantly, forming dark puddles around the uneven concrete floor.

"Look at this," Paulie Cronin said, tapping the newspaper. "Liz and Dick are reuniting after two divorces and that's just two divorces from each other. They've had plenty of other ones. I'm happy for them," he sighed audibly.

"You lost your fuckin' mind, Paulie?" Chris Kiley fumed.

From the front, Marty, Timmy, and Ray Horan stepped through the glass door inset in time to hear this last exchange.

"Don't underestimate the value of mental illness, Chris," Marty said smiling, walking toward their semicircle. "It makes living life a lot easier."

"I can vouch for that," Paulie Cronin giggled.

Ray noticed right away how accepted Marty was. It was only one month since Jack had died of the heart attack, and day by day he could see the growing respect for the nephew. When he entered the room, the bullshit ceased, the papers were put aside quickly, the eyes of the beholders became riveted on their new leader.

He had dressed in a charcoal black business suit, white shirt, and plain red tie, his cousin Tim, like a bookend, garbed in a silver grey suit and a blue shirt with a maroon tie.

Marty sat on a heavy keg next to Chris Kiley. "Timmy and I have a meeting at the auto dealership at 10:30 so I'm hoping we can do our business in an hour or so. Chris, before you cover your stuff I want Ray to update all of you about the consolidations and how they're going."

Ray cleared his throat. "I've been working with the Italians to put in place the arrangements Jack made with them before his death. With Sally Cardoza's demise, the guineas have a new leader, too. He's Rocco Apostoli, brought in from Providence where he was passed over as the head of the whole New England gang of guineas. I haven't met him, but I've been dealing with his lieutenants. The good news is they've been giving us back our territories, the sections in Boston, Lynn, Lowell, Somerville, Cambridge we lost last year. We're back up to controlling 12-1/2% of the interests again."

"That fits," Stevie Guptill, who handled the prostitution piece, said. "I've seen their whores leaving the areas over the last couple of weeks."

"Our guys are being hired on the waterfront," Chris Kiley volunteered. "Our accountants are moving back in, gettin' a better look at the books."

"Our numbers runners are back out there too," Joey Dunn said.

"How about the drug trade?" Timmy asked.

"That happened fast. Except for the maverick operations, which will always be there, their dealers are out of the old areas," Ray Horan said.

"What do we know about this Apostoli?" Chris asked.

Marty stood and walked toward the coffee urn. "Not a cool guy, the way I hear it. Flies off the handle. Did the dirty work, though, for Gennaro Biggio in Providence. They bypassed him and sent him up here. So he's not a happy camper, but he's following through on the peace agreement. I've got a dinner date with him next Saturday night. I'll get a better handle on him then."

"Anything else, Ray?" Timmy asked.

"That's it for now. So far, so good."

Marty sat back down, sipping the coffee. "So what do you have, Chris?"

Chris Kiley reminded Marty of the actor Humphrey Bogart. He possessed the same trim proportions; long, toothy face; the cynical manner, even the slightly nasal speech pattern. He was dressed in a flannel shirt and chinos. On the waterfront, the enforcers either dressed to kill or, like Chris, understated. Now in his early fifties, he had been with Jack from the beginning, along with Ray Horan.

"With all this good news, you might not like to hear what I got," he snickered in his Bogart mode.

"I'm all ears," Marty replied.

"Terry Cavanaugh leaves Walpole this week. His five to ten stretch is up. He put in four and they're cuttin' him loose."

"Four fuckin' years for armored car robbery?" Freddie Quinlan asked, astonished.

"He caught one of the those dumb ass liberal judges who bought the sob story about his humble beginnings," Timmy responded. "So he's coming out, huh? Not good news."

"So who gives a rat's ass about him?" Joey Dunn asked.

Marty swallowed the last of the coffee and placed the cup on the floor. Terry Cavanaugh, he thought. A loose cannon about to come back into their midst. Would he join up with Bulger and Flemmi, start off on his own, or just disappear from the area entirely? It was difficult to project.

What they didn't need right now was another splinter group, another Irish gang jeopardizing the new peace, maybe even giving the Italians an excuse to terminate the agreement. Bulger and Flemmi had their piece of the overall pie and were content and under reasonable control. Cavanaugh was never under anyone's control for as far back as Marty could remember.

"Set up a meet for me, Chris. Tell Cavanaugh I want to see him as soon as he's settled back in over in Southie," Marty directed.

He looked around the warehouse and then over at Stevie Guptill. "You been checking for bugs in here regularly, Stevie?"

"Our communications guy is here every day. He goes over the whole place. We're clean, Marty."

"Keep on top of it, Stevie. You know we're being watched."

He stood and pointed toward the roll-up door. "Let's leave in twos. Every five minutes. I'll be in touch."

3

Terry Cavanaugh listened to the doors slide closed for the last time. He stepped out onto the second tier and waited for the two guards to lead him toward the processing area. As they moved along the walkway, fellow convicts yelled out final greetings and best wishes. "Good luck, Cav!"

He looked neither right nor left but focused entirely within himself. He was getting out, and he didn't need any problem at this particular moment. The guard on his right—Paul Swanson—pointed to the stairwell and started to descend. Swanson was all right—bright, not full of himself, fair, a talker. But Victor Rodriquez was another matter. The fat bastard on his left ought to have been behind bars himself. He enjoyed taunting the men, playing with their psyches, picking on the weak. Sometimes in a physical way mind you, but mostly baiting them, letting them know he was in control as if they needed reminding. He enjoyed breaking their spirits, claiming he treated them all the same. What was it Jerry Kramer had said about Vince Lombardi? "He treats us all the same, like dogs." That was Rodriquez.

What was there about certain people that you sensed immediately they didn't like you and vice versa? That was how it had started with Rodriquez. Mutually exchanged looks conveying animosity. And then a period of anticipation, Terry sensing the guard simply looking for an excuse to land on him.

Just over a year ago, Terry had run into a mound of trouble with the screw. He had been eating lunch in the mess hall when the two men next to him started shouting obscenities at one another. Suddenly they were at each other with fists swinging. Terry had interceded, trying to restore peace before the screws arrived on the scene. He managed to wrestle one of the combatants to the floor before Rodriquez, the first guard to appear, pummeled him between the shoulders with a sap. He had gasped and rolled over in pain, unable to think or speak. In the resulting confusion, Rodriquez had identified him as the perpetrator, not the peacemaker. And if not for the fact that the captain of the guards himself had observed the entire episode from the walkway above, he would have been in deep shit.

Since then, Terry had taken every opportunity to give Rodriquez the evil eye, to demonstrate his animosity while staying within the Walpole code, giving the guard no chance to implicate him in any situation that could lead to an extension of his sentence. But then, just two weeks ago, Rodriquez found another way to get at him. His cellmate, a fragile Irish kid named O'Blenes, had been alone with Rodriquez in the laundry room at the end of a shift, and, according to Rodriquez, had both sassed him and become physically aggressive toward him. Chandler O'Blenes ended up in the prison hospital and, that night, the guard had paused outside Terry's cell, winked, and said, "How do you like them apples, Cav? Your friend don't look too good right now."

Terry had just stared back at him, saying nothing. Not with just days to go.

In the processing room, Terry put on the same clothes he had walked in with four years ago. While

Swanson and Rodriquez stood in the background, Terry stared into the mirror, his face stolid, the grey eyes expressing no emotion. He parted his blond hair on the right allowing the cowlick to fall halfway down his forehead. He stepped away and studied his frame in the full-length mirror. He had come in at 6'0 and 180 pounds and would be leaving the same way.

"Ain't you the fuckin' pretty boy, Cavanaugh," Rodriquez taunted.

Terry turned and braced himself, keeping his balance evenly distributed. He made sure Rodriquez was locked on him. "Go fuck yourself, you spic piece of shit," he said evenly.

As Rodriquez advanced on him, Swanson stepped between them. "Hey! That's enough! You don't need another episode with this guy, Victor." He shoved Rodriquez backward. "And you don't need trouble on the way about the door, Cav!" He extended his baton between them.

"Keep that fuck away from me, or I'll shove that baton up his ass," Terry replied, exploding, the veins in his neck expanding, his lips becoming thinner, the inner rage no longer contained.

Swanson turned toward Rodriquez. "Victor, leave. That's an order. I'll handle the rest of this myself. Go now!"

Rodriquez muttered something under his breath, turned and slammed the door on the way out.

Terry leaned down to the bench and slowly picked up the duffel bag containing his small number of personal effects. Enough time to put the rage back in the bottle, keep the genie under control. Be disciplined, he reminded himself.

"You calmed down?" Swanson asked, agitated.

Don't show your his intentions on the way out, Terry thought to himself. "He pushes too hard, Swanson. Look, I'm sorry. I'm fine now."

"Then go, Cav. And let's not see you back here." He extended his hand, and Terry accepted it.

Swanson escorted him through the gates out to the lot. "Someone coming for you?" he asked.

"My sister's over there in the Buick Century," he replied.

"Good luck, Cav."

"Thanks, Swanson. I won't be seeing you again."

Swanson gave him an I've-heard-that-before look. "I hope not," he said emphatically.

As Terry Cavanaugh breathed in the early winter air, he walked briskly toward the Century. Along the way he kicked at the wet, moldy leaves still clustered on the road. He looked above the canopy of trees to a blue bowl of sky. Free. Free to go back to Southie. And in a week or so he would shut down the engine of one Victor Rodriquez for good.

4

Marty Kelly left the garrison he had inherited from his Uncle Jack and strolled across Lynn Shore Drive to the walkway above the beach. On this cold December night, only a very few strollers or runners elected to brave the elements, but he enjoyed the briskness, the smell of the salt water, the stillness of the early evening.

He pulled the collar of his cashmere coat up and quickened his step in anticipation of seeing his cousin Bobby once again. In a short period of time, Bobby had established himself as a impending star. What was it Roger Ebert, the film critic, had said about him? "Sean Kielty is an up and coming young actor. He displays the range and versatility that so many of his peers lack. The camera simply likes him."

Marty looked out to the sea at low tide, the waves barely undulating, the ocean like a plane of flat glass extending from Lynn toward Swampscott and beyond the rocks to Marblehead.

He thought of the call from the Globe reporter. What was her name? Judy Goodman. Yeah, that was it. Would he give her some time regarding a story she was working on?

"What story?" he had replied.

A story about the great increase in the theft of stolen cars in the Boston area, she had replied. In a calm, even voice, she indicated that because he owned the largest Chevrolet dealership north of Boston, she hoped to gain his views on the subject.

Was she fuckin' serious? he had wondered. Was that the topic, or was it just a scheme to gain a personal interview with the nephew of the notorious Irish crime boss and recently deceased Jack Kelly? The Globe, among others, had been carrying stories recently about the fading influence of the Mafia and the ascendency of Irish gangs in and around Boston.

He had acceded to the request, and he wasn't exactly sure why. Maybe the irony of the situation—Martin Kelly commenting on crime. Maybe her voice, the perkiness there, the youthful lilt. Whatever, he had agreed to see her in a day or two.

He approached his Aunt Marjorie's brick edifice on Puritan Road in Swampscott with mixed feelings. Bobby and Timmy would be here, but so, too, would be that new boyfriend of Marjorie's, the fuckin' Jew doctor she had taken up with a few months ago.

He knocked on the front door and within seconds, Marjorie Kelly, Jack's ex, held her arms aloft, beckoning him into her embrace. "Marty, come in! How are you?" she squealed.

He walked into the foyer to Sinatra's out-and-out jazz rendition of "Night and Day," the 80's Sinatra showing signs of his vocal deterioration, losing it on the high notes.

"Happy birthday, Aunt Marjorie," Marty said, extending a package toward her. "And I won't even ask you how many."

"Well young man, aren't you the perfect gentleman!"

She moved with ease as she asked for his coat, her blond hair tucked to her ears, her calves sleek and fiercely brown, her body trim, the shoulders broad for her frame. Marjorie Kelly may be in her early fifties, he thought, but she looked ten years younger.

"David, come greet Marty," she yelled toward the kitchen.

From that direction the pompous ass appeared. What the hell does she see in him? Marty wondered, not for the first time. She had been divorced from Jack for more than fifteen years, but David was the first man she had dated seriously since that time.

"How are you, Marty?" Dr. David Aronson asked. As if he gave a shit, Marty thought.

"Good, David. And yourself, boyo?" He liked to fire out Irish expressions just to help the good doctor understand he didn't belong to the right tribe.

"How's business?" Aronson asked as they moved into the living room.

"Bobby here yet?" Marty asked, not answering the question.

Marjorie brightened as she pointed downstairs. "He's down there with Timmy, leaving the old folks to their knitting. Go down, I'll call you when your mother and father arrive."

"Is Sean Kielty really down here?" he teased as he descended the spiral, carpeted staircase.

"Hey, Marty!" Bobby replied, springing from the bar, nearly spilling his drink. He playfully dug a left hook into Marty's mid-section and then hugged him, slapping him on the back.

"Seriously all the girls are lined up all along Puritan Road out there waiting to see the matinee idol," Marty asked.

"Yeah, sure," Bobby replied.

"What do you want to drink?" Timmy asked.

"A fuckin' double shot after seeing the good doctor up there courtin' your mother," Marty said, moving behind the bar.

"Fuck him," Timmy said. "But it's her birthday so let's not spoil it."

Marty put his hands in the air in a posture of surrender. "No problem from me," he said. He mixed the VO with ginger ale and then sat down in a green easy chair.

"So which starlet are you dating now, cousin? I read about a different one every week or so in the gossip columns," Marty said.

Bobby broke into a broad grin and pointed an index finger in Marty's direction. "You're just jealous," he replied.

"That's for sure," Timmy said.

"Well, he could bring one of those femme fatales back to Lynn with him and introduce us," Marty laughed.

"Generally speaking, there are people of good taste out there. I don't think so," Bobby grinned.

"Boys! Come up right now. Jerry and Sheila are here!" bellowed Marjorie from above them.

"How long you staying Bob?" Timmy asked.

"Just a few days. I want to be around out there and see what might be coming up. In this business you're only as good as your next picture, that is assuming there is a next picture."

They paraded up the stairs to the living room, Marty in the rear, anticipating seeing his father for the first time since Jack's funeral.

Jerry Kelly sat on the couch next to his wife and made no effort to acknowledge his son when they entered the room. He sat impassively, his hands folded together on his knee, his eyes cold. His body language connoted he really didn't want to be here, not in the presence of a son who had become the new leader of the Irish Mafia.

He came alive only when Bobby approached him, standing and embracing his nephew. And then, he was back on the couch, averting Marty, making it perfectly clear he was here only because of Marjorie.

"Time to cut the cake," David Aronson announced from the dining room, an intruder in their midst not having brains enough to stay in the background.

Marty bit his lip and headed for the bar. Lately, whenever he was around family, he needed lots of double shots.

—

On Saturday evening, Marty drove north on Route 1, past the honky tonk of motels, sports bars, pizza joints and country dancing barns, to the Hardcover Restaurant in Danvers. He had chosen it because it was a bit noisy and because he and Rocco Apostoli could find some privacy in the area devoted to small tables just off the bar.

Always meet in public, he had reminded himself. And always in a busy place where the clientele would have its own interests. Here young lovers sat sipping wine, enjoying the excellent food and outstanding service. Occasionally, the wait staff would congregate, singing out "Happy Birthday" and providing the celebrant with a reduced check.

He spotted Apostoli sitting alone at a table for two just beyond the bar. He looked very much like the pictures of him that had appeared in the Boston papers. Middle-aged, he was rail thin with hair gone to grey. Above his right eye, a small scar ran near the brow. He was reading the sports pages, paying little attention to the movement around him.

"Rocco Apostoli?" Marty asked, stopping at the table.

"Sit down, Kelly, sit down," Apostoli said, signaling to a young waitress.

"Thanks for your willingness to see me," Marty said as he sat across from the new head of Boston's Mafia.

Apostoli didn't answer right away. Instead he slowly set aside his paper. "So what can I do for you?" he finally said.

A pretty young lady with a scrubbed clean look took their drink order and wandered away.

Marty sat back in the chair and surveyed the crowd, mostly people his age, in their late twenties, holding hands, absorbed in their own conversations.

"I want to express my good feeling for our new arrangements. Before he died, my Uncle Jack agreed to the return of our territories with your predecessor..."

"Predecessor?" Apostoli interrupted. "You a college kid or somethin'?" He didn't smile.

"Something wrong with that?" Marty asked.

Apostoli shrugged. "You sound fuckin' funny is all."

Marty could feel his lips thinning but he held his temper. Get on with the business, he urged himself.

"Mr. Apostoli, I'm glad we're back to where we were. I don't need any trouble from anyone, and we're happy to have our share of the pie back. I thank you."

Apostoli sipped his red wine and thought for a moment. "New York and Providence insisted on these new arrangements so we really had no choice did we, Kelly? So why thank me or express your good feeling?" His voice was both strong and taunting.

Marty threw down the last of his highball and signaled the waitress for another. He then leaned across the table and stared at Apostoli.

"What's your problem?" he asked.

"My problem?" Apostoli repeated. "My problem is I don't agree with those mealy mouths in New York and their peace agreements. If I had my way, we wouldn't be carvin' up territory with some dumb Irish fucks—college or no college. What we would be doing is keepin' what we got and givin' you turnips a fuckin' bone, if even that."

Jack had always stressed to him the importance of poise, encouraging him to always listen carefully and never display what he really felt to an enemy or a potential enemy. He had learned that lesson, only to a point.

He picked up the menu and studied it for a few seconds. "Why don't you try the corned beef and cabbage? It's delicious here. I highly recommend it. And when it gets here, Rocco, stick it up your ass."

Apostoli sat upright in his chair. "Who the fuck you think you're talkin' to?"

"A first class asshole," Marty replied. "I invited you here as a courtesy, as my guest." He started to stand. "You know Rocky, Rocco—whatever the fuck your name is—we have an agreement whether you like it or not. If you dagos can't stick to it, that's going to be a problem—for you, not for me."

He signaled to the waitress who hurried across the room. As she approached, he handed her a fifty-dollar bill. "Give my friend here whatever he wants." He turned without another word and left the room.

5

On that same evening, Timmy Kelly and Paulie Cronin watched the dancers whirl around Hiberian Hall in Boston, six teen age girls beautifully aligned, demonstrating their agility as the small band played the traditional Irish step dance. Around them, the neighborhood groupies—most of them in their twenties—clapped in rhythm, the young men trying to balance their beers, the flitty Irish girls in their company demonstrating their new found independence by matching them drink for drink.

"Christ, I can't imagine my mother swirling down the beer like these dipsos," Timmy said as he and Paulie leaned into the bar. "Women's rights gives them the right to act as much like assholes as the men, I guess."

As the performance ended, the band immediately began playing "My Wild Irish Rose," and the young men—most of them members of the ironworkers union—quickly searched out a partner, for fear that something much faster would be played next.

Timmy turned to the bar and ordered a boilermaker and, while he waited, craned his neck to study the crowd in the huge mirror before him. And that's when he saw her for the first time, angling directly for him, her frizzy hair running down to her shoulders, a bounce to her step as she approached.

"Hey, you, would you like to dance?" she asked him as he turned at the sound of her voice.

Paulie Cronin flicked ash from his cigarette and laughed out loud.

Timmy looked at her long before responding. She had deep-set green eyes the color of emeralds themselves, dramatic cheekbones, and sensuous lips.

She extended her hand. "Maureen Cavanaugh," she said.

"Hello, Maureen Cavanaugh," Timmy nodded. "Do you know who I am? I mean do I know you?"

"Are we going to dance before this tune is over or not?" she asked, a hand on her left hip.

"You're on, Maureen Cavanaugh," he replied.

He placed an arm around her waist and guided her to the edge of the dance floor as the band started into "How are Things in Glocamora?"

"So who are you?" she asked. "Am I supposed to guess or what?"

"Anyone ever tell you you're a fresh little broad?" he said, telling her, more than asking.

"All the time," she smiled back. "But it doesn't bother me. Am I going to find out your name before my hair turns grey?"

He looked down to her, studying her. "It's Tim. Tim Kelly."

"And where are you from Tim Kelly?" she asked, a lilt in her voice.

"Lynn."

"Lynn, Lynn, the city of sin."

"The city of firsts," he corrected.

"What's that's supposed to mean?" she asked.

"It means people from Lynn appreciate the fact that the first jet engine was manufactured there, the first night baseball game in America was played there, the first..."

"What are you, Tim Kelly? An historian?" she interrupted.

He laughed out loud. "No, I'm an auto dealer. In Lynn," he added.

"Good news. I might be in the market. That fuckin' old Century I have is falling apart."

He let the swearing go by without comment, but he had to admit the girl was full of surprises.

"Where you from?" he asked as the band segued into "When Irish Eyes are Smiling," the national anthem.

"Southie. Over on L Street."

"And what do you do besides asking men to dance and then doing your best to aggravate them?"

From the bar, Paulie Cronin raised his drink in salute and laughed at him.

"I'm a teacher," she replied.

He almost stopped in his tracks. "You got to be shitting me."

She bumped into him hard. "Hey, you're with a lady. Watch the language."

"Really?"

"What really?"

"You're a teacher?"

"In Boston. At the Tobin School over on Mission Hill. Third grade."

"As my Irish aunt is so accustomed to saying, 'Jesus, Mary, and Joseph. May the saints preserve us'."

"Hey! I'm a good teacher." She poked an index finger into his stomach.

As the band closed the set, he smiled broadly at her. "Y'know, I'm glad the dance is over so now I can get myself to the hospital."

"Stop being a wise ass and buy a girl a drink, will you?"

"What do you want?" he asked as they crossed the floor.

"Whiskey sour," she replied.

"Maureen Cavanaugh, meet Paulie Cronin," Timmy said, as they reached the bar.

"You sell automobiles, too?" she asked.

Paulie looked at Timmy before responding. "I boost them," he finally said.

She sipped the whiskey sour and then turned to the mirror. "You guys ought to do stand-up at the comedy clubs, you know?"

Paulie saw him first. "Look what the cat just dragged in," he said.

At the entrance, a young man stood passively surveying the crowd. Terry Cavanaugh's long, thin, blond hair was now tied back into a neat ponytail. He was dressed casually in faded jeans, a white cotton shirt, and a leather jacket.

She followed their eyes toward the door. "You know my brother?"

Timmy looked at her, astonished. "Your brother?"

Terry Cavanaugh walked toward them, his eyes shining. "What are you doing here, Sis?"

She embraced her brother. "One of my regular hangouts, Terry. A working girl's got to have some fun."

"How are you, Cav?" Timmy extended his hand.

"Fine, Timmy. Paulie. It's good to be back in circulation, you know. How's Marty?"

"Good. You get the message he wants to see you?"

For just a moment the grey eyes flickered and then they expressed nothingness. Cavanaugh reached for his Newports, pulled one from the pack, and lit it. "I did. Tell him I'll be in touch as soon as I'm settled in."

Timmy decided to let it go, not push it. The guy was probably in need of an adjustment period. He decided to change the subject.

"Maureen Cavanaugh. I didn't make the connection."

"How do you know these two?" Maureen asked her brother.

"I used to run with Timmy and his cousin down on the waterfront. What were we Tim? Seventeen?"

"Full of piss and vinegar," Timmy laughed.

"Remember the time you and Marty took on a couple of those teamsters after work hours. You put one asshole's head right through the fuckin' windshield."

Timmy picked up his shot glass and finished it off. He followed it quickly with the last of his beer. "We need to hit the road, Cav." He offered his hand. "I'm glad you're out, Cav. See you soon."

He looked for the barkeep. "Give this gentleman a drink on me," he said as he slapped a twenty on the bar.

"It was nice meeting you, Maureen," he said.

She shook his extended hand. "You too," she replied.

As he and Paulie moved toward the exit, Tim wondered what Cav might be telling her.

6

"Look at that crybaby, will you?" Gino Petrelli picked up the remote and pointed it at Rocco Apostoli. On the screen a curly-haired man in god-awful short shorts was asking his audience to shake their booties.

"You don't like Richard Simmons?" Rocco replied.

"Fuckin' crybaby is what he is," Gino said, aiming the remote at the set. The head of the New England Mafia sat in a thick terry cloth bathrobe, his face pasty beneath the tan. At seventy-one years old, he respected doctors and health experts, but not this fairy passing out medical advice. He cleared his throat of the phlegm from the medicine.

His legitimate business holdings included fourteen bars, six restaurants, and a catering company. All of these businesses were profitable in their own right, but they were also used to launder the approximately $50 million generated each year through drug trafficking, union activities, the whores, extortion, and gambling all through the six New England states.

He sat back on the couch and sipped his orange juice. "It's no fun gettin' old Rocco. You know that? Here it is almost noontime, and I can't get this old body going. This all-night work will be the death of me yet."

Rocco smiled. He should be in such good health at Petrelli's age. The old bastard was always moanin' about his health, and eating like a pig, one of those guineas like Danny Aiello's old mother in "Moonstruck." A fuckin' hypochondriac.

"So what brings you to Providence?" he asked Rocco.

Petrelli's condominium was one of thirty-six spread over three buildings shaped like the letter A. Each unit had a small fenced patio at ground level and centered between the buildings was an elongated pool. A pleasant but not an overly ostentatious place to live.

"I want your permission to move on that fuckin' harp in Lynn—Kelly," Rocco replied, the anger mounting with each word.

Petrelli sighed and clicked his tongue. He reached for the orange juice.

"Why?" he finally asked, glancing at Rocco.

"The fucker doesn't respect me, Gino. I met with him the other night—you know, just to break the ice on these new arrangements—and it didn't go well, not at all." As Rocco thought about it, he could feel the wetness forming under his armpits.

"So what happened? And, by the way, you requested this meeting?"

Rocco responded without hesitation, trying to make his voice reasonable, letting his tone assure Petrelli that he was a man in control.

"Well, Kelly actually called for the meeting to tell the truth."

"And?" The old guinea sat there sipping his juice, acting for all the world like it was his fault, not Kelly's, not even yet knowing what had occurred.

"The asshole walked out on me!" Rocco proclaimed, the vein now pulsing in his throat.

"Why would he do that?" Gino asked, as calm as a May day.

"Why? Because I told him I didn't favor these arrangements, Gino. That's what I told him, and I don't. We're bringing this unproven Irisher back into full partnership with us when Jack Kelly's dead. We don't need to, Gino. All bets should be off now that this punk's runnin' things."

Petrelli didn't say anything right away, and when he did, Rocco didn't understand where he was heading.

"You go to the movies often, Rocco?"

"What the fuck's that got to do with this issue, Gino?"

Petrelli's voice came back calm and collected. "I'm just asking. What do you do to relax?"

Rocco winced and shifted his attention to his hands. "I don't have much time, not with the businesses, and my ladies." Gino wouldn't know much about the ladies. Probably hadn't a hard on in the last ten years.

"You know what your problem is, Rocco?"

"No, but I think I'm goin' to find out."

Petrelli laughed. "Relax, Rocco. The point I'm trying to make comes from a movie. You see 'Godfather II'?"

Rocco shook his head. "I got no time for that Hollywood gangster bullshit."

"Well, make time. You can learn. There's a scene in there where Al Pacino tells his subordinate what I'm gonna tell you. His subordinate—some fuckin' wound-up guy, like you Rocco—wants to ice this guy and Pacino tells him what I'm gonna tell you. 'Leave him alone,' he says. 'I have bigger business with Hyman Roth'—that was the name of this Jewish guy in Miami..."

"What business you got with that fuckin' Irisher?" Rocco interrupted.

Petrelli bit his lip, showing irritation for the first time. "When I'm ready to divulge it, I will." He shifted on the seat. "You know, Rocco, we had the fuckin' murder of our boss, Gennaro Biggio, the murder of your predecessor, Salvy Cardoza, the murder of our friend Nick Rizzo from Revere—all in the last few months. Then we got the FBI watchin' all of us, armed with the new Rico laws..."

"Half of them on the take," Rocco interrupted again.

Petrelli decided to let him have it, both barrels. "That's the second time you interrupted me. Do it one more time and this conversation is over." He said the words calmly but with menace in his voice.

Petrelli reached for his coffee. "With all the recent trouble right now, we're in no position to move on anybody. What's the matter with you Rocco? These orders are straight from Forelli in New York. They want us at peace with the Irish. With Reagan in as president pushing policies favorable to our interests, we can't afford these vendettas. So the answer is no. Leave Martin Kelly alone. Understand?"

Rocco's lips thinned. "I don't like it," he said, the anger still there in his voice.

Petrelli sipped his coffee. "You know Rocco, and I know, you're not happy New York chose me over you to run things from here. You ought to accepts things as they are. Enroll in one of them anger management workshops. Calm your piss down and get with the program. That's my advice."

Rocco Apostoli rose slowly, determined to control his famous temper for once. "I have to get back to Boston. Let me know when you can get up there. I want to introduce you around, y'know?"

Gino Petrelli rose and extended his hand. "Thanks for your understanding," he said.

Unsmiling, Rocco shook it and quickly left the room. "Fuck anger management," he muttered to himself once he was on the elevator.

7

Terry Cavanaugh had extremely fond memories of Quincy. During summers, he would sometimes stay overnight with his Aunt Alice and Uncle Bill at their apartment on Summer Street. He recalled waiting for his uncle to return from work at the Fore River shipyards so they could play catch in the backyard. And as he swung over the Furnace Brook Parkway, he remembered the movie houses downtown that Alice Meade would take him to—the Wollaston, the Adams, the Quincy.

He turned right on Hancock Street, the main thoroughfare, and then made a quick left onto Merrymount Road. Victor Rodriquez did not live in a quiet residential area, not with the Registry of Motor Vehicles utilizing the street every day for driving tests. He had reconnoitered the area very carefully and decided the best approach was definitely at night in bad weather, especially after he had indentified his intended victim as a creature of habit.

For more than a week, he had observed the screw, always being sure that he boosted a different car or borrowed one from a friend so as not be arouse suspicion. In the evenings, he had cruised back and forth, sometimes stopping and parking, just another person practicing for the driver's license.

At 11 P.M., virtually every night, Victor Rodriquez left the old Victorian and drove to the convenience store up near Quincy Square. On his return, he would park his late model Buick Park Avenue in the driveway adjacent to his home. At Walpole, he had often bragged about living alone following his divorce. He didn't need anybody, he would brag to the convicts. Who would want the miserable prick, Terry had thought.

The light, cold rain ran down his windshield, blocking his view, but, like clockwork, he observed Rodriquez descending the steps, entering the car and heading south toward Quincy Square. If history was any precursor, he would return in ten minutes with a small shopping bag. It appeared as if he bought the next day's groceries, hopefully just for himself. Terry didn't need any fuckin' wild dog running at him, but, to date, he had not seen any sign of one.

He moved the stolen Ford up to a point thirty yards from the house and opened the glove compartment. He took out the pistol he favored so much—a Colt .45 Model 1911 that he had had tuned up by a friend who was an armorer. It was large, ugly, and very fatal. It only held seven bullets, but one of those big heavy bullets could knock a fuckin' sumu wrestler off his sticks. In contrast, a .38 or a 9mm might not do that. The Colt .45 was a killing machine for sure.

He waited five minutes and then turned up the collar of his black raincoat and left the car. He crossed the dark street, being sure to stay as much out of the light as possible. Not so difficult to do with Quincy, like most suburban cities and towns, practically using flashlights for street lamps these days. He passed close to the hedge in front of 91 Merrymount Road and slipped into the open driveway. In the rear, a gate separated a huge swimming pool from the driveway itself. No sign of a dog.

He edged behind an old oak tree next to the high fence dividing Rodriquez's property from his neighbor's. He peered through the light rain and studied the working-class neighborhood. At 11:10 P.M. very few homes were lit, and from his position behind the tree, he felt he could not be seen, either by neighbors or by the headlights of Rodriquez's vehicle when he returned. There was virtually no traffic on the street at this hour, but he did not want to linger too long. Get it done, and get out of there, he told himself.

Suddenly a car appeared heading east toward him. Rodriquez? The vehicle slowed and a right directional signal flashed. Slowly the car swung into the driveway, its lights appearing to search the darkness.

Rodriquez cut the engine, then the lights, and stepped out. A bag of groceries in his hand, he headed back toward the top of the driveway.

"Hey screw," Terry whispered softly from the shadows. As Rodriquez turned, Terry moved out from behind the tree. He wanted to be sure the guard knew who he was.

"You remember me, screw?" he said.

"What the fuck you doin' here, Cavanaugh?"

"It's payback time, screw. You remember how you messed up Chandler O'Blenes and a few other cons along the way, asshole?"

He raised the Colt and fired, sending Rodriquez backward onto the concrete. Standing over the body, he fired another round into his forehead and then walked briskly out to the street.

8

They met at the Pine Grove Cemetery in Lynn because dead people can't talk. Long ago, Marty Kelly had learned from his uncle that when decisions had to be made and assignments rendered, it was preferable that business be conducted in the open air, most often in a public place. What with the new audio and visual technology the police possessed, precautions most definitely had to be taken.

Two days before Christmas, he and Ray Horan meandered among the grave markers in the best-kept cemetery on the North Shore. They headed from west to east toward Manning Bowl, the 20,000-seat football stadium rising above them from across the street.

"I think we should set an example right away with Doucette," Ray was saying. "He's been skimming on us for sure."

"How much?" Marty asked, blowing hard on his knuckles, the cold, dry and relentless.

"$2,000 a week, maybe for the last two months," Ray replied.

They paused near the main entrance and studied a headstone depicting a young man dressed in a Red Sox uniform—Harry Agganis, the legendary football and baseball player, Lynn's all-time best athlete, buried just yards from the scene of his football greatness.

Marty moved away. "That's $16,000," he said calmly. "Where was our accountant on this?"

"Asleep at the throttle. You want I should fire him? I could send one of our legbreakers to send George Doucette a message."

"How long's he been with us?"

"Back to 1970 with your uncle."

Marty looked across to Manning Bowl and then turned, heading back to their vehicle. "Have him iced, Ray. Put a bullet in his head and bury him down in Bourne deep in the woods."

Ray almost lost his breakfast. "You serious?"

Marty stopped at the Caprice and leaned against the hood. "I'm serious as hell, Ray. And never mind firing the accountant. Sounds like he just missed it. He wasn't involved with Doucette, right?"

"No, but why ice Doucette?" Ray persisted.

Marty bent down, picked up a chestnut, and tossed it down the walkway. "What do you think Jack would have done, Ray?"

Ray answered without hesitation. "He would have had Doucette killed."

"So what's your problem?"

"You're kind of new, Marty. It's only been a month, y'know? Doucette's been with us a long time. Maybe you should go slowly."

"What time you got?" Marty asked, looking at his own watch.

"It's 8:25," Ray replied.

"I've got the date with that Globe reporter at nine o'clock."

Ray looked at his shoes and tried one more time. "Why ice him, Marty?"

Marty smiled at his uncle's oldest friend, the most loyal member of the Irish Corsicans gang. "Because of the very fact that I am new, Ray. Doucette took advantage of Jack's death and my newness. When we needed him most, during the transition, he let us down.

We can't have the others know he got away with it. It's got everything to do with my being new, Ray. Ice him."

"He's got a wife," Ray replied.

"Children?"

"No."

"Be sure the wife's taken care of," Marty said, opening the car door. "And the accountant, let him know he fucks up again—can't catch these things—he'll be joining Doucette."

—

They crossed the city, Ray driving, heading toward the car agency on the Lynnway. On Washington Street the triple-deckers bent at the waist, their porches soft, their steps in dire need of paint. The tenants had changed since the early 60's when he and Timmy would roam these downtown neighborhoods. Asians and Hispanics had replaced the Greeks, the French, the Italians and the Irish of his youth, but still, like the immigrants of old, they yearned for opportunity, a piece of the economic pie, a chance at a new life.

As they approached the agency, Marty looked down the Lynnway toward the sea. New storefronts—law offices, real estate agencies, a popular restaurant, other car agencies—lined the boulevard as it curved toward Lynn Beach. He was proud to be a part of the transformation of this part of his city. When they stopped, he said something to Ray, left the car, and stepped through the door cut into the huge showcase window.

As he headed toward an office facing the showroom, an overweight, middle-aged woman dressed in a maroon outer coat approached him. "Are you the owner?" she asked.

He stopped and faced her. "Yes. I'm Martin Kelly, part owner of Kelly Chevrolet. What can I do for you?"

"Viola Sheperd, Mr. Kelly. What you can do for me is get me another new car. I bought that lemon Impala out front there from you people three months ago, and it's been back here four times already. I told your sales manager..."

"Come into my office, Mrs. Sheperd, and let's talk about it." He touched her elbow and directed her forward. He didn't notice the shapely young lady sitting at a salesman's desk across the room. When he entered his office with Mrs. Sheperd, the younger woman stood, ostensibly to study the new 1983 Impala rotating in the center of the room. She craned her neck to hear their conversation.

"You're telling me you've been back here four times?" Marty was asking.

"That's right, Mr. Kelly. It's a lemon for sure, and your guys think I got nothing to do with my time but come back here every twenty-four hours. I..."

"Did you talk to our sales manager?" Marty interrupted.

"Yes, Mr. Craig. You know I work for a living, I'm a widow, I work in an office and wait on tables part-time." She paused for a breath, her lips trembling.

Marty picked up the phone and dialed. "Bill? Marty. You've been dealing with a Mrs. Sheperd regarding a new Impala that she brought back. What's the problem?"

There was a long pause while he absorbed Craig's explanation. Viola Sheperd tried hard to compose herself, but a small tear formed in the corner of her eye.

Marty finally spoke. "Bill, I'm going to send Mrs. Sheperd back to see you right now. I want you to give her a new car. That's right. Take back the other one. We'll deal with that issue later."

He hung up the phone. "You're all set, Mrs. Sheperd. Mr. Craig is going to take care of you."

"You're going to give me a new replacement?" she asked, amazed.

"I'm sorry for your trouble," he replied, standing, steering her toward the door.

"Well, thank you so much Mr. Kelly. I really don't know how to thank you. I..."

"Mrs. Sheperd, if you're satisfied, you'll tell others to come here. That would mean a lot to me." He smiled, little signs of wrinkles-to-be forming at the corners of his mouth.

And then he saw her as she turned to face him. She was almost a foot shorter than he was and should have been overwhelmed but her dark skin and even darker eyes and long straight hair parted in the middle made her appear taller. She wore a simple blue suit and carried a tape recorder in her hand.

As Mrs. Sheperd moved away, she approached him, extending a hand. "Mr. Kelly? I'm Judith Goodman from the Globe. We have a date."

Judith, not Judy, he noted.

He looked her over. Her eyes were steady and cool, her manner very direct. All business, she was. "So we do. Come on in," he said, motioning toward the office.

Moving behind his desk, he pointed to one of the two straight-back chairs in front of him. “Have a seat, Mrs. Goodman.”

“It’s Miss,” she replied with a small smile.

“How about some coffee?” he asked, his gaze becoming a stare.

“No thanks,” she replied. “That was quite a nice gesture,” she said, an index finger raised, pointing toward the showroom. “I didn’t think you auto dealers had hearts,” she said, practically blinding him with the smile.

“You observed that?”

“I’m trained to observe.”

“So maybe your powers of observation can help you see what an honest car dealer I am,” he grinned broadly.

“Seriously, why did you do that?”

Marty leaned back in his leather chair and laced his fingers together. “It’s simple. Like I said, we run an honest business. She doesn’t deserve to be jerked around, and now that she’s satisfied, she’ll tell many others she was treated right here.”

Judith Goodman smiled, this time for effect he thought. “You’re very convincing, Mr. Kelly. By the way, do you mind if I use a tape recorder?” While she was asking, she was also readying the instrument.

“Yes,” he replied.

“What?”

“Yes, I do mind. No tape, at least if you expect to interview me,” he answered with quiet composure.

She shrugged her shoulders and removed the recorder from the desk. “You agreed to this interview, Mr. Kelly. You didn’t set any conditions at the time.”

"The recorder implies I'm not to be trusted, Miss Goodman. If you want to talk, let's do it in the normal way. Take notes if you want."

She weighed his answer and then flipped open her notebook. "To begin, can you confirm a few things for me?"

He nodded. "Shoot." He used the word deliberately.

"You're the son of Gerald Kelly, the owner of Kelly Food Enterprises in Wakefield."

He nodded again.

"You graduated from North Shore Community College and took some night courses at Northeastern University in business administration."

"That's right."

"You and your cousin Timothy run this business which actually belongs to his mother."

"Correct."

Be careful she doesn't lull you to sleep, he thought. His uncle had always insisted that he stay focused in situations such as this one. The ax would be falling any question now.

"Your uncle Jack Kelly ran this business before you. He was the leader of the Irish Mafia in Boston before his death. Now..."

For the first time, Marty leaned toward her. "Says who?" he interrupted.

She didn't flinch and pressed on. "Says a number of people, Mr. Kelly. It's generally accepted by my police sources, by..."

He interrupted her once again. "Alleged, Miss Goodman, not accepted. If you're a reporter for the Globe, you ought to know the difference. Now my uncle is deceased. He died, as I'm sure you know, of natural causes. In his lifetime he was never arrested or ever publicly accused of any crime. He was a legitimate businessman."

"Mr. Kelly," she protested, "your uncle Tom was murdered just a few weeks ago. Found hog-tied in a car."

He just stared at her.

"So there appears to be some connection to organized crime." She tried to relax him by utilizing the smile once again. "I'm only saying there appears to be."

Marty could feel his lips thinning. "Miss Goodman, you told me you wanted to do a story about stolen car rings, but somehow I'm getting the impression you're going down other roads. What exactly do you want from me?"

She studied him carefully. "I'm eventually doing a story on the entire Kelly family—you and Tim, your other cousin Sean Kielty, your father, your deceased uncles, your..."

"My father?"

"We want to show the interconnections of all members of the Kelly family, their businesses, their influence..."

Marty stood and walked to the window behind his desk. He looked out at the harbor, and at the seagulls swooping toward the pier, dipping their wings in search of prey. He turned to face her, and when he spoke, his voice was calm, a slight smile on his face.

"Miss Goodman, I'm not a person to tell someone else how to do her job. You and you alone decide that. But if you write a story that somehow draws connections of legitimate businessmen—my father, Tim, my cousin Sean, myself—any of us—to organized crime, then you better get some advice from your paper's lawyers.

"My uncle Tom was murdered, and his murderer was never found. You want to widen the story to suggest my family—any of us—is involved with crime, then be ready for a problem. Not one of us has ever received a parking ticket, to my knowledge. You draw even an inference, you've got a problem."

He sat down. "Now do you have any other questions I can help you with?" he said dismissively.

She raised a quizzical brow. "You know, Mr. Kelly, I consider myself a good reporter who can usually tell when I'm being threatened. With you, I'm not so sure."

"I'm not threatening you, Miss Goodman. I just expect fairness. You media people ought to put yourselves in the position of the people you're writing about. You want to talk about stolen car rings, we'll talk about it, but not about my family."

She flipped the notepad, stood, and picked up her shoulder bag. "You're an interesting guy, Mr. Kelly. Thanks for your time."

"Can't interest you in a car?" he teased, trying for a light ending note.

"Only if I can get a free one like Mrs. Sheperd," she laughed.

"I'll be watching for your story, Miss Goodman," he said. "I'll see you out."

As he walked through the showroom, he wondered where she was coming from. She was as measured in her responses as he was. Fuck her and the shore patrol too, he thought.

She shook his hand and strolled out into the morning sun. He watched her walk toward her car, hips swinging, she knowing he was looking, he anxious to look.

9

"Good to see you, Cav. Sit down right here," Marty said, sliding over one seat in the booth, Timmy across from him.

Three days after New Year's Day, 1983, only a few regulars sat along the bar at 3:00 P.M. He preferred the Continental Restaurant, Route 1 North in Saugus, for that reason. He liked meeting at places that were located at the intersection of major roads making it easy to come and go. And he liked mid-afternoon meets. An hour from now and this popular eating place would be humming with foot traffic, but for now he could easily detect the presence of the FBI or the Boston Police.

In the background the piped-in voice of Karen Carpenter permeated the lounge adjacent to the main dining room. In a beautifully modulated alto tone she sang "Goodbye to Love." Recently, the papers had gossiped about her suffering from an eating disorder, anorexia nervosa. Marty hoped that was just more media bullshit.

"What will you have?" Marty asked right away.

Cavanaugh was dressed in a blue woolen sweater and light gray slacks. "Boilermaker," he answered.

Timmy signaled the lone waitress.

"You meet in nice places, Marty."

Marty laughed out loud. "Not always, Cav. We alternate a lot, with the fuckin' Feebs everywhere these days. How you doing?"

Cav shrugged his shoulders. "Now that I'm out of the pen, I'm doin' a lot better. I'll tell you that."

The waitress took their order, which killed all conversation for the moment. When she left, Timmy asked, "Did you know that screw from Walpole that was iced down in Quincy the other night?"

Cav shook his head. "No, I didn't."

"Cav, let me cut to the chase here," Marty said. "Timmy and I would like you to join up with us. We got a spot for you."

Back quickly, the waitress deposited the drinks. "All set for now?" she asked.

"Fine," Timmy replied, smiling.

Marty looked across at Cavanaugh and knew the answer they would get before the reply came. Terry Cavanaugh belonged to no one, to no group. Marty remembered back on the waterfront when Terry would sit alone at lunch break. The kid weighed the same then as he did now. While the others rested, telling fuck-them stories, bragging about drinking or sex or both, Cavanaugh would just stare off into space or flex a hard rubber ball into his hand, even get down and do a series of push-ups. But whatever he did, he did it alone.

Cav answered the question with a question. "You guys got back your territories?"

Timmy swallowed some beer and nodded. "The guineas agreed to reinstate them after the last troubles. We're back to where we were."

"Keep your fuckin' guard up," Cav replied.

They were drifting off the subject, Marty thought. "We could use you, Cav. We need a guy to hold our clients in on the extortion piece. There's always someone trying to intrude, especially the spics or the blacks now. They're moving heavily into Lynn, the whole North Shore, over in Somerville. We need someone to help hold them in line. What do you say?"

It wasn't what he answered that troubled Marty; it was how he answered. The words were fine, but the expression was cold, unfeeling, maybe even calculated.

"I'm not sure what I'll do, Marty. Right now I'm thinking of going it alone. I appreciate the offer, but no thanks."

Marty nodded in acceptance.

Timmy asked, "So what will you do?"

"Maybe even get a legitimate white-collar job like you guys," Cavanaugh replied, a smile touching his lips for the first time.

"A good-looking guy like you could sell some cars. Join up with us," Timmy pressed.

Marty studied Cavanaugh as he responded. "I'll make my own way, Tim," he replied firmly.

Marty leaned forward and placed his hand on top of Terry's. "You do that, Cav. And I wish you luck. But I don't ever want to hear of your crossing into anything that's ours."

Terry lifted his hand and shook off Marty's. "Worry about the dagos, Marty. That's where your trouble's goin' to come from."

He stood and started fumbling with his wallet. "I got to go," he said.

"The drink's on us," Timmy said, waving his hand.

"See you guys around," Cav said.

"I hope not," Marty replied, putting the proper tone of wariness in his voice.

10

What beats a weekend in San Francisco? Not much, Bobby Kelly thought as he strolled with Jason down Taylor Street, heading for Fisherman's Wharf. In front of them the wind buffeted the Bay as seagulls swooped around the fishing boats at anchor.

It had been a short flight from Los Angeles to the City, their favorite city. Last night—Friday night—they had visited the trendy coffee shops over on Fillmore, had strolled by the renovated Victorians along Lower Pacific Heights, and had ended up at the Top of the Mark, enjoying one another, free from prying eyes, light years away from the artificiality of LA, with no one remotely recognizing a budding young star. It would be different when "The Big Chill" hit theaters, Jason was reminding him as they walked.

"Maybe. Did I tell you what happened to my friend Kevin Costner on the film?" Bobby asked.

"What?"

"He plays the suicide victim whose funeral drives the whole plot, right? Well, after he rehearsed this fifteen-minute flashback sequence for maybe two months and filmed it for five weeks or so, the scene was cut from the movie."

"Jesus!" Jason cringed, showing a little bit too much of his effeminate side. "I'd be furious!" he wailed.

Bobby loosened the knot on his wrap-around sweater and thought he might put it on, the wind now swirling through Ghiardelli Square. On the little hill before them, a juggler tossed apples and oranges on high while small children screamed in glee as a little monkey raced around an organ grinder.

"It's the nature of the business, Jason. He'll bounce back. Maybe someday he'll be a big star. He's got both the looks and the talent. I'm telling you the story because the same thing could happen to me. I could end up on the cutting room floor as well."

Heading west, they approached Aquatic Park, observing the swimmers moving parallel to the shore, the undulating waves pulling them toward the piers. Most wore coats of grease and bathing caps of white, reminding Bobby of the L Street Brownies back home in South Boston.

"How was your trip home before Christmas? You haven't said anything about it," Jason asked.

Bobby frowned. "All right. It's always good to see them all."

He looked across at his friend and lover. Jason wore faded blue jeans, running shoes, and a bomber jacket over a black T-shirt. At six foot three, with his blue eyes and angular features, he looked more like a movie star himself than a public relations executive who trained politicians, CEOs, and aspiring businessmen in media relations.

"I haven't told them about us, Jase. I could never do that. My mother, my brother Tim, my cousin Marty—they're as Irish as Paddy's pig and so fuckin' prejudiced that anyone different from them is an enemy and by different I mean anyone not with blue eyes and black hair."

"I have blue eyes and black hair," Jason teased.

"But you're not straight as an arrow," Bobby added, laughing.

"Well, I'm not that," Jason agreed.

"And like I've told you, some of them use guns."

Jason was silent for a minute. "On second thought, maybe you shouldn't tell them." He burst out laughing.

Bobby placed an arm around Jason's waist as they walked. In the most socially liberal city in America, nobody much noticed and nobody much cared.

It was here in the city about two years ago that he had first met Jason Ellison. Bobby had been filming a scene for a television play just outside the majestic Fairmont Hotel on Nob Hill when the young executive had stopped to observe the action. Their eyes had locked for an instant and Bobby had the feeling that he needed to know the man.

Later, when the day's shooting was over, Bobby had walked through the main entrance in search of a bar. The crowded lobby looked the size of a soccer field. A dark maroon carpet and lush velvet chairs filled the area. He entered the New Orleans Room and found a small round table in the corner. At the twilight hour, the tables were just beginning to fill when the attractive stranger approached and asked to join him.

For close to two hours, they had discussed Los Angeles—each surprised to hear the other lived there—occupations, world politics, any number of subjects. At the time Bobby felt as if he were on a date—hoping to impress, eager to connect, a feeling of want and need permeating his body. He had found a soulmate.

When the evening crowd gathered and the Dixieland jazz band began to play, they adjourned across the street to the Top of the Mark at the Mark Hopkins Hotel. From there they joined small groups of gawking tourists looking down at all sides of the city, pointing out various landmarks to fellow travelers. Among the Japanese groups, it seemed as if every other person possessed a camera. Close to midnight, Jason invited him back to his room at the Fairmont.

During his days as an actor on the soaps in New York, Bobby had experimented with both women and men. But until that first night with Jason, he had never really known love.

Now, two years later, although living together in Los Angeles, they always found reasons to return to their city, at least once every couple of months.

11

Timmy Kelly could smell the rain coming as he pushed his Impala up Mission Hill toward the Tobin School. The late afternoon grey of January darkened the sky, making it feel more like 6 P.M. instead of 2 P.M. Crazy Boston, he muttered to himself. Just one grey day after another. But the sun had appeared yesterday, which meant there were maybe only three good days left until May. He pulled in front of the school, just down from the school bus lanes. A female crossing guard stopped snapping her gum long enough to give him a dirty look.

He had timed things perfectly. From the doors, hordes of young people came rushing toward him as if the building had caught fire. Every tenth one carried a book, which made him reflect on his own childhood back at St. John's in Swampscott. There had been more of a sameness back then. He and his white classmates had all worn a uniform and marched quietly from the school, loaded with books, led by the nuns and the lay teachers. This swarming horde was dressed in everything from shorts to Mackinaws, maybe a third of them white, the rest Black, Hispanic and Asian. The whole scene approximated a Chinese fire drill.

From the side of the building, two boys, about eleven years old, tumbled more than stepped out the door, exchanging fists and rolling into a puddle of slush. Suddenly Maureen Cavanaugh was between them. Dressed in a long blue raincoat, she separated them, holding one boy while she ordered the other to leave.

As she bent to wag a finger in the face of the alleged perpetrator, her frizzy hair covering part of her face, he noted she was slimmer than he thought, but the bounce was perpetually there. Energy oozed from her.

He lowered the passenger-side window and leaned on the horn. When she stood, he waved. She raised her index finger indicating that he wait one minute. For a brief time she spoke to the errant offender who then ran off probably to assassinate his sister, Timmy thought.

As she approached the car, he yelled out, "How you doing, Slim?"

"What brings you here?" she asked, the smile on her face indicating his being there wasn't really a problem for her.

He decided to keep the mood light. "You made a pretty good referee there between Ali and Frazier."

"And you're pretty glib for a guy on the sidelines," she retorted.

Irish feisty, that's what she was. There had been really only a few types of Irish-American women over the last few decades. Back in the 40's, there was the subservient woman who catered to her husband, took care of his food, and drink, his wash, and his pecker. Then came the sweet and demure lasses of the 50's and 60's, prim and seductive, cock-teasers, they had called them in his youth. Now there was the new women's lib types of the 70's and 80's, feisty and tough, but only to a degree. It wasn't so much they were Irish; the Italian women acted the same, he noted, but your Irish girl knew you knew she was putting much of it on. Your

Italian was different. Fuck you was said with vengeance, not a lilt.

"How about a cup of coffee?" he asked.

"You came all the way up here from Lynn to ask me for a cup of coffee?"

"I came to Casablanca for the water," he said, smiling broadly.

"There is no water in Casablanca," she retorted playfully.

"Then I was misinformed," he followed through, quoting Bogart. "Get in."

Ten minutes later, they sat in the booth of a McDonald's over on Boylston Street, the green spheres of Fenway Park hovering above them, the restaurant quiet at this hour. In the corner, an old man poured mountains of ketchup onto a fish sandwich while his distraught daughter tried to dissuade him. From the loudspeaker Neil Diamond sang of "Yesterday's Songs".

"You know Tim, you really know how to treat a girl. McDonald's on our first date," she grinned.

"Next time it'll be Pier 4," he replied.

"Who said anything about a next time?" she retorted haughtily.

She studied him carefully. "My brother knew you from the waterfront, he says," she added.

"Yeah, back about eight years ago he and I and my cousin Marty all worked down there unloading."

She blew on her coffee. "Coffee's so hot you would think it's for radiation treatments," she said. "Terry says you do more now than sell cars."

"Yeah? What else did he tell you?" Timmy asked, irritation creeping into his voice.

She looked over his shoulder, out to the corner of Boylston and Jersey, where two motorists at the stop sign were fuming at one another, ending their loud discussion with middle fingers saluting one another in the universal language of disdain.

"Not much else. He said I can do better. You don't come very highly recommended."

He nodded. "I'll have to personally thank Cav for his good words."

She sipped her coffee and ran her hand through her hair. "Look. You seem like a good guy to me so let me be blunt."

What had she been to this point? he thought.

"My brother just got out of Walpole, and I want to see him stay out. My mother died of heartbreak with all this Irish macho shit. My father left us when I was ten, and he was a big gangbanger himself. So, Tim Kelly, I'm not sure I want to get involved with another problem man."

He smiled at her, the Kirk Douglas dimple on his chin broadening. "I wasn't suggesting marriage, Maureen. Maybe you're making more of this than I intended."

"What did you intend?" she smiled back.

He finished the coffee off and balled the paper cup. "What I intended was just to get to know a very pretty girl a little bit. Maybe have some dinner some night."

She rolled her eyes. "You have other girls you date, Tim Kelly?"

"One or two," he replied.

"Don't give them up."

"Huh?"

"I'll go out to dinner with you, but maybe that's it. Don't go giving up your day job."

He laughed out loud. "As my Irish aunt always says, 'May the saints preserve us'."

12

"Fuckin' The Donald. Look at the arrogant prick," Chris Kiley ranted, pointing to the news photo of Donald Trump preening in the lobby of the Trump Tower, leaning against a piano.

"Hey! Who says you can't have it all?" Joey Dunn answered. He flicked ash from his cigarette into an empty paper coffee cup.

"Remember when we were young and the nuns would say money can't buy you happiness? Remember that, Freddie?" Paulie Cronin asked.

Chris Kiley considered himself better read than any of them. He cast a disdainful look at Paulie Cronin. "Nuns always teach that shit. You can find love with someone who's poor is what they preached. My ass. You guys know what era we're in today?"

Paulie Cronin sought an answer from Joey Dunn or Freddie Quinlan. Behind them, Steve Guptill stood at the entryway peering out at the street through the glass in the middle of the roll-up door.

"Error?" Paulie Cronin asked.

"Era, you dumb asshole," Chris Kiley answered. "This is the fuckin' 80's, an era of conspicuous consumption."

"What the fuck's that mean?" Freddie asked.

"Here comes Marty and Tim," Stevie yelled from his position.

"Ray, can you believe these guys?" Chris asked Ray Horan, sitting by himself in a fold-up chair, trying hard not to laugh out loud.

"We had heroes back in the 40's and 50's, guys like John Wayne that we looked up to. Then in the 60's, John Lennon, Jack Kennedy, guys you could admire. We started downhill in the 70's with that mope Jimmy Carter and people worrying only about themselves. The "Me" decade, that's what the 70's was about."

"What the fuck has that to do with the nuns?" Paulie interjected.

"It means what they taught has no meaning today. This guy here—pointing to Trump's photo—represents the move from "heroes" to "me" to "greed". Today it's the dash for cash that life's all about. Guys like this smug bastard don't care about what the nuns said. He knows he can buy happiness. We're in a gilded age, I'm saying."

Chris Kiley stopped long enough to stare at Paulie. "And if you fuckin' ask me what gilded means, I'll open your head with a fuckin' meat hook."

Ray burst out laughing just at the moment Marty and Timmy came into the cavernous room. The others joined in, as Freddy Quinlan playfully threw a left jab at Paulie.

"Let's not wake up the dead people of Charlestown," Marty said. "What's so funny?"

"Nothing," Ray replied, tears forming at his eyes. "We're just talkin' about The Donald."

"Is that right?" Timmy said.

"About how greedy he is, and how greedy the times are," Chris added.

Marty and Timmy sat together on the kegs at the front of the semicircle. "We got a few things to talk over," he said, by way of gaining their attention.

The ritual always proceeded in the very same way. Despite the fact that security was checked every time they met, Marty spoke as if they were being overheard. Never would he issue an incriminating order in front of the entire group. When the group met, he provided an overview of recent events or upcoming situations that could have some bearing on their lives, or he asked for news regarding people or events that might effect their firmament.

"I spoke with that Globe reporter," he began. "She claimed she wanted to discuss my view—you know, as a dealer—regarding the big increase in stolen autos around Boston, but she quickly moved into a bunch of allegations about Jack. The fuckers can't let the dead rest in peace."

"There's been no stories in the papers, Marty," Chris volunteered.

"I know, and I'm surprised," Marty retorted. "Maybe no news is good news. Tell them about Cav, Timmy."

Timmy stood and moved toward the coffee urn. "He's not interested in joining our club. He may go his own way it looks like."

Stevie Guptill tapped his foot on the floor, partly to alleviate the cold. "There's talk on the streets that he's extorting money from people over in Malden."

Right in the territory of the Italians themselves. Not good news at all. Either they or the Italians controlled 95% of the action around eastern Massachusetts. Even if Cav planned to stay out of his territory, Marty knew the Italians would not be pleased.

"Keep your eyes and ears open. Be sure we know what Cav is up to," Marty directed.

Ray Horan lit up his cigarette and blew a stream of smoke skyward. "I got a call from Luis Gomez. He wants a meet with you guys."

The cousins glanced at one another. Luis Gomez, Marty thought. Why would he want to see them?

Gomez was an up-and-comer in this age of affirmative action and greed. At eighteen, he had been asked to leave Chelsea High School and spend a little time at Cedar Junction after tossing acid in his high school English teacher's face. Upon his release, now more hardened than ever, he had formed his own group over in the South End—the Slick Spics, the Irish called them. They had their own share of the action, about 2% of the total take gifted to them by the Italians, essentially to keep them under control, which was easier said than done. Gomez was into prostitution, loan-sharking, and extortion, the staples of every crime family, but he was also a free-lancer, dabbling into armed robbery and home invasions if the payoff were there.

"He say why?" Marty asked.

"Just said he had an interesting business proposition," Ray replied.

"Tell him we'll meet him over at the Mass Avenue Bridge Saturday morning about nine."

"Any problems with the guineas?" Timmy asked.

They all shook their heads at the same time. "Things are quiet, and they're abidin' by the rules," Chris Kiley said.

Marty nodded pensively. "Maybe too quiet," he finally offered. "Anything else?" he asked.

There was no response. "Then let's leave by twos," he said, standing.

13

"Judith Goodman here."

She answered briskly, in a business-like tone, in the manner of the new career-working women of the last ten years. Marty caught himself. But if a man answered in the same way, that was all right. Asshole, he called himself under his breath.

"Miss Goodman, this is Martin Kelly over in Lynn."

She was quiet for a moment, measuring her response.

Actually, he didn't know why he was calling her. Ostensibly, he had a reason ready. If the truth be known, he just wanted to hear her voice again, see her in person, watch her walk again.

"Yes, Mr. Kelly. What can I do for you?" she asked, more friendly now, maybe sensing a story.

"I'm just curious, Miss Goodman. I..."

"Please call me Judith," she interrupted.

"Not Judy?" he teased, immediately regretting the comment.

"It's Judith, not Judy," the ice princess shot back. "What are you curious about, Mr. Kelly?"

"Marty," he replied.

"Marty, what are you curious about?" she said, the ice melting, the warmth kicking in.

"I haven't seen the story, Judith. Any reason why not?"

"I decided not to print it," she replied, almost too quickly.

"You or the Globe's lawyers?"

As soon as the words were out of his mouth, he knew he had made a mistake. That was not the way to progress with this woman.

She sighed audibly. “Marty, it was my decision—all the way. I didn’t feel we had enough to run with it.” She paused for a moment. “You were right. There’s no need to involve your family at this time.”

“Thank you,” he replied sincerely.

“You’re welcome,” she laughed. “You’re much nicer when you’re not threatening,” she added lightly.

He laughed back. “I didn’t threaten you, Judith. As a matter of fact, I enjoyed talking with you. Then and now.”

When she didn’t immediately respond, he plowed ahead. “Would you like to have dinner with me?”

“Yes,” she replied with virtually no hesitation.

“How about next Saturday night?”

“I could make that.” No pretension, no bullshit about her schedule. He liked that.

“Then I’ll pick you up at seven. Okay?”

“Okay, but let me tell you where I live.”

“I know where you live,” he replied.

“You do?” she said, surprised.

“At the Prudential on Huntington Avenue,” he replied. “I also conduct investigations,” he added.

“I guess so. See you then, Marty.” More neutral. Less ice, but also less warmth.

“See you then, Judith.”

14

Terry Cavanaugh waited until it was almost closing time at Nick's Cafe before making his play. He stood along the bar next to Mickey Riley, as good an intimidator as anyone he knew. Down at Walpole he had once seen Riley break a man's head open with one swipe of his open hand.

He looked out the neon window toward Granada Square, just around the corner from this neighborhood hangout. At this early morning hour, most of Malden was sound asleep. He studied the long bar, the timeworn paneling, the scarred, heavy tables—all of which gave the place a feel of a home away from home for the many Italians in the area.

"We're closing in five minutes," the short, balding bartender/owner announced from his station to the patrons still remaining—aside from Terry and Mickey, just two old men arguing about who was the better ballplayer, Williams or DiMaggio.

"Fuckin' Pete Rose and George Brett could out hit and out hustle those two," Cav whispered to Mickey. "Half their careers, those old ballplayers never even played against a smokey or a spic. And today there's a different relief pitcher every inning. Those old timers played in the daylight against starting pitchers whose arms were falling off. Maybe after eight innings and 200 pitches, they might take the guy out," he added.

The two old men slowly wandered to the front door as Nick Angelo spoke. "That's it for tonight, fellas!"

Terry and Mickey made sure the old men had left before speaking.

"Nice place you have here, Mr. Angelo," Terry commented as he finished off his Bud.

"Do I know you?" the owner asked curiously.

"I don't think so," Terry replied. "I'm Terry Cavanaugh. Most of my friends call me Cav, and this here is my friend Mick Riley."

"What's a couple of harps doin' in an Italian neighborhood?" Angelo asked, half in jest, a hint of irritation there in his voice, one eye on the clock, anxious to close up.

"Business, Mr. Angelo, business," Terry replied. "Your business, actually."

Angelo lifted an eyebrow and snorted. "My business? What are you talkin' about?"

"We're insurers, Mr. Angelo. You realize this place could go up in flames some night? Or maybe some hard-ass guys get into a fight, destroy the whole place. You could lose your license, y'know? Or maybe your delivery guys have troubles in the alley back there and hundreds of bottles get busted. In these days anything can happen. There's a lot of assholes out there."

Angelo stared right at him. "Yeah, and I'm lookin' at a couple of them right now. This isn't Southie or Charlestown. This is Malden, Rocco Apostoli's territory. I already pay him for protection. My best advice to you two is to leave now and stay the hell out of here and out of Malden. You're out of order."

Slowly, Cavanaugh picked up his empty beer bottle and threw it against the large mirror behind the bar. At the same time, Mick Riley moved toward the front door and slid the bolt into place.

In one motion, Cav placed a hand on the bar, braced himself, and leaped. Frightened, Nick Angelo stepped back as Terry approached him.

"Mr. Angelo, I don't really give a shit about Rocco Apostoli or any other guinea hood you're paying. You want to pay him, fine. But you're going to pay me for sure."

Angelo started to protest once more. "But I..."

Cav raised an index finger to his mouth. "Listen, Mr. Angelo, and listen good. One of my guys will be by every Monday from now on. You'll present him with a check for $2,000 a week for our services. Understood?"

Angelo nodded. Later, he would take this up with Apostoli's people who would know how to handle these crazy harps. "I understand," he finally replied.

"Then we'll have a drink to cement our new relationship. Okay with you, Mr. Angelo?"

"Sure," he stammered.

"Then I'll help myself to a little hair of the dog. What'll you have?"

"Nothing, not a thing," Angelo answered.

"You won't drink with us?" Terry asked indignantly.

"Give me a beer then."

"Mick, get Mr. Angelo a Bud."

They all stood behind the bar, Terry helping himself to straight whiskey and a beer chaser, the other two sipping from the longnecks.

"Hey, Mr. Angelo," Terry said. "What's the picture in your mind of an Italian going to war?" He hesitated a moment and then threw his hands above his head in a posture of surrender. "Get it?" he laughed.

Angelo tried to smile. Apostoli and his people would soon change the smiles on these two assholes' faces.

15

The wind whistled across the Charles River pushing along the few runners crossing the Massachusetts Avenue Bridge heading east, and stinging the faces of those heading toward Cambridge. Below the bridge a sheet of ice covered the Charles, except where it turned to grey water at the stanchions supporting the structure. In the distance, bundled runners, dressed in Gore-tex or heavy flannel, looped around the Charles on the Cambridge side.

Marty and Tim stood sipping coffee, looking back down Mass. Avenue. "Here he comes," Timmy said.

A tanned, well-dressed man in his early thirties blew on his gloves as he moved toward them. Luis Gomez both looked and talked like the wild and crazy star of Saturday Night Live, John Belushi. His cheeks were puffy, the nose straight, the sideburns long with his hair full. Although only about five-ten, his attempt at an erect bearing and his obvious posturing gave the impression that he was taller.

"What the fuck are we, polar bears?" he greeted them. He not only looked like Belushi, he was as edgy as the crazy bastard, Marty thought.

"It's quiet here, and we can see any surveillance coming," Marty answered.

"Yeah, if we don't freeze right here in place first," Luis said.

"Let's walk. It'll be warmer," Timmy said, pointing north to the Boston side. They descended the stairwell to the walkway below, Storrow Drive on their right, the Charles on their left. The sun beamed from a cloudless sky, preventing the temperature from becoming bone chilling. They were all dressed to fend off the severity of the day—soft fedoras, business suits, and long outer coats.

"I hear you guys did Doucette," Luis Gomez said, as they walked toward the Hatch Pavilion.

A dumb comment, one not to be answered. And this guy wonders why we want to meet him in a public place, Marty thought.

"Huh?" Gomez asked when he received no reply.

"I don't know any Doucette," Marty finally said. "What can we do for you, Luis?"

Luis Gomez pulled his collar up and yanked his fedora lower. "Play it your way, Marty."

An older man, probably in his sixties, jogged toward them accompanied by a Vanna White look-alike.

"Will you fuckin' look at that pervert." Louis exclaimed.

"It could be his daughter," Timmy said.

"Yeah, and they don't boo Santa Claus in Philadelphia," Gomez retorted.

Ahead of them, the golden dome of the State House loomed in the hills above Beacon Street, the sun reflecting like a laser ray off its top.

"Are we going to hear about your business proposition anytime today, Luis, or should we make another date so I can freeze my balls off then too?" Marty asked, a lilt in his voice.

"You know Marblehead?" Gomez asked.

"Like the back of our hands," Timmy replied.

"There's a place there near the harbor on Darling Street. One of them Victorians that's been in the hands of an old Yankee family until about six months ago. A sand nigger name of Mustafa Talik bought it."

"What are you in the real estate business now, Luis?" Timmy asked.

Luis stopped short. "I'm in a lot of businesses now, Tim. I bought a few properties around Boston, you know. I'm an investor," he bragged. "But what this is about is a fuckin' Egyptian, a very wealthy camel driver who's got maybe $4 million in jewelry in this house."

"How do you know that?" Marty asked.

"Sources. I got sources."

Marty stopped just a few yards short of the Hatch Shell. "Let's turn back," he said.

"This guy's just waitin' to be separated from his jewels," Luis said.

"We're not into house robberies, Luis," Marty said evenly.

"House robberies?" Luis repeated indignantly. "I'm talkin' about a major league heist with $2 million in it for each of us."

"It's a cowboy operation, Luis. And we long ago stopped being cowboys," Marty said.

Luis laughed. "I can remember not too many years ago when you two heisted the Mystic River Bridge."

"That wasn't us," Timmy said firmly.

"Yeah, right," Luis retorted, forsaking the handkerchief protruding from his topcoat pocket, stopping to clear his nose by placing his index finger against his nostril and blowing. So much for fashion, Marty thought.

"It sounds like you have the mark all laid out. Why involve us?" he asked.

"For one thing, I need white guys. We Hispanics aren't really welcome in downtown Marblehead. What is it you say—we stick out like a sore thumb. And then I need someone who knows how to plan, not only for the house but ways in and out of the town. If you know Marblehead, you know the streets are small and winding down near the harbor. It's not easy to get in and out. I also need someone that can fence the jewelry. I only know small timers. We'll need a good fence."

"Who's the "we" in all of this?" Tim asked.

"Just the three of us is all. This is a freelance operation. We give nothing of this back to the guineas. It's like our—what did they call it back at Chelsea High—our extra-curricular activity." He snorted rather than laughed.

"Who's this guy Talik?" Timmy asked.

"A very rich Egyptian like I said. He got driven out of Egypt by Sadat's people. He was involved in some attempt to overthrow the government. They kicked his ass out."

"How do you know about him?" Marty asked for the second time.

"Sounds to me like you guys are a bit interested in this cowboy enterprise," he said derisively.

"Before we are, we're going to need to know a lot more," Marty replied.

"Talik is a doctor, some kind of surgeon. He performs operations only on women."

"A plastic surgeon?" Tim asked.

"Yeah, that's it. He turns some scag into a better looker and, with the fat ones, cuts the rolls off so they can eat to their heart's content. I know about him because he has a bad habit. He likes to snort lines of coke, and one of my compadres is his supplier. From him, I've heard about the fuckin' Arab being loaded. They've become drinkin' buddies. When he's on a high, he brags about stealin' half of Cairo and bringin' it here with him. Says he doesn't trust banks. Keeps his stuff in a safe in the house."

Marty watched the cars flying down Storrow Drive, lane switching in the traditional Boston manner, most acting as if they did not want to miss out on the Oklahoma land rush.

"It could be bullshit," he finally said.

"What do you mean?" Gomez said indignantly.

"Maybe he has no money and maybe there's no safe," Marty answered.

"Elvis is very reliable. He says the sand nigger ran off with the family jewels."

"Is he married? Who's he live with?" Tim asked.

"The wife and him are the only ones. She's an American. Once in a while an aunt visits. My guy says the aunt walks all over Marblehead with a veil so nobody sees her face. Probably 'cause she's a fuckin' beast."

"That's not why they cover their heads, Luis," Marty rejoined.

"Whatever. There's no kids, just the guy and his wife."

"Has your guy been to the house?" Marty asked. "Has he actually seen the safe?"

"That's what I'm tellin' you Marty. This guy has you come to his house. Talik ain't wandering around on Mission Hill lookin' for a line. My guy didn't actually see the stuff in the safe, but he saw a fuckin' safe. The A-rab and his wife both shoot up and are high as fuckin' kites so my man walks one time right into the library and sees the safe behind this picture of some naked bimbo with a big ass. It's there all right."

"You do any casing of the scene?" Timmy asked.

"You think you're dealin' with some dumb-assed spic, Tim? In the dark, three times, I looked the place over. 21 Darling Street."

"I'm asking about the house and the neighborhood, Luis."

"The neighborhood's quiet. The good doctor and his wife have been home every Friday night. I went back three Friday nights in a row. Never any sign of company. That's the night to hit him."

"I'm a long way from hitting him," Marty replied.

"You're not interested then?"

"We're not safe crackers, Luis," Marty said.

"Who said anythin' about cracking a box? We put a gun to the asshole's head and tell him to open the thing, or he'll be joinin' his ancestors in one of those mummy cases."

"And what if he still won't open the safe?"

"We grab his wife and tell him we'll shoot her first."

"Who takes care of your source?" Tim asked.

"I do. I already told him he'll get 10% of my $2 million."

They climbed the stairs back to the Mass Avenue Bridge and paused together at the top. With the wind increasing, there was now very little foot traffic along its span.

"So what's the verdict?" Luis asked.

Marty extended his hand. "We'll talk about it and get back to you, Luis."

Luis frowned, disappointment crossing his face. "Don't take too long, Marty."

"We won't. I'll call you in a few days."

Luis Gomez didn't reply. He turned east and sauntered off, lowering his head as the wind riffled his back.

16

"There's a guy says he's an old friend of yours out here," Rosie O'Shea announced from the doorway.

"What's his name?" Marty asked, rising from his chair.

"Dan Slattery," she replied.

Marty smiled, the tiny crow's feet at the corners of his eyes widening. "Send him in, Rosie."

His thoughts circled back to a time long ago. Dan Slattery. How long had it actually been? In the 50's, Dan's father Leo had been Jack Kelly's best friend and tutor. He had been killed in 1962 in New York City when one of the Ryan brothers, leaders of the Westies gang in Hell's Kitchen, then involved in a vendetta against the Kellys, had gunned him down near Columbus Circle.

Dan Slattery was now an FBI agent, stationed in New York City and married to a Manhattan police officer.

"Danny! Now look at you!" Marty bellowed, his clear voice carrying a trace of Irish lilt, as the handsome young man stood in the doorway.

Danny Slattery grinned and met Marty halfway across the room, embracing him long and hard. "Marty, it's great to see you again. You look great!" He was dressed in a charcoal grey business suit with a white shirt and a burgundy tie.

Marty laughed as he stepped back and looked Danny over, measuring him with affection. He noted his slight frame and thatch of chestnut hair. "Two years?"

"That's about right," Danny nodded.

"How's your wife? How's Christine?"

"Just great, Marty. We can't complain."

"Well come on. Sit down. How about some coffee?"

"You got time to talk for a while?"

Marty glanced at his watch. "Sure. Plenty of time for you, Danny."

"Then let's take a ride," he suggested.

"Sure." Marty reached for his topcoat and pointed toward the door, banking his anxiety. As they passed through the circular showroom, he spoke to Rosie. "Be back in an hour."

They drove in Danny's Fairlane toward the Nahant Rotary, cruising full around the circle toward Swampscott. On their right, huge whitecaps pounded the sea wall, the water bounding above it, drenching the walkway. On a late January morning there were very few people moving along Lynn Shore Drive. A beautiful golden retriever barked at the waves as an old timer wrestled with him, trying to edge him away from the sea wall. Marty studied the old man, envying his time, the time to just walk alone, play with the dog, be at peace with nothing much to worry about. He smiled to himself. Probably the old man didn't see it that way.

"So how's New York?" Marty asked, wondering about the ride, guessing that Danny probably feared some form of surveillance back at the dealership.

"It's been crazy there since Reagan took over in '81. The Bureau, the New York police, they've all been concentrating on the Mafia, with good results, but something new's happening. Have you ever heard of the Vigilantes?"

Marty shook his head. "No."

"They're a gang of about thirty guys, formerly musicians. They dress in green military outfits and black boots. They wear hatchets on chains around their necks. For a while, they took control of the crack trade. Can you believe that? A gang of thirty guys who started in the music business took over the crack trade from the Mafia?"

"How did that happen?"

"Down there, all kinds of small gangs are fighting for control. It's a new day. They're hard to catch because, unlike the Mafia, they have no well-defined structure. But you know what? These small gangs of crackheads kill more people in one year then the Gambinos and Luccheses in twenty."

No real surprise, Marty thought. The same thing was occurring in Boston. The Mafia was under fierce attack from the Feebs while smaller gangs of the newly enfranchised were forming—different strains of the Hispanics, led by Gomez and four or five other cowboys; the Asians; the fuckin' out-of-control Jamaicans; various Irish gangs challenging his position; and on top of it all, the Mafia organized the same in 1983 as they had been in 1940, and probably in 1740.

"Crime's up worse than ever in New York, Marty. The criminals are peein' on our heads, and the politicians are telling us it isn't raining. How are things with you, Marty?"

Marty cast him a sidelong glance. "Are you asking as an FBI agent or as a long time friend?"

Danny considered him and frowned. "As a friend. And that's really why I wanted to see you, Marty." He paused for effect. "You're a prime target of the Bureau, you and Tim."

Marty didn't answer right away. Instead, he stared out the window at Seaside Park as they entered the center of Marblehead. Far to his right, a wooden semi-circular bleacher stretched behind home plate from the right field to the left field foul lines. Directly in front of him, the outfield ended at a step incline. When he was at Lynn English High School, back in '71, he had crushed a long home run right out here to the street and across to the front steps of Star of the Sea Church.

When he didn't reply, Danny grimaced. "I don't know what surveillance systems they might have already set up, that's why I didn't want to say much back in your office. There's going to be a concerted push..."

Marty raised a hand in protest. "Danny, do you remember what Jack said to you two years ago?"

Danny pulled to the curb outside the Warwick Theater. One movie theater in Lynn, Saugus, Swampscott, Nahant and Marblehead combined, Marty thought, as he studied the old movie house.

"I remember, but I also remember what he did for me and my mother after my father was killed. He took care of us, Marty, made sure I got to Holy Cross. He..."

"He also told you to feel no obligation to us. Do your job. You don't owe us..."

Danny frowned, unwilling to drop the subject. "What do you know about the killing of a guy named Doucette?" he interrupted.

Marty shrugged his shoulders. "As far as you're concerned, I don't know anything."

"Both the FBI and the Boston Police think you do. They're working it hard."

"Is that so?" Marty replied, disinterest in his voice.

Danny let out a loud sigh. "Marty, I'm tellin' you they're on the case. They've taken down some good crews, and the more structured your organization is, the higher their success rate."

"Fuck them," Marty replied.

"Marty, listen to me. You know it's not easy for me..."

"Yes it is, Danny. It's very easy. They have nothing on me, no evidence of any involvement in any crime..."

"You sound like you believe your own press," Danny interrupted. "They'll turn someone. They'll find a way..."

Marty reached for the ignition key and turned it off. "Listen to me, Danny. You have a wife, a wonderful wife, and a lovely mother, and you're down in New York. I appreciate the information, but I don't want it, and I don't need it. Don't you think your bosses know of your connection to the Kelly family?" His voice rose audibly. "Of course they do. They'll be watching you as much as Tim and me. Just leave it. Don't press it."

He playfully tapped Danny on the jaw. "Understand?"

Danny stared into the rearview mirror rather than look at him. "If that's how you want it, Mart."

Marty nodded. "That's exactly how I want it."

—

Neither of them said much of anything. They stood at the window of her loft looking down on L Street, Day Boulevard visible in the long distance, the islands of Boston Harbor an outline in the early dark. Maureen leaned into him, kissing his cheek as he placed his arm around her.

She stroked the tiny scar above his upper lip. Tim must have been a beautiful baby, she thought, studying him now, lifting her head toward him. There's a time, she considered, when you just look at one another with no attempt to explain, knowing that it is just right. She turned him toward her bed and started taking his suit coat off.

"You okay?" she whispered. He nodded, letting her take the lead. She undid his Stephano Ricci tie and started to unbutton his shirt. And then she asked him to lift his arms so she could remove his T-shirt. She sensed the man-smell of him, a touch of Drakkar Noir, which she liked.

She knelt down and pulled at his shoes. Then she stood again and unbuttoned his pants, letting them drop to the floor. Slowly, he stepped out of them. She pressed her lips against his chest. He was her beautiful man, strong, gentle, his skin warm. I'm in love, she told herself. It's crazy but I am.

She slipped out of her clothes.

"What about birth control?" Tim asked.

"I'm on the pill," she whispered." "Lie down."

She was wet, she realized, as she straddled him. She squatted on her haunches instead of resting on her knees. "Yes!" she screamed, moving up and down the full length of him. His rhythm was perfect. He penetrated far inside of her, his huge hands holding her hipbones gently. He moved them to her breasts, rolling his finger in loops around her nipples. And then he turned over on top of her, not breaking their rhythm.

"Oh!" she cried.

"Am I hurting you?" he asked, gently.

"No, no. It's just so good."

He pressed into her more rapidly, and she let her hands travel up his smooth back until they were around his neck and then she lifted her head ever so slightly, looking into his wide-open eyes that glowed blue even in the dark, and thrust her tongue into his mouth.

She loved him, now and forever, she thought. She wanted to give herself to him now and always. And she wasn't fooling herself, she thought, seeking reassurance. Suddenly he increased his pace, going fast and hard, and then the tension within her rose as they reached climax together.

Then they lay under the sheets for almost an hour, lovers saying very little. He cupped his hand behind her neck and pulled her close. "I love you, Maureen Cavanaugh."

"And I you, Tim," she replied. "God, do I love you."

Yet, as she lay quiet, staring at the ceiling, reality, not ever far removed from her, returned. Tim Kelly was a dangerous man involved in a dangerous business. What future did she have with him?

17

Whenever he visited San Francisco, Bobby chose to use the cable cars, either the Hyde-Powell line or the Powell-Mason. He had read somewhere that the cable cars were the brainchild of a London mechanic named Andrew Smith Hallidie, who came to California for good back in 1852. Like everyone else, he sought his fortune in gold, and in the process developed a system of wire ropes to transport his findings. Later, the city fathers wondered how they were going to transport the snobs up and over Nob Hill, so in 1873 Hallidie stepped in, again utilizing his wire ropes. In its first trial run the car had cruised down Clay from Jones to Kearney and back again, successfully bringing joy then and for decades to come to millions of visitors.

Bobby jumped from the car within the 2800 block of California Street and headed for Eliza's. At noon, the usual lines were forming out the door to sample their classy Hunan and Mandarin dishes. He cut through the crowd toward the maitre d's station. In front of him, tasteful neon lights blended with large groupings of absolutely beautiful hand-blown glassware, both on the tables and above the bar.

He spotted his agent immediately. Ross Crombie was a short, plump man, whose most distinctive feature was unkept eyebrows which headed off in all directions.

"Hey, Sean!" he greeted Bobby, standing.

"How are you, Ross?

Crombie shrugged his shoulders as he sat. "Could be better. My ticker is to be watched says my doctor. I have to cut down on the cholesterol. Might as well die."

Bobby smiled across at him. "This place will help you along."

"And that exercise shit is for the birds. Did you see that photo the other day of Reagan lifting weights over his head? Supposedly, he's setting an example for the rest of us. The only exercise I want is the walk to the refrigerator."

A pert, young Chinese waitress approached them. Her face had an unformed prettiness to it.

"I'll have the vegetable moo-shi with lots of plum sauce," Crombie ordered. "And bring me another mai tai."

"The egg roll and boiled rice for me," Bobby said. "And a Coke, please."

"That's not enough for a bird," Crombie said.

"Tis enough. T'will serve," Bobby rejoined.

"Hemingway, right?"

Bobby shook his head. "Shakespeare. 'Romeo and Juliet'."

"Whatever," Crombie replied, diving into his mai-tai.

"Any news on the part?" Bobby asked.

"I talked to Ulu Grosbard the other day."

"And?"

"He's thinking about it. He saw you in "The Big Chill" and liked what he saw. The new picture's tentatively titled "Falling in Love". He's signed Bobby DeNiro and Meryl Streep."

"Will he want a screen test?"

"For sure. DeNiro's finishing up "The King of Comedy" in New York. Then he goes into the new one. So the test will be in New York. Can you fuckin' imagine "Raging Bull" didn't get the academy award?" he added disdainfully. "Ordinary People" is an ordinary movie. Someday—you watch—Scorcese's picture will be rated the best film not only of the year but of the whole eighties."

"Well, at least it was the best picture of 1980," Bobby responded.

"I'm pushin' it hard, Sean. I can tell Grosbard likes you for the part of Streep's husband."

"Anything else on the horizon?"

Crombie scooped one of Bobby's egg rolls onto his plate. "Maybe. 'La Cage Aux Folles' is holding tryouts in New York. There may be a part there. George Hearn and Gene Barry are going to star. Any objection to playing a queer?"

"No," Bobby answered. "Of course not," he added, a bit too defensively.

"Then good. While you're in New York for the screen test, we'll have you tryout for a couple of roles in the play, too."

He looked down at his plate. "I ate too much," he grumbled.

Bobby smiled broadly at him.

"And, Sean, put on a couple of more pounds will you? You're supposed to be an up and coming movie star. Ladies of the 80's prefer heft."

"I hear you, o master," Bobby grinned.

18

"What's the answer going to be?" Ray Horan asked. They sat in Jack's old house, now Marty's, right across the street from Kings Beach in Lynn.

Marty stood at the bow window looking out at the ocean. Undulating waves crashed against the sea wall and breached the rail on the walkway. To his right, Red Rock Park looked bleak in the early winter night. He sipped some of the highball and turned toward Tim. "What do you think?" he asked.

"It's your call, but it's really not our thing."

"The answer is no," Marty replied calmly, sitting down next to Tim on the couch. "Gomez is flaky, and it's too much of a crapshoot."

"Did you guys look over the place?" Ray asked.

"I did," Tim said. "Darling Street runs from downtown to the waterfront itself. The street's one way and narrow, like Gomez says. The best way out would be by boat across Marblehead Harbor to the Neck."

"In the fuckin' winter?" Marty asked, incredulous.

"It would be a surprise," Tim laughed.

"Yeah, like Washington crossing the Delaware," Marty said.

"Getting out by car is another problem. That is, if anyone in the neighborhood got suspicious, saw something, it would be tough getting away. Too many side streets along the waterfront to maneuver on the way out of town."

Marty waved his hand. "Tell him we're not interested, Tim. Let him go ahead on his own if he wants. It's not our thing."

He ran his fingers through his hair. "Anything else?"

"Just one other thing," Ray responded. "One of the city council members over in Southie is askin' us to put his kid on."

Marty placed the drink on the table. "On where?"

Ray took a swig from his longneck. "On the waterfront. He says he'll cause problems if it doesn't happen. Guy named Donovan."

Marty poured some more Canadian Club. "How's he know about us?"

"Probably the rumor mill. Says one Irishman should take care of another," Ray said.

"What do you know about him?" Marty asked.

Ray leaned forward in his chair. "He's a wild man. Popular over in Southie with the residents. Never saw a black man he liked. Wants to send them all back to Africa. He gets re-elected by the old timers. Attends every wake and every funeral, a complete pol. The kid's an asshole too. Dishonorably discharged from the army for harassing some woman private. He says if we don't put his kid on and keep him on permanently he's going to demand the mayor and the police commissioner investigate the rise of Irish gangs in Boston," Ray concluded.

A hardness pervaded Marty's face. "Ray, give Donovan two messages. One, I'm a businessman, and I don't know him, and I don't have a knowledge of or a concern with jobs on the waterfront. Second, tell him if he causes me any trouble, he'll find his son on the waterfront all right—in a fuckin' body bag in the not too distant future. And then tell him he should learn to ask nice."

Ray studied Marty. In the early months of his ascendency, he was making good decisions. He was demonstrating that he possessed the same ruthlessness as his uncle, the same decisiveness after weighing alternatives, the same Irish sand. Two years ago, he would have been all for joining Gomez. He was growing, maturing. There was still the Irish temper there. In that respect, he was less like Jack and much more like Tommy. With Jack, you never knew what he was thinking if he didn't want you to know. Marty still had to learn that.

But all in all, it was like Jack was still there. They were in good hands.

—

He placed his feet up on the edge of the coffee table, making triangular arches of his legs. Judith faced him, her back resting against the sofa arm. Barefoot, she stretched her legs toward him. He tried hard to appear as if he hadn't noticed. But not for long. He decided to chance it, particularly with Willie Nelson plaintively singing "To All the Girls I've Loved Before" in the background. He rested his arm lightly on the top of her ankles, and then he leaned forward to pour more wine into her glass and then more CC into his own.

"Martin. That's a pretty name," she said softly in that sexy voice, the effect of too much wine obvious. "Do many people call you Martin?"

He shook his head, smiling. "I like Marty better."

They sat silently for a moment. His arm was still on her legs. "I'm glad you're here," she said tenderly. "This wine's gone right to my head."

He laughed loudly. "Well, it's a good thing we're home already. Wouldn't do to have you arrested. You know, you with the Globe and all."

He decided he wasn't going to take advantage of her. "Look, it's getting late, and we both have to get up early in the morning. I hope you enjoyed the dinner."

He stood up, placing his half-filled glass on the table and headed for the door. She followed him and stood next to him. "Thanks again," he whispered into her ear.

She leaned into him, and he held her and they kissed, loose and intimate immediately, definitely not a goodnight kiss. She pushed hair back from her face. He didn't move at first, but just continued to hold her tightly, one hand running along the side of her breast. She kept leaning against him, almost as if determined not to start anything else. But he had more patience than she did, even though he was still trying to make up his mind whether he wanted to get involved. He did, and he didn't.

Then she reached down to his trunk, and it became evident to them both that he was interested. He tried to restrain himself. A fuckin' newspaper reporter. He really didn't know about this. Then why had he approached her? he wondered. And was her interest sincere or was it due entirely to the wine? Calculated to gain his confidence for a future story? All of the above?

Just enjoy it, he told himself. He started to undress. In no more than a shimmer of time, she was wrapping her legs around his, pressing against his hard chest.

She didn't take him to the bedroom, just back to the sofa. Marty kissed her breasts as she stroked his back and ran her hands up his thighs. Then she lay back, lying partially on the arm of the cushion, a leg extended along the top of the sofa and guided him. "Go slowly," she murmured, but she really didn't have to tell him.

Later, much later, he started to think again. Driving from her apartment, he thought of his confusion. He liked her, he liked being with her, smelling her smell, enjoying the light repartee, the back and forth teasing. But as the dawn's early light showed itself on the horizon, another light came on in his foggy brain. She's a newspaper reporter, and she also could be one hell of an actress.

—

Nick Angelo waited his turn by playing with his soft fedora, twirling it nervously in his hands. The offices of Rocco Apostoli Inc. were abuzz on Monday morning as subordinates appeared in the waiting room and then quickly disappeared behind the twin doors leading to the inner sanctum. Outside on Atlantic Avenue, huge trucks roared from the alleyway, which led to the rear of the massive warehouse. The red and white fleet of Rocco Apostoli Meat Packers was on the move, delivering goods all around the Boston area.

A lone secretary sat outside the gateway to Apostoli himself, her gums churning as she attacked her bubble gum. It's a damn wonder she doesn't blow some bubbles too, Nick thought. Where had professionalism gone?

Suddenly she beckoned him forward, the gesture probably necessary because she couldn't talk through the pink wad in her mouth. The lump moved to the corner of her face. "He'll see you now," she barely muttered.

When Nick Angelo appeared in his doorway, Rocco stood, came out from behind his ostentatious desk, and walked across the red Oriental rug.

"Nicky, how are you?" he gushed. "What brings you here?"

"Rocco, thanks for seein' me," Nick said, fumbling with his hat.

"Sit over here with me, old friend." Rocco said. He led Nick to a sprawling leather couch. "What's the problem, Nick? I only got a few minutes," he said, looking at his watch.

"You got troubles I think, Rock."

"I got troubles? What the hell you talkin' about?"

"I meant we got troubles," Nick countered.

"Am I gonna find out what these troubles are, Nick? I mean sometime today would be nice. Maybe before I die of fuckin' old age."

"You know a harp named Terry Cavanaugh?"

Rocco shook his head. "Should I?"

"Him and another mick came into my place Friday night lookin' for business. He wants $2,000 a week from me for protection services."

Rocco mulled it over for a second. "Just throw his ass out. You tell him you're covered?"

"He broke up my place! Talked about torching it."

"You tell him about me?"

"He said fuck you, too. I still have to pay."

Apostoli practically leaped from the couch. "He what?"

"Rocco, I can't afford to pay twice. You got to get him off my ass. He looks dangerous to me. I didn't feel good about him."

"What's the turnip's name again?"

"Cavanaugh. Terry Cavanaugh. I never saw him in Malden before."

"Fuckin' harps are out of control in this city," Rocco fumed. He moved to the huge plate glass window and looked out to Atlantic Avenue. He turned back toward Angelo.

"I'll take care of it, Nick. In the meantime, go about your business and make sure you pay this asshole zilch. You got it?"

Nick Angelo stood, knowing it was time to leave. "Thanks for seein' me, Rock."

Apostoli placed an arm around Nick's neck and walked with him toward the doorway. "Call me right away if anythin' else happens, right?"

As Nick passed through the huge waiting room, he heard the sound of a bubble bursting.

19

Luis Gomez sat across from his driver, Felipe Pichardo, and dug his gloved hands deeper into his pea jacket. "It is fuckin' cold!" he exclaimed as they slowly cruised down Darling Street, being careful not to rush.

"Where'd you boost this Caddy?" Luis asked.

Felipe grinned broadly. "You know that garage around the corner from the Boston Garden? I walk in there all dressed up, y'know? I take the elevator to the third floor lookin' prosperous, y'know? I just walk up to this one and it takes me just a second to jimmy the lock. I tell the dumb guard I lost my ticket. Had to pay the max. I figure a Caddy's good. Fits right in, in Marblehead, y'know. What you think? We look like a couple of Yankees from Marblehead, right?"

"Give me a hit from that fuckin' pipe," Luis answered.

As Felipe slowed the vehicle, he handed the pipe across. Luis blew in the good Mexican stuff and sat for a moment waiting for its full effect.

"You ready, Felipe?" he asked, looking at his subordinate.

"Man, I'm ready to tackle the fuckin' world. Let's go kick some A-rab ass."

Luis liked the buzz, the fuzzy feeling. He didn't buy the theory that you needed a clear head when big things were going down. The crack hit made him fearless, exaggerated his sense of power and control. The fuckin' Arab better not cause any problem. "Pop the truck," Luis ordered as they stopped completely on the street outside number 17, a small driveway separating them for Talik's Victorian.

They moved to the rear and reached their gloved hands into the trunk, Luis choosing the .38 with the suppresser, and Felipe the Glock nine he favored. Felipe picked up the duffel bag.

The Victorian was lit up like a Christmas tree, the television volume up a bit too loudly for this upper middle-class neighborhood. A soft, fluffy snow fell about them, not really troublesome but enough of a nuisance to keep pedestrians off the roads this late at night. Weapons down low and close to their sides, they walked to the old home and climbed the steps. They approached the locked outer screen door, a leftover from summer. On their frequent drive-bys, Luis could not believe that residents would still have screen doors operational in February. Not just here, but on many of the surrounding streets. Old Marbleheaders daring winter? Whatever, it was a godsend.

Luis pulled his knife from his jacket and ripped a huge slit in the screen. He looked behind him but saw no movement either on the street or in the home across from them. Felipe stepped through the hole, placed the ski mask over his face, and knelt at the side of the main door on their right. He pushed the screen back together as best he could. As they had planned, Luis then rang the bell and lowered his head, his .38 in one hand, the ski mask in the other.

The main door opened and Mustafa Talik appeared in view, dressed in an open necked white dress shirt and grey slacks. He stepped out to the porch and started toward the screen door. "Yes?" he asked. "What can I do for you?"

"What you can do is get the fuck back into the house!" Felipe ordered, pressing his weapon against Talik's spine. He positioned himself behind Talik and reached for the lock on the screen door, allowing Luis to enter.

Talik muttered something in Arabic but obeyed Felipe and entered the house. For a moment, Luis stood on the porch, donning his mask, facing the street, gauging whether any neighbors had been alerted. Close to midnight, there was no sign of alarm, no cause to be concerned. He entered to a hallway, which led directly to a living room on his right. Across the hall, a stairwell ran upstairs.

"Who is it?" a female voice called from the kitchen, the last syllables of which indicated the individual was moving toward the living room.

Ellen Talik was an American, with olive skin, maybe Italian or Greek, Luis thought. Maybe thirty. She stopped on the spot when she saw them. "What!..." she uttered in surprise.

"Shut the fuck up and sit over there," Luis directed.

"Check the rest of the house," Luis directed Felipe.

"What the hell is this?" the woman persisted.

Talik hadn't said a word since they had entered the house. He looked both scrawny and stoned and acted as if he were floating off in space somewhere. And the wife didn't look much different, Luis noted. Two fuckin' cocaine addicts ready to be had.

"What you want?" Talik said indifferently as he joined his wife on the sofa. "I have no money."

Gomez pointed to the picture on the wall—a Van Gogh imitation of a nude woman. A fuckin' fatso, Luis thought. "We want what's in the safe, Mr. Talik. You open it carefully and quietly, without incident, and they'll be no problem. Understand?"

Luis stood in the middle of the room feeling more unsettled than he liked. That last hit had his head reeling.

Felipe came back toward him. "Nothing upstairs or down. These two cokeheads have a line out on the kitchen table is all."

Talik sat impassively, not answering Luis's question. Something was wrong. Why was he so calm? The coke? Maybe just because he was an A-rab.

"You hearin' me?" Luis asked.

"I am connected," Talik said softly. "You must now go before I call my friends."

Luis looked to Felipe who reacted as if someone had just handed him a bag of dogshit.

The American wife smiled at them, her eyes gray and wide. "You two better get the fuck out of here while you still can."

Their words made Luis focus through the hit. He wanted another belt as soon as they got back in the car, but first things first.

He walked toward the sofa and pressed the .38 against Talik's temple. "Open that fuckin' safe, or you're dead and so isn't she."

"Fuck you!" Ellen Talik shouted.

"Fuck me?" Luis said. "Fuck me?" he repeated. "No fuck you," he said, firing the .38 directly into her chest, the suppresser preventing any noise.

She fell back against the sofa, blood oozing from her chest cavity. Talik reached across, half standing, through his fog, not quite comprehending what had happened.

Gomez shoved him back and placed the .38 against his forehead. "One more fuckin' time. Open that safe!"

Talik nodded almost inperceptively and stood. As he rose, Luis shoved him toward the wall. "You have ten seconds, asshole!"

He hadn't meant to shoot the wife, maybe only scare her. Why did she have to aggravate him? He hated to be aggravated, especially when he was on a high.

Talik pushed the picture of the bimbo aside and revealed the safe. He stood awkwardly, squinting, thinking through the fog.

"We haven't got all day, Mr. Talik," Luis said tersely.

"I am trying to remember," Talik replied evenly.

Then he spun the dials and the box popped, opening ever so slightly. He opened it fully just as Luis pushed him aside.

Luis reached in, his fingers touching emeralds, rubies, jewels of all sizes. "Give me the duffel bag!" he ordered Felipe.

Talik stood to his side. "You will not get away with this. I have friends. I..."

Luis really didn't want to kill either of them. In fact, for a few seconds he couldn't remember why he had killed the wife. Then he remembered. Her mouth. Her big mouth. Now that he had the jewels, there was no need to off Talik. As Felipe scooped the jewels into the bag, he thought about Talik a bit longer.

Suddenly Luis lifted the .38 and shot him through the heart. The Arab fell backward to the floor, almost knocking over a floor lamp in the process.

"Ready?" Luis asked Felipe.

"Yes! Let's go!"

"Slowly, my friend. Let's not panic!"

Before they walked out to the porch, they shut down most of the lights. Even through his haze, Luis knew that could buy them time. A darkened house meant people were asleep, and were not to be bothered.

Felipe kept the lights off in the Caddy until they had turned off Darling Street. Looping along the waterfront, he headed back toward the center of town.

"Fuckin' A-rab!" Felipe ranted. "What's that shit about being connected?"

"He ain't connected no more," Luis countered.

20

The gunmetal gray of the Atlantic seemed never-ending as Terry Cavanaugh drove down Day Boulevard. Uninterrupted, it ran all the way to wherever the fuck it ended, probably in China, he thought.

He watched the flatness of it in the rearview mirror as he drove up East Broadway to where it intersected with L Street. On the radio Roy Orbison was singing "Oh Pretty Woman" in that distinctive voice. Nervously, Terry tapped his index finger on the wheel, really not enjoying the song, not with his stupid sister acting like such an jerk. He switched to WBZ where the newscaster was discussing the mayoral plan to redefine Mission Main into Taj Mahal. Yeah right, he thought, another urban renewal project for the smokies to wreck.

He parked outside her building and climbed the steps to the third floor. This early on a Saturday morning she should be home. He rang the bell impatiently.

"Who is it?" Maureen called in that breezy way of hers.

"Count Dracula."

She peeked through the eyehole and then released the lock and unlatched the chain.

"You found a job yet?" she asked as he entered.

"And good morning to you too."

She rose to peck his cheek. "Sorry," she said. "It's on my mind, you know?"

"I'm workin' at Tower Records over on the Fenway. Near Boylston."

"That's great, Terry. Really great. Want some coffee?"

"Thanks. That would be good."

He sat down at the kitchen table and looked around. She kept the five-room apartment clean and eye catching. Pink curtains covered the kitchen window and the linoleum was spotless. Not one thing out of place in the whole damn kitchen, he noted. They sat on high stools around a semi-circular kitchen table.

"The parole officer got me the job," he finally said. "It sucks."

"It's a job, Terry," Maureen said, placing the coffee in front of him.

"I stopped by to talk about you, not me."

"Me? What about me?"

"You were seen the other night at the Red Coach Grill over on Stanhope Street with Timmy Kelly."

She cast him a disdainful look. "I was seen, Terry? I was seen? Give me a break."

"Wouldn't Ma be proud of you, Mo? Hanging around with one of the biggest fuckin' gangsters in Boston."

She walked back toward the kitchen window and dumped the remains from her cup down the drain. "Remember when we were kids, Terry? Ma would say to us, MYOB. That expression still applies today."

Terry slammed his hand down hard onto the table. "It is my business, Mo! Ma didn't sacrifice to send you to college to have you end up with the likes of Timmy Kelly."

"That's the pot calling the kettle black," she retaliated.

"Maybe it is, Mo. Maybe it is. But I got your interest at heart. You're headin' down the wrong road with Kelly. Who was it warned me years back about hangin' with the wrong crowd? Huh?" He stood and walked toward her.

He placed his cup on the counter. "The coffee's bitter," he said, his voice softening . "Don't you go bitter on me, Mo."

She rested her head on his shoulder. "You don't always have to play big brother, Terry," she whispered in his ear.

"Yes, I do, Mo. I love you, and Ma's not here now. What do we have? Each other, right?"

She shook her head firmly. "You got that right."

"I'm not gonna say any more about Kelly."

"Yeah, right."

"Just think about it, huh?" He cupped his hand gently under her jaw and lifted her eyes toward him.

"I can do that," she replied.

—

"She's dead, Rocco! My baby's dead! And Mustafa too!"

Victorio Apostoli was wailing so loudly that Rocco had a difficult time understanding him.

"Vic, calm down. What the hell you talkin' about?" He glanced at the clock on his desk. 10:05 a.m.

"I stopped by this morning to take her to breakfast like we planned. Like every Saturday," he sobbed. "I found Ellie on the floor with Mustafa. And the jewels—$4 million of jewels gone! The safe open..." He couldn't continue.

Rocco looked at his clock once again. His older brother was in a state of shock, the words strung together, the sobbing making him almost incoherent. "Where are you now Vic?" he asked.

"Back home in Ipswich. I called you as soon as the police let me go."

"I'll be there in forty minutes," Rocco replied.

His favorite niece dead? Along with that fuckin' Arab she had met in Cairo at the American University. He hadn't fully accepted the Arab, but Ellen was family and so then was Mustafa. He had warned the two cokeheads about keeping those stolen Egyptian jewels in the house, but they wouldn't listen. Now they were both gone. Whoever murdered them was as good as dead himself. The killer or killers had to be someone associated with the drug trade. He would squeeze his sources and find out exactly who was responsible.

21

The empty swimming pool was a clear symbol of the season. Around the perimeter of the cavernous hole, deck chairs were piled together. Beyond the fence the Danvers River looped toward the town, its banks crusted with light snow.

But at least in the winter, you could find a seat at the Danversport Yacht Club, Marty thought. On a late winter Tuesday, he sat beside Timmy enjoying the drinks at the circular bar, the only other customers two dykes trying hard not to show their affection in public.

"Will you look at that?" Timmy said, chasing the amber with the beer.

"What?"

"The two lesbos over there. Sickening."

The probable male member of the tag team cast them a derisive look and exhaled a stream of smoke in their direction.

"Chris vouches for him?" Marty asked, stirring his ice cubes.

Timmy nodded. "He went to East Boston High with him."

"What's a couple of Irishmen doing at East Boston High?" Marty asked, laughing.

"You shittin' me? After Judge Garrity put out the court order, there's Irishmen and everything else at East Boston High. No more just dagos."

"Did you meet this guy Gil Rafferty?"

"I did," Timmy replied. "He seems legit. Good lookin' guy with no record. Just what we want, Marty.

We need some help with the enforcement, you know it as well as I do."

"Then pair him with Ray and Paulie. Let's see what he's like."

"You want to meet him?" Timmy asked.

"If Chris vouches for him, and you liked him, I'm okay with it, but make him pass some tests. Earn his bones."

Across from them, the gay couple seemed absorbed in one another. They drank wine, a pansy drink, which befit the occasion, Timmy felt. Through the huge plate glass window, a functions manager squired what looked like representatives of a senior class and their advisor through the grounds, stopping occasionally to point out how things would look so different come their June prom night.

"So Gomez went ahead, huh?" Timmy asked.

"You knew he would," Marty replied.

"They fuckin' killed the Arab and the wife."

Marty sipped the CC. It made him feel both relaxed and complete. "We were smart to stay out of it. Something must have gone wrong. But he got the jewels."

"Can I tell you something personal without you getting pissed?" Timmy suddenly asked.

Marty nodded. "Go ahead."

"I've been seeing Maureen Cavanaugh."

"I know," Marty replied.

"You know?"

"Half of Boston knows."

"And?"

"And that's your business, Tim. I have no problem with it."

"The brother might," Timmy said.

"Fuck him," Marty rejoined. "What's the word on him lately? I'm hearing he's still causing the guineas some trouble."

Timmy nodded. "They'll straighten him out any day now."

The two dykes tittered at some story the more feminine one was telling.

Marty glanced at Timmy. "Terry's not to be underestimated, Tim. He's building his own little business."

"He won't be allowed to operate," Timmy said. "They'll kick his ass and close him down."

"We'll see," Marty replied. "I don't really give a shit as long as he stays out of our territory."

On the television above the bar, President Reagan looked resplendent in an olive suit as he deplored the conduct of two members of the House of Representatives who had been censored for having sexual relations with Congressional pages.

Suddenly the bartender approached Marty. "Someone wants you to call this number, Marty."

Marty glanced at the piece of paper. "It's Saladna," Marty told Timmy. "I'll be right back."

He found the wall phone just off the main lobby. He dialed the number of Rocco Apostoli's number one operative on the North Shore.

"Hello," someone grunted.

"Chuck, it's Marty Kelly. Dominic called."

A pause for a moment, and then Dominic Saladna's cheery voice came across. "Marty, my lad. The big man wants to see you ASAP."

"Like when?" Marty replied.

"Like how's tomorrow morning over at Atlantic Avenue about nine."

"I'll be there."

22

Huge silver birds queued up on the runway at LAX, the line extending practically back to San Diego, or at least as far as the eye could see. Sitting in the lounge with Jason, Bobby really didn't care. He felt so upbeat and excited about the trip to New York that he could wait forever.

They sat on rounded bar stools, Bobby facing the large plate glass window looking out to the airstrip, Jason watching the crowd forming in a long line for McDonald's choicest.

"When's the audition?" Jason asked.

"Tomorrow morning. Grosbard has three or four of us coming in." There was a high rise to his voice, an enthusiasm for the challenge. He glanced at his watch.

"You still have a half hour," Jason said, almost too rapidly, fidgeting with his hands.

"Something wrong?"

Jason didn't answer right away. Instead he averted his eyes and looked over to the counter where one Black teen was showing another the new break dance steps while the large crowd waiting for orders began to applaud.

"I need to tell you something, but it seems there's never a right time or place," Jason finally sighed.

"Tell me? Tell me what?"

Actually, Jason had been waiting for just this very moment. Tell him, and then let him get on the plane. Let him dwell on it while he was in New York. He would be more accepting of it in a day or two, after he had time to think on it.

"Jase?"

"Sean, I haven't been totally honest with you. I..."

"You're seeing someone else?" Bobby interrupted, an edge in his voice.

Jason nodded slowly. "Yeah. A guy I met a few months ago over in West Hollywood."

Bobby raised a shaky hand. "Wait a minute. A guy you met in West Hollywood? I thought we agreed to be monogamous? Didn't we, Jase?" He tried to subdue the anger, unsuccessfully. "What the hell are you talking about?"

Jason shrugged his shoulders and averted his eyes. The Black kid demonstrating the new break steps took off his baseball cap, displaying hair standing on ends like porcupine needles from heavy gel usage.

"I don't know what to say, Sean. I didn't start out to become involved. It was just another affair like any other to begin. It..."

"An affair? Another affair Jase? Am I hearing this right? One guy, Jase? Two? What? How many affairs are we talkin' about?"

The crowd around them was focused on the guys making like Astaire. Otherwise, the anger in Bobby's voice would have drawn more attention. Jason ground his paper cup into a ball and looked directly at Bobby. "All right, Sean. There's been more than one. I admit that. I'm trying to be honest here. But this guy—Brian—we want to be together. It just feels right. I was hoping you could understand, y'know, based on our history."

Bobby could feel the quiver down in his loins. Not a sexual stirring, as he usually experienced with Jase, but a fear, the fear of loss, loss happening right before his eyes. When you don't see it coming, it devastates you, he thought. The world turns, but it is never the same again.

"What I'm saying," Jason continued, "is that when you're in New York, I hope you think about us. I'm willing to move out, but maybe you might want to and then Brian and I..."

Bobby raised his hand again. "Jason, fuck you." He started to stand.

"Sean, I was hoping you would understand!" Jason reached for his arm.

"I'm going to my flight, Jase. When I get back from New York, you be gone from the apartment."

He turned toward the concourse, never once looking back.

—

"Good morning, Dominic."

Marty folded his topcoat over his arm and walked into Rocco Apostoli's office. The great man himself sat behind his ornate desk, making very sure he kept the desk between them. I'm more important than you, was the message being conveyed.

As Dominic closed the door behind them, Marty strolled confidently toward one of the straight back chairs in front of the desk. He glanced at Rocco but said nothing, playing the same game as Apostoli. Fuck him, and any sign of respect. When he got it from Apostoli, he would return it.

Apparently Apostoli had decided on a new strategy, other than his normal pillage and burn, because he suddenly stood and started to move around the desk. "Thanks for coming by, Marty. You want something to drink?"

"Coffee, if you have some. Black."

Rocco picked up the phone and spoke to the secretary. He then pulled the other straight back over to the side and sat down. "We got off to a bad start a couple of weeks ago," he began. "You riled me up and I...No, let me say that a different way. Let's just say we got off wrong. From my view, I say let's forget that..."

What the hell does he want? Marty wondered.

There was a knock on the door followed by the entry of a young woman chewing what looked like either a wad of tobacco or bubble gum and holding a tray. She placed it on the coffee table next to the desk, turned and left.

Marty decided to play along. He extended his hand. "Let's forget it."

Rocco nodded toward the coffee. "Help yourself."

Dominic Saladna sat alone on the couch at the side of the room, saying nothing, waiting to speak only when spoken to. Marty stood, poured the coffee, and sat back down. Rocco never moved from his chair. He leaned forward. "I need your help on a matter, Marty."

"How can I help?" Marty asked warmly.

"It's a North Shore problem," Rocco said. "That's your territory and Dominic's here."

"What problem?" Marty asked.

"You know my brother Vic don't you?"

Marty shook his head. "I don't think so."

Rocco waved it off. "No reason you should know him. He's not in the business. He's my older brother. Lives down in Ipswich. He's one of them environmentalists. Has a home with fuckin' signs all over the bathroom, y'know? So you can't even take a leak. Sign says 'If it's yellow, let it mellow. If it's brown, flush it down.'

"He's a good guy, though. Except for worryin' about some asshole shark gettin' bitten by a human. Shit like that. Too bad he didn't worry more about his fuckin' family instead of some squirrel gettin' his ass kicked. He's got a daughter Ellen. She flunked out of BU and he sent her on a world tour to find herself. Only problem with that is she decided to find the supply everywhere from Cartagena to Cairo along the way instead. When she got to Cairo, she found some rich sand nigger and married him—a guy by the name of Mustafa Talik."

Marty swallowed some of the coffee, trying to hide his surprise.

"You heard about him?" Apostoli asked.

"He was murdered in Marblehead the other night," Marty said.

"And my niece with him," Apostoli replied.

"I'm sorry to hear that, Rocco."

"You know anythin' about it?" Rocco asked.

"Why should I?"

Rocco gave him his hard stare. "It's your territory, Marty...the North Shore, Marblehead," he said almost too emphatically.

Marty bit his lower lip while he considered a reply. Jack had taught him the importance of careful responses to difficult questions or situations, to evaluate always and not feel the necessity of a quick answer.

He decided to challenge the inference in a calm manner. "It's my territory, Rocco, but I have nothing going on in Marblehead. You know that. We're not into house invasions. My action's in the big cities."

Rocco wouldn't let it go. "Last I saw Marblehead is still on the North Shore. You and Dominic here are responsible for what goes down around there, far as I'm concerned."

Leaning forward, Marty reached for the coffee cup. "Is that right, Rocco?"

"What do you hear?" Rocco persisted.

"Nothing. And unless I hear a little friendlier tone from you, I won't be hearing anything soon either."

Rocco sat forward in his seat. "Who the hell you think you're talkin' to?"

"You really want an answer to that?"

Dominic decided to speak for the first time. "Hey, we're all friends here."

Rocco pointed an index finger at his subordinate. "You shut the fuck up. You talk too much anyway. My niece's dead, there's millions in jewels missing, and I expect you guys to find out—and fast—what happened."

Marty stood to leave for the second time in his two meetings with Apostoli. "I can't help you, Rocco, and I don't work for you. Your people got iced, so it's your problem not mine."

"Sit down you lousy harp!" Apostoli screamed.

Marty turned on his heel and walked straight to the door.

23

Terry Cavanaugh whirled her around the floor of the Palace nightclub near the Saugus/Malden line, while Billy Joel's new song, "Uptown Girl" blared through the loudspeakers. He liked that video on television, the one where a well-dressed Christie Brinkley strolled through steam and smoke and mixed with the blue-collar guys.

When the number ended, he searched out Mick Riley and his girl over near the bar. If they left soon, they could drive over to the Breakheart Reservation and get laid and still get home in time to beat his curfew. Usually that peckerhead of a probation officer called him a couple of times a week around midnight.

"Let's split. Go get somethin' to eat," he said, squeezing the hand of the stacked blond he had met earlier in the evening.

"You're on," Mick replied. "You hungry?" he asked the redheaded friend of the blonde.

"Starved!" she screamed above the din.

They walked out to the parking lot, heading for Terry's car. Laughing among themselves, they didn't notice the four men studying them as they strolled deeper into the lot. Suddenly the men stepped out of a green Cadillac parked just two spaces to the right of Terry's car.

"Hey!" their leader yelled in the direction of the group. The four held baseball bats along their sides, the weapons partially hidden by their long coats. They paused a few yards in front of Terry.

"What can we do for you guys?" Terry asked, stopping dead in his tracks.

"What you can do, smart-ass, is get rid of the girls," the burly leader replied. He did the talking, but he looked like the weak link. The other three looked like exactly what they were—in-shape enforcers.

"Why?" Terry asked. "Why ruin the night? We have places to go." He felt behind his short leather jacket for the knife, the only weapon he had.

"Get rid of them!" the leader commanded.

"Go wait over there for us, girls," Terry said, pointing to a large empty space at the rear of the lot. "We'll be right along."

As they half walked and half ran away, Terry turned, a huge smile on his face. "What's the problem, gentlemen?"

"You. You're the fuckin' problem, Cavanaugh," the leader said. "We're goin' to break your balls so you'll know enough in the future to stay out of Rocco Apostoli's territories. Cabeesh?"

Terry laughed out loud. "Talk's cheap, fucker. Come right ahead," he beckoned.

Brandishing the bats, the burly man and one of the muscle men moved toward him, while the other two advanced on Mick. As the leader lifted his bat high to strike, Terry grabbed it with his left hand and with his right stabbed the second man in his shoulder just as his bat struck Terry high on the shoulder. He tried not to think of the pain as he withdrew the knife. He wrestled the bat away from the leader and saw his horrified look as his friend sank to the asphalt.

Terry swung the bat full force into the leader's body, causing him to topple. He turned quickly and advanced on the other two, who had Mick on the ground swinging their weapons across his back. With both hands he swung the bat across the legs of the one about to strike Mick and then as the fourth man turned to face him, raised his leg and kicked him in the groin. He swerved around, but there was no other action. All four lay on the ground, either unconscious or moaning. He bent toward Mick and helped him to his feet. It looked as if his left arm had been broken.

He unlocked the car from the passenger side and assisted Mick to the seat. He closed the door and looked around the lot. No sign of the girls now, and no sign yet of the police. He had a few more seconds.

He walked back to the attackers and kicked each one in the head before he returned to the car. His shoulder throbbed with pain, but he could move the muscles. Nothing was broken.

He drove past the lobby and headed out Route 1 back to Boston. He felt pretty good, and he hadn't even gotten laid.

—

He hadn't seen his mother this happy in a year. Sheila Kelly lifted her mai-tai—the only one she would allow herself—and offered a toast.

"Judith, it is such a pleasure getting to know you." She smiled effusively and placed her other hand on top of Jerry's.

As the highly efficient wait staff bustled about the aisles of the largest volume Chinese restaurant in New England, Marty thought he saw a quick, passing smile cross his father's face. They sat in a booth just off the dance floor at the Kowloon in Saugus. In the background the three-piece band warmed up by playing a few bars of "Let's Hear It For the Boy." Next to them, two little children tossed pennies into the reflecting pool that ran from the main dining entrance right down the center of the restaurant.

"Thank you so much, Mrs. Kelly. I..."

"Sheila. And Jerry. Don't make us sound so old," Sheila admonished.

Shortly after New Year's Day, Marty had brought her to Copeland Road to meet his parents. And they had taken to her right away. Probably because she was a professional woman, and probably because they hoped she could change him. For his part, he only knew that more and more he felt whole, coalesced, when they were together. Across the table, with the subtle lighting, Judith's face looked like no other. To him, she was the most beautiful woman in existence. Tonight she was wearing a black dress with thin shoulder straps. She turned her wine glass by the stem and smiled across at him.

"How's the food services business these days, Jerry?" she asked.

His father sipped his mai-tai and grinned. "Couldn't be better, Judith. We're getting new contracts to supply some of the new hotels being developed or renovated around Boston—The Westin, the new Copley Plaza."

"Let's do a story," she suggested. "Sounds like it could be really interesting."

"I forgot to ask you last time we met what kind of reporting you do," Jerry replied.

"City. I'm involved with the City section. I cover almost anything that concerns Boston. New hotels and how they're serviced would interest our readers."

"Then why don't you come out to our headquarters in Wakefield right along Lake Quannipawoit, and we'll sit down and talk."

"You've got a date," she said coyly, jabbing an index finger toward him.

Whatever else she was, she was helping him reconnect with his family. They liked her, who wouldn't?

Did she know of his "other business" his father had asked him when they were alone recently. Not in any detail, but yes she knew he was involved.

"Another lemonade, Marty?" Bobby, the lead waiter asked, appearing, as always, right on time, teasing his long time customer about his propensity for mai-tai's.

"I'm set, Bobby," Marty replied, covering the glass with the palm of his hand.

He decided it was time to make his announcement. "Mom, Dad, your anniversary's coming up in April. Judith and I have a little surprise for you." He reached into his sport coat and pulled out the airline tickets.

"We're going to Ireland in April. For a week. And we both want you to accompany us as our guests."

Sheila placed both hands along the side of her face. "Oh, Marty. We haven't been in years! What with the press of business for your father and all..." She beamed her radiant smile of twelve months ago—before she had learned that her only child was the heir apparent of the Irish mob.

Jerry looked at her silently, just for a moment. He turned to Marty and raised his glass. "Let's do it. I need a break, and I'm sure you do too."

Marty winked across at Judith and held her eyes. He loved those eyes. And he loved her and the way she moved. The way she held herself. What was the name of that old song the band was now playing? "Love Is a Many-Splendored Thing." He had to agree.

24

"You haven't said anything, have you?" Luis Gomez asked apprehensively, his eyes darting around the basketball court at the Lynn YMCA, acting as if the Frankenstein monster were about to pay him a visit.

Timmy stood at the foul line, perspiration dripping from his brow as he brought the ball to eye level and let it fly. Swish. Marty retrieved it and tossed it back to him. They always ended the three on threes or one on ones with a foul-shooting competition. Twenty shots. Whoever finished second bought breakfast. At 8:00 a.m. there were only a few others utilizing the basketball court, most choosing the track or the pool instead.

Beyond the end line Luis stood with his arms folded across his chest. "Have you?" he repeated.

"No. What went wrong, Luis?" Marty asked softly.

Gomez was dressed in cream-colored slacks and a forest green polo shirt in anticipation of spring. He had called last night, asking to see them as soon as possible. The Y was as good a place as any, Marty had felt.

"Ten out of thirteen so far," Timmy yelled out.

"The broad was on coke. She was out of her fuckin' mind and set me and Felipe off."

"Were you and him using?" Marty asked.

"What difference does that make?"

"Lower your voice, Luis," Marty directed. "Did you know the broad was Apostoli's niece?" he added.

"Now I fuckin' know. Then I didn't. Fuckin' scag wouldn't shut up so I popped her."

"Fifteen out of eighteen!" Timmy announced.

"How about him?" Marty asked.

"He wuz blabbin' some A-rab talks about bein' connected. We decided to ice him, too."

"You still have the jewels?" Marty asked as Timmy joined them.

"Sixteen of twenty. Let's see you beat that, cousin," he bragged.

Marty walked to the line and flexed. He bounced the round ball a few times and then released it.

"I got 'em, and I'm not doin' anything with them right now."

"Good. That would be my advice," Timmy said.

"I came to find out what the word is, y'know, out on the street," Luis said, his eyes dancing.

"Apostoli's inquiring," Timmy replied. "Jesus, Luis, you never told us the Arab was tied to Apostoli."

"My fuckin' research was wrong, is all."

"Yeah, I guess so," Marty said from the line.

"Do I have to worry about you guys?" Luis asked. He looked around the gym as if expecting Apostoli at any moment.

"The hell with Apostoli," Marty said. "Our discussion is strictly between you, Tim and me. That's ten out of fourteen," he added.

"He's never going to hear anything from us," Timmy said.

"We told you before Luis. We're out of it. We were never in it. Your business is your business," Marty said.

Luis Gomez relaxed noticeably. "I'm gonna wait till the heat dies down. Then fence the jewels."

"You do whatever you have to do, Luis," Timmy said.

Gomez nodded and headed for the stairwell.

"That's fifteen of twenty," Marty said, grabbing the last rebound and putting it back in.

"If Sister Drucilla back at St. Joseph's was right, fifteen doesn't beat sixteen," Timmy laughed. "You buy."

—

Bobby came home because he needed to come home. What was that poem he had learned back at the Stanley School in Swampscott when he was a kid? "Home is the sailor, home from the sea and the hunter home from the hill," it had gone.

He wanted to be around the people who loved him, he thought, but as he sat in the dining room of his mother's home, she gushing all over her oldest son, that slug Dr. Aronson pontificating, he wasn't so sure. At least Tim was here.

"Eat, Bobby dear," his mother was saying, making too much of him as always, so proud of his stature—her son the movie star. Timmy winked at him to show his understanding. The favorite son was home.

David Aronson carefully placed three strawberries on top of his ice cream and added just a dollop of cream. At the moment he was intent on exhibiting his vast knowledge of the arts, particularly the theater, and, in his own way, letting Bobby know he worked in an inferior venue.

"Olivier is indomitable. What's he now? 75? Yes, probably 75." He answered his own question to be sure no one else had the chance to speak. "And look at him. I read the other day he's over in London now, at 75, carrying the crushing weight of playing King Lear on the stage. Amazing. There are lines from the play that fit him—Lawrence Olivier—to the tee. 'No, I will weep no more. In such a night/To shut me out. Pour on; I will endure!' And he has endured. He's the absolute best."

"Do you agree, Bobby?" his mother asked. Bobby really didn't want to get into a discussion with the asshole. He glanced at Tim who was giving him a look that read that he, too, wondered why their mother had taken up with this bore.

Bobby was sure he knew why. Marjorie had always loved the arts, and culture, and professional people—Aronson fit a category. Unfortunately, in this case his mother could not distinguish the wheat from the chaff.

Sensing his discomfort, Timmy spoke up, trying to change the subject. "So you had a break in your schedule?"

Bobby nodded. "I was in New York for a few days."

"What's happening down there, dear?" Marjorie asked.

"There's a new movie going to be filmed in New York and Waterbury, Connecticut. 'Falling in Love' with Robert DeNiro and Meryl Streep. The director—Ulu Grosbard—and DeNiro asked me to read for the part."

"DeNiro's rather pedestrian," Aronson said.

Bobby didn't respond.

"Did you actually meet him?" Marjorie asked.

"I did," Bobby nodded.

"Did you get the part?" Aronson asked.

Bobby shrugged his shoulders. "I don't know. The way it works is they test a number of people. They liked my work in 'The Big Chill'. We'll see."

"DeNiro has talent—no question about that. But he's become lazy recently. He wastes his talent," Aronson said, not letting it go.

"You think so, Bobby?" his mother asked.

Enough of this bullshit, Bobby thought. "I think DeNiro is our greatest living actor."

Across the table, Dr. Aronson scoffed and set his napkin to the side. "Greater than Olivier? Come now, Bobby," he laughed.

Bobby was the only one to note the change in Timmy's countenance. A hard look came across his face, his lips thinned, his eyes focused.

Bobby kept his voice even. "Could Olivier play the alienated psycho in 'Taxi Driver'? Could Olivier play a jazz saxophonist like DeNiro did in "New York, New York"? Could he change his weight drastically and play a boxer as DeNiro did in "Raging Bull"? I don't think so. Olivier can play the classics, a bit of comedy, but he has none of the range of DeNiro."

Aronson started to jump right back in. "My analysis..."

"Fuck your analysis," Timmy interrupted. He spoke softly. "You don't know shit from shinola about the movie business so why don't you just shut the fuck up and learn something."

Aronson looked like someone had shot him with a Glock.

"Timmy!" Marjorie practically screamed.

Timmy pushed back his chair. "Ma, you want to listen to this know-it-all be my guest. I'm leaving."

"I really have to go, too," Bobby said, standing.

Aronson sat there, slumping forward, a hurt look on his face, playing for sympathy. The Olivier of Swampscott, Bobby thought.

Marjorie stood and rushed to the doctor's side. "David, I'm so sorry. I..."

David raised a hand. "I'm all right," he finally sighed.

Bobby moved toward his mother and embraced her. "I'll call you in the morning, and we'll have breakfast."

Confused, she stood and then glared at Timmy. "We need to talk—and soon young man. I won't have my company..." She started to sob and left the room.

Out on the front porch, Bobby asked his brother for a ride into Boston. They drove down Humphrey Street, past Blockridge Field, toward Lynn, the ocean on their left.

"I'll make it right with her tomorrow," Timmy finally said.

"What she needs to hear is that she's dating a complete asshole, but she won't accept that," Bobby replied.

"Sorry I spoiled the party," Timmy said.

"If you hadn't, I would have."

Timmy looked across at him. "You seem awfully preoccupied tonight, Bob. Something wrong?"

Bobby didn't reply right away.

"An affair of the heart go wrong?" Timmy teased.

He could talk with his brother about anything—about acting, his dreams, his aspirations, even about Timmy's involvement in the crime and corruption. But he could never talk to him about a gay life, about his love for another man, his hurt at the break-up of that love. There was no way Timmy would ever understand those feelings.

"Something like that," he replied.

"There's lots of fish in the ocean," Timmy said.

No, there isn't, Bobby thought..

25

"I'm tellin' you, you gotta talk to Forelli in New York. You can do it, Gino. You can convince him to let me ice that son of a bitch."

Gino Petrelli let out a long sigh and looked for their waiter. Through the huge plate glass window of the Ritz dining room, he could see long-legged women carrying briefcases pushing against the wind that was rushing down Newbury Street. Occasionally old Yankee women from the neighborhood would walk by, most of them accompanied by a string of dogs, not your fuckin' manly looking dog but those little yapping Chihuahuas. Half of the one million-dollar plus condos in the neighborhood must contain those little shitters, Gino thought.

"What happened this time?" he finally asked Rocco.

"He walked out on me again, right in the middle of the discussion," Rocco fumed.

"Tell me about this so-called discussion," Gino said.

"What? Now you don't fuckin' believe me?" Rocco replied indignantly.

The waiter—the one that walked like he had a pole up his ass—approached them carrying the afternoon tea service.

Rocco watched Gino come alive when the pansy food arrived. Whenever he was in Boston, he wanted to meet at the Ritz. Not the North End, mind you, where they could be among their own, maybe have some nice antipasto and a glass of wine at mid-afternoon, but here in the middle of bankers, old crows with noses held high in the air, yuppies living off the old man's change. He looked at the waiter who, with gloved hands, poured tea as if he were delivering fuckin' pieces of gold. From a huge tray, he placed some scones, some cream and then some fresh strawberries in the center of the table.

"Take some," Gino directed, his eyes gleaming in anticipation.

"Fuck that shit," Rocco replied, the waiter acting as if he hadn't heard him. "Bring me a double scotch. You got any cheese and crackers?"

The waiter stood taller. "Sir, we have cheeses from Russia, Switzerland, Scandinavia..."

"How about America? You got any American cheese, like Kraft's?"

The waiter gained another half inch. "I believe we can find some, sir," he finally sniffed.

"Good. And try to deliver my double scotch sometime in the next half hour, will you, pal?"

As the waiter glided away, Gino Petrelli shook his head. He plastered his scone with cream and then pointed it in Rocco's direction.

"See the fuckin' attitude you have, Rocco? Look at you. Always up tight. Look around you. What do you see? People enjoying themselves is what. No one giving anyone a hard time except you, Rocco. I'm willing to bet your so-called discussion with Kelly was more like you giving him marching orders. That's what I think."

For a moment Rocco thought about pouring the bowl of strawberries over Gino's head. Just for a moment. Instead, he opted for a softer approach. Anger management, Gino had called it.

"Gino, he's pissin' in my face. I lost my niece, her husband, there's $4 million in jewels out there somewheres. You don't think Martin Kelly should be helpin' me with this problem?"

Gino dropped some cream onto his cloth napkin and looked disappointed at the loss. He paused, as the waiter delivered Rocco's drink and a tray of cheeses.

"Jesus! Will you look at this? A fuckin' fancy tray complete with Ritz crackers. Probably costs $25.00. I could buy fifteen boxes of crackers for what this is gonna cost."

Gino sighed audibly, but decided to stick to the subject. "You don't need Martin Kelly's help with this problem, Rocco. I want you to leave him to me. You find whoever killed your niece on your own. My guess is Kelly knows nothing about it. That cokehead of a son-in-law of yours probably talked too much in front of too many people about the jewels."

Rocco downed half of the double in one swallow. "I'm thinkin' the same thing. I'm lookin' at people who could have sold him the stuff. But it's a long list." Gino spooned out some more strawberries.

"Why do you keep hesitating on Kelly?" Rocco asked calmly.

Gino picked up another scone and dipped it into the cream. That's more like the way we do it in the North End, Rocco thought.

"First of all, he's protected by Forelli himself, and neither you or I need trouble from New York. Secondly, he's been producin' for us, or haven't you noticed? He keeps his people in order, and we get our cut of the businesses. He produces more from his territory than your pal Dominic Saladna over in Revere and as much as any of the rest of our guys all over New England."

"He shouldn't have those territories. Italians shouldn't be leasin' out their turf to an Irisher," Rocco replied.

"I agree," Gino said.

"You agree with me?"

"I always have."

"Then what are we arguin' about?"

Gino placed his elbows on the table and tented his fingers along the side of his mouth. "You trust my judgment, Rocco?"

Not if you keep eatin' this fag food and acting like some century old Brahmin, Rocco thought. But he answered diplomatically. "Of course, Gino."

"Then do me a small favor. Play this subtly. You know what I mean by subtle?"

Rocco thought for a moment. "To not show my true feelings?"

"Close enough. Calm down with Kelly. Smile at him once in a while. Help him to worry less about us. Get his guard down."

Rocco signaled to the waiter who stood against the wall, getting ready to pounce on anyone who let their water glass drop below three-quarters full. Too bad the fucker wasn't as fast with the scotches, Rocco thought. He held up his glass and pointed to it.

"Well?" Gino asked.

"I can do that. I can do subtle. But why are we waitin? What do we care if he's relaxed or not?"

Gino leaned forward across the table and lowered his voice. "My sources tell me Kelly's soon to have trouble with the feds. Both in New York, and up here they're going after the Irish gangs. God knows they've ragged our asses for years now. Broke up Raymond Patriaca, got some of our people on tax evasion, and now they're lookin' at the rise of other groups—the Irish, the chinks, the spics. And it's better for us that they are.

"When they're on him—and they will be—we show Forelli he can't handle it. Either he makes a big-time mistake out of impetuousness—he's not his uncle, you know, he doesn't have Jack's coolness—or we make one for him. Convince Forelli he's backin' the wrong pony. The kid's not the uncle, we tell him. Right now, he doesn't look all that bad."

Rocco nodded. "You want to fuck him up and have no blame back to us."

Gino pointed his index finger at Rocco. "Bingo!" he said. "But I need you to calm down for a while, let events transpire. Cabeesh? Besides which, I hear you got other problems."

Here comes the shit, Rocco felt. "Such as?"

"Such as some other harp kicked four of your guys' asses down in Saugus the other night way I hear it."

Rocco sat up straight. "Who told you that?" he replied indignantly.

"Never mind who told me. What I heard was a guy named Terry Cavanaugh shoved four bats up four guys' asses. Karate kicked one guy's ass across Route One."

"It'll be taken care of," Rocco said defensively.

"I'm sure," Gino replied derisively, searching his plate for a third scone.

26

Only in Boston does late winter begin on March 1 and stretch right to May 1. Whatever the calendar says, there is no such thing as spring. On March 17 the noonday showed bright but chill. A heavy snow had fallen over night, and clung still to the sidewalks outside Catherine Slattery's home in Jamaica Plain.

Inside, Marty, Timmy, and Ray Horan sat in the spacious and tastefully decorated open kitchen while Catherine cooked corned beef and cabbage at the stove. "I'm so glad to see you all," she was saying, so pleased they were honoring the tradition that Jack had initiated—visiting her on St. Patrick's Day.

At fifty-six, the woman herself was still striking. She stood tall and erect, with sculptured features, a straight nose, wide-set hazel eyes and glossy black hair piled high on her head. Leo Slattery's widow had never remarried, and all of the men there knew why.

"I saw Danny when he was in town recently," Marty said.

"Really? I didn't know that," Catherine responded. "What did he have to say?"

Marty considered her. "Not much. Just the usual family stuff. He says Christine is doing fine."

"Imagine. Two policemen—husband and wife—in the same family. Leo and Jack would turn over in their graves," Catherine laughed.

There was a small, appreciative chuckle from the men.

"To Jack and Leo," Ray said, raising his longneck on high.

"Cheers," Timmy said.

"How are you doing, Catherine? You need anything?" Marty asked.

"I keep busy volunteering my time over at Beth Israel. Danny and Christine come in from New York at least once a month. I'm doing all right," she smiled.

She placed the heaping platter of corned beef and cabbage on the table. "Help yourself to more beer if you like."

"Now how about your meeting a nice Irishman, someone to hug you, to take good care of you?" Timmy said, embracing her playfully on his way to the refrigerator.

"Just what I don't need at my age. Why is it that men always feel that a man is the answer to every girl's dream?"

Ray pursued it half in jest. "We want you to be happy, Catherine."

"Do I need to tell you what I think all three of you already know? I have my memories." For some reason she wanted to tell them directly. "I've been very lucky. I had a good marriage with Leo until he was killed. We raised a good son in Danny, and thanks to Jack after Leo was murdered, we didn't want for anything, including Danny's college education."

She stopped for a moment and locked her eyes on Timmy. "After Leo, I fell in love with your father, Tim. Oh, I don't think Jack knew that I loved him over all those years. He was more interested in other women after he and your mother were divorced. But, you know, just before he had that fatal heart attack, we began to spend time together and..." She stopped and dabbed at her eyes.

Timmy moved to her and placed an arm about her. "Catherine, don't be sad. Not today."

She raised her head, her smile overcoming the tears. "That's just it, Tim. I'm not sad. I loved your father, and after him, I only want the memories, not another man. There couldn't be another man, not after Jack."

Later, they sat in the living room, the television announcer interviewing that sportscaster, Bob Ryan, who was making the case that there had never been a better front line than Larry Bird, Kevin McHale, and Robert Parish in the entire history of the National Basketball Association.

"You need any money?" Marty asked Catherine.

"I'm fine, Marty. Really."

There was a momentary silence as the men focused on pictures of Bird driving the baseline, stopping dead in his tracks, and hoisting his shot over the outstretched arms of Magic Johnson.

"I need to say something to you," Catherine suddenly announced. "Could we turn that down just for a few minutes?"

Ray stood and killed the picture.

"Marty, you said when Danny visited you recently he talked about the family. Could I ask you—is that all he talked about?"

Marty studied her for a moment. "You don't need to get into this, Catherine."

"Did he tell you about the FBI focusing now on the Irish gangs?" she asked stridently.

Marty looked across to Timmy and Ray. "He started to, Catherine, but I discouraged his talking about it. I don't want to compromise his position with the Bureau. I..."

She raised a hand, looking exactly like the nuns back at St. Joseph's, the gesture a demand for silence. "That's bullshit, Marty, and you should know it. Danny is family. He owes you..."

Marty shook his head. "No, he doesn't."

Catherine persisted. "He does, and I do. Maybe you won't talk to him about it, but he still talks to me."

Marty cocked his head toward her. She wouldn't stay silent. "The word in New York is that the FBI has either infiltrated your crew or turned a member. No one knows his identity except the big mucky-mucks. But it has happened, Marty."

—

Terry Cavanaugh tried to sip the boiling lava they were selling as coffee, but then had to put it down quickly. Outside the restaurant across the street from Bunker Hill Community College, the mid-morning traffic wound its way across the Gilmore Bridge toward Boston and Cambridge. Even at 9:30 A.M., it would take most commuters an hour and a half to make the trip from a point ten miles north of Boston, into the city itself. In their frustration, motorists greeted the new day and one another by leaning on their horns and punctuating the air with middle fingers held on high.

From his booth in the rear, Terry rotated his shoulder, the pain still there, although nothing had been broken. Mick Riley had been less fortunate what with his left arm fractured in two places. Terry smiled to himself as he rubbed his shoulder. He now had almost fifteen clients paying him protection, a stable of whores out working the streets, a small amount of loan-sharking which would grow with the vigs each day, and the crack selling real good. He was progressing. The guy over in Malden—Nick Angelo—still refused to pay so just this morning he had instructed Mick to torch the fucker's place.

He looked at his watch. Mo should be here almost any minute.

Through the plate glass window, he spotted her Camry making the turn from Rutherford Avenue. She parked facing in and sat there momentarily, adjusting the rearview mirror, fixing her lipstick. And then he saw them. Two men dressed in down parkas pulled in two spaces away from her and studied her closely as she exited the Camry and headed toward the entrance.

As she walked into the restaurant, Terry riveted on the two men. They did not move. He guessed they would wait for a period of time, making sure of the logistics before following her inside.

Maureen practically flopped down in the seat across from him. "It's too early for a working girl to get up, it being school vacation week and all, but whenever my brother's willing to pay, I can be here," she sighed.

He looked over her shoulder toward the parking lot. They didn't have much longer.

He touched her hand. "You trust me, Mo?"

She smiled her Irish smile, the heartbreaker one. If Helen could launch a thousand ships, a smile from an Irish colleen could launch a million. "Of course," she replied.

"I want you to get up and leave."

"But why?"

He squeezed her hand. "Mo, just do as I say. Right now."

With an angry look, she stood and walked briskly across the restaurant floor. As she reached the front door, he felt behind his back for the Glock nine. He watched while she entered her car and then backed away. The two men acted exactly as he thought they would. They made no attempt to follow.

He stood and walked casually toward the men's room, pushed the door open with his foot, and entered. Quickly he checked the action on the Glock and chambered a round. They had followed her here from Southie. A clever tactic, he thought. Let his relatives and friends lead them right to him.

He estimated that by this time they would have entered the restaurant. He opened the door, his weapon at his side. Hugging the wall, he peered around the corner toward the front. The two men were now standing near the entrance, scanning the restaurant.

Terry dropped to a knee and sent a spurt from the semi-automatic across the room. As the two men fell backward, he stood, the weapon still at his side, and walked deliberately toward the door. He stepped over the bodies. He could hear the screams and the wailing of the customers, but never once looked anywhere but at the front door.

Once outside, he crossed the street and ran quickly down the steps into the underground subway station.

27

Dr. Paul Devlin certainly held one's attention. Tall and slender, he possessed a fine chiseled face, with gray hair swept back over his temples, and Irish blue eyes that were very pale. He studied Bobby Kelly with that translucent gaze from behind his metal desk. Outside his West 62nd Street office, a fiery orange sky had pushed the early morning fog out and harbingers of early spring could be seen virtually everywhere. Across the street, Central Park wrestled with the upcoming changes, buds appearing now on the trees, robins chirping away at the runners looping the roadway below them, the runners themselves dressed in shorts for the first time in months.

"I first thought it was mono, what with your having a sore throat, some fever, and the rash," Dr. Devlin was saying. "That's why I prescribed the antibiotics."

"Then why aren't they working, Doctor? I've been missing from 'La Cage aux Folles' for two weeks now. Thank God they're delaying the start of that new movie I was telling you about because I don't feel great right now."

Dr. Devlin's pale eyes were thoughtful. "I'm afraid I have some bad news for you."

Bobby sat forward in the chair and knitted his brow. "I'm listening."

"You're HIV positive, Sean." The doctor let it hang there in the air for a long moment.

Bobby shrugged his shoulders. "What does that mean?"

"Have you been reading at all about AIDS?"

"I have AIDS?" Bobby asked, astonished.

Devlin raised his hand from the desk. "No, I didn't say that. What you have is a virus. Let me take this from the beginning.

"In the late 70's this HIV infection probably first appeared. We're just learning now—some four years later—that when the infection enters a human cell, it becomes directly incorporated into that cell's DNA and can rest there for years. The real name for the infection is human immunodeficiency virus. Blood transfusion researchers first got a clue to the severity of the virus this year. Just two months ago, the researchers discovered through a study that infected patients all had received blood transfusions. So now we suspect that AIDS can be transmitted through blood products."

Bobby winced noticeably. "You're losing me, Doctor. What is the difference between HIV and AIDS?"

The doctor stood, came around, and sat on the edge of the desk. "AIDS is not one disease, Sean. We're early into this, but what AIDS is is a susceptibility to many diseases. It is caused by HIV. The virus destroys one type of the body's white cells which, in turn, weakens your immune system, lowering resistance to some infections and certain types of cancer. These 'opportunistic' diseases are rarely found in a person with a healthy immune system."

Bobby stared at him for a moment. "But I haven't had any blood transfusions in the last ten years," he protested.

The doctor nodded vigorously. "Then I have to lead in to a very critical question. We've known about AIDS since 1981. What we didn't know is that the

HIV infection could be transmitted by blood donors." He paused for a moment and studied his hands. "We've also known for some time that the HIV infection can be transmitted through semen or vaginal fluids. Here in New York and practically in Los Angeles and San Francisco, we've seen among the homosexual population—people who theoretically should be healthy—a surge in the number of HIV infections and, subsequently, in AIDS. The same thing is happening among drug users. Are you homosexual, Sean, or could you have used any infected needles when taking drugs?"

Bobby paused before answering. Out in L.A., drugs were everywhere. He had been at party after party where spoons and needles—two of the requisite tools for mixing speedballs—were easy to come by. But he had never been tempted.

"I've had a male lover—one—for the last two years. But it's been over for three months now," he finally replied.

"That's probably how you contacted the virus," the doctor said quietly. "I suspected something was wrong when your symptoms didn't clear up."

"But I don't have AIDS, you said." Bobby said it too rapidly, the fear showing in his voice.

"No, you don't," the doctor replied gently.

"What do I do then?"

"There's a drug I'm going to prescribe for you—AZT or Zidovudine. It's new, but I believe it delays the development of AIDS in the case of many HIV-positive patients like yourself. There's not a lot of history here yet, Sean. But you should have hope. In the early research studies that have been conducted, we've found that some people move rapidly—in say a year or two—and develop AIDS while others do not. There can be a prolonged period of relatively good health."

Bobby realized that he really wasn't hearing the doctor as he continued to talk. HIV positive. There were so many questions to ask that he didn't really know where to begin. He stood and walked to the window while the doctor babbled on—some more about hope, something about the condition not necessarily being a death sentence...something about the medication.

Over in Central Park, he observed a teacher directing a column of small children to hold hands as they traversed the walkway. Their youth made him suddenly feel both very sad and very cold.

"What you're telling me is that I'm going to die," Bobby blurted it out, trying hard to hold his composure.

"There's good reason for hope, Sean. You can't lose hope. We'll watch your CD4 cell count in the months ahead," Dr. Devlin said. "I'll want to see you every two weeks, sooner if you have any signs of a problem."

"Like what?" Bobby asked, focusing once again.

"You could remain in otherwise good health for years, or you could experience symptoms such as fatigue, fevers, a dry cough, weight loss. Will you be in New York for the near future?"

Bobby nodded. "I'll be here. Between the play and the new movie, I'll be around. Funny, I just heard I got the part in the new DeNiro movie and now this."

"Sean, one more thing. I realize I'm hitting you with a lot at one time, but you need to tell your partner..."

"He's not my partner anymore," Bobby interrupted.

The doctor paused for a beat. "Even so, he needs to know—if he doesn't already."

"What do you mean?"

Devlin raised a quizzical eyebrow. "How long since you've seen him?"

"Three months," Bobby replied.

"You may want to look him up," Devlin said. "See how he is. Let him know of your situation."

Bobby did not respond.

—

Maureen Cavanaugh flipped through the incomplete papers and passed them over to Maria Goncalves. "I've asked him to stay after school so that I might help him, but Willie refuses. Can you influence him, Mrs. Goncalves? Help him to understand that with a little effort he can be a good student?"

Maria Goncalves looked like thirty going on fifty. She was missing a front tooth and her eyes wandered, her pupils dilated, another urban renewal mother, almost incapable of taking care of herself, let alone her four children. But she had come by when she had received Maureen's note, which was more than most of the mothers and fathers did.

"As I said, I'll speak to him, Miss Cavanaugh," she said quietly. "Right now he seems to want to run with the gang."

"I'll be here for him, Mrs. Goncalves. If we could work together..."

She was interrupted by the school secretary standing at the open classroom door. "Miss Cavanaugh, there's an urgent personal call for you. What would you like me to do?"

"Put it through to the teachers' lounge. I'll be there in a minute," she replied.

She turned to Maria Goncalves. "Do you have any other questions for me, Mrs. Goncalves?"

"No, and please call me Maria."

Maureen smiled at her. "Maria, I look forward to working with you. You get him here, and I'll provide the extra help. Together we'll show him he can do the work."

She stood and walked with Maria down the first floor corridor. "The gangs will do nothing for him. We need to help him understand that," she added.

She stopped outside the teachers' lounge and offered her hand. "Thank you for coming, Maria."

Nodding, Maria Goncalves headed to the front door, turned, and mouthed "Thank you" before exiting.

Maureen entered the lounge and picked up the phone. "Yes? This is Maureen Cavanaugh."

"Mo, it's me."

She kept silent for a minute. "Terry, what happened?" she finally asked quietly.

"Two fuckin' Italians had a grudge against me."

"They're dead! And you killed them!" she screamed.

"Calm your water down, Mo. What was I supposed to do? Let them fuckin' shoot me?" he screamed back.

For a moment Maureen toyed with the telephone cord, twisting it while she tried to regain her composure. "Why did they have a grudge against you, Terry?" she finally asked, calmly.

She could picture him shrugging his shoulders, taking his time so that he could manufacture more bullshit. "It's a territorial problem," he finally said.

"Territorial?" Her voice shot up an octave. "Is that what you said, Terry? What are you, fuckin' dogs?"

"Sis, listen to me. I'll get this problem under control. In the meantime, I won't be around for a while. It's better that way."

She started to cry. "Terry, what's going to become of you? You've shot two men..."

"Defensively," he interjected. "I'll be fine, Mo. I'll be in contact." And then he hung up.

She sat there alone, thinking—of Terry, and of Willie Goncalves, and of mothers like Mary Cavanaugh and Maria Goncalves, and of the ugly pull of the city. And then she thought of Eugene O'Neill's line from "A Moon for the Misbegotten."

"There is no present or future—only the past, happening over and over again—now."

28

"So you see, Marty, I come to you. I come for justice, which I hope you can provide. For old times' sake."

It was a good weekend, Marty felt, except for the dead husband. He sat with Ginger Dalton and Ray Horan in his living room on Lynn Shore Drive. Ginger was still something to see, and he knew he was not the only man in the city with eyes for the job. She was dressed in a blue woolen suit, cut at the knee, exposing thigh, which he knew she knew he had noticed. Her lips were too maroon, and there were lines along her mouth. She's still pretty, but worn, he thought.

"You and Charlie were so close, Marty, like brothers. When we were all at Lynn English—when was it? Just a little more than ten years ago? When you and I broke up, I took up with him."

She smiled as memories came flowing back. "Do you remember we had open campus at English at that time? The dumb school people felt we could learn more by leaving the building part of each day and talkin' with the store owners or the businessmen. Half of them were peddling pot to us, remember?"

Marty smiled at her and laughed. "Ray, would you get Ginger another drink," he said.

From the doorway Ray unfolded his arms and moved toward the kitchen.

"Those were good times, Ginger. Charlie was a terrific basketball player, and we had a great coach in Ron Bennett," Marty said.

"We had a ball, didn't we?" she said.

Ray handed her the scotch and soda and quietly moved to a corner seat.

She got right back to it. "You're busy, Marty, and I appreciate your seeing me. Did you know Charlie served time?" she added, too quickly, the memory of it all over her.

"Yes," he replied quietly.

"For fraud. Oh, he was guilty all right. He became a lawyer and started bustin' into people's estate trusts. You read all about that? We were living in Sudbury then, high off the hog. He started with the drugs, y'know? That's what changed him."

She straightened her dress as she uncrossed her legs. "While he was in prison in Pennsylvania—one of those minimum security facilities—he got into trouble with this drug dealer peddlin' stuff right within the walls. He took a lot of stuff and then didn't have the money to pay the guy back. The dealer was some Roxbury businessman. He had Charlie killed, Marty. Oh, it was made to look like an accident. A vehicle backed into him, crushed him against a wall. He was murdered, Marty. One of his close friends in there told me the story when he got out of the slammer."

"Is the Roxbury guy still in there?" Marty asked.

She shook her head. "No, he's back home operating a real estate office over on Dudley Street."

"What's his name?"

"Dana Carter."

Marty sipped his highball and then placed it back on the table. "And what do you want from me, Ginger?"

She touched her eyes with the handkerchief she had been twisting in her lap. "Over the years, I've been reading of your uncles and the allegations about them. I don't know whether you're a part of the life like people say you are, but if you are, Marty, I'm asking for your help."

The anger flared in her eyes. "I would like him dealt with Marty. He took my Charlie's life and left me with nothing. Charlie was a good man, a thief yes, but he wouldn't hurt a fly. It's wrong what happened, and I want justice. I don't have anything now, but..."

He raised a hand. "That's not necessary, Ginger."

"Will you help me?" she pleaded.

He didn't reply right away. "I'll get word to you," he finally said.

As if on signal, Ray stood to help her with her coat. A few seconds later, Marty walked her to the door.

"Will you?" she asked once more.

"I'll get back to you," he repeated, as he opened the door.

He walked through the kitchen and made himself another CC and ginger. Ray stood in the doorway, arms folded. "What do you think?" he asked.

"You check out the whole story through our sources. Charlie Dalton was good people when I knew him. He was my best friend growing up. He lived right below Copeland Road on Lynnfield Street. I was always in his home, and he in mine. And Ginger was my first serious girl. My mother loved her. We were all close. When I knew Charlie, he was no troublemaker. I lost touch over time, you know? Check out the story."

"And if it checks?" Ray asked.

"Make sure this Carter's dealt with."

"Who do you want on it?" Ray asked.

"You been looking into what Catherine warned us about?"

"Carefully. So far, I don't see anything. There's no word or sign of an informer or any infiltration of our group."

Marty sat down at the kitchen table. "We need to see it coming, Ray. The new guy—Gil Rafferty—that Chris brought in, how's he doing?"

Ray smiled. "Because he's new, I've been payin' extra attention to him. He seems legit. Moved here from New York where some people vouched for him, friends of Chris's."

Marty ran his index finger across the bridge of his nose. "If Ginger's story checks out, assign Gil Rafferty. Let's see him make his bones on this one."

Ray remained silent for a moment. It was highly unusual for anyone except Marty to meet alone with the individual assigned to do murder. Such matters were never discussed at group meetings and the leader was the only one who would both designate and order a kill.

"You're not going to meet with him?" Ray asked, surprise in his voice.

"You tell him," Marty said.

"I don't get it, Marty. Why the change?"

Marty moved to the counter and poured another shot of CC. "Let's just go step by step. I have a hunch as to how he might react."

—

Early the next morning, he decided to take a drive, partially to clear his head of the amber and partially to think. Jack had often stressed the importance of time alone. Time alone to either forget about problems, or to think about them and weigh potential solutions. His uncle would use running for this purpose. He preferred basketball.

Marty dressed himself in a fleece top and bottom over a Polo sweat shirt and drove across downtown Lynn, heading toward the outdoor basketball courts at the Meadow.

His city had changed so much in recent years, he thought as he crossed by the scene of the Second Great Lynn Fire. Just two years ago, the night sky had been illuminated as entire blocks of the downtown had been leveled, with brick leather factories and apartment houses collapsing into the streets. It had taken two weeks to put out the fire, and it had left behind emotional scars still felt today. Seventeen buildings had been destroyed, with the prospect of economic recovery grim.

He summoned a faint, sad smile. Jack had taught him to love Lynn, regaling him with stories of his youth when, during the war years, the city had truly flourished—100,000 people, many of them employed at the huge General Electric plant, turning out the very first jet engines, joining together to defeat the Japanese and the Germans. People unified for a purpose—the Irish, the Greeks, the Poles, the Italians. He had sat at his uncle's knee, fascinated by his stories of the immigrants who had traveled to Lynn's shores and how, when they all pulled together for a common purpose, they had improved the quality of life for all.

Clearly, there was a tear in that fabric today—people interested now essentially in themselves, split by a me-tooism that hurt his city, as well as the nation.

The drive toward suburbia sprawl had also hurt the city, the downtown of his uncle's youth now lost to the new malls that had arisen in neighboring Peabody and Burlington. He turned down Chestnut Street, taking note that the children and grandchildren of European immigrants no longer inhabited the two-family houses or three-decker apartment dwellings along the route. Instead, Asian-Americans, Blacks, and the Hispanics had taken over the center of the city.

Could they lead Lynn's resurgence? Jack had taught him to believe they could. It might take twenty years of so, but the city will come back, he had insisted. The new minorities will become empowered eventually, and a new common purpose will emerge to unite them.

He pulled to the curb next to Lynn English High School and the Meadow, a flat parkland stretching for blocks with the school lying on its western edge. As a boy, Marty had participated with other "Meadowlarks" from Lynn's multiplicity of neighborhoods in games of football, baseball, and basketball, the action transpiring over the different locations in the park, the boys organizing themselves in the 70's, disdaining the need for parental involvement.

He stood alone on the court, the weather still a bit cold in late March for most to partake. He had his routine, and he followed it. Dribbling from out beyond the foul line, he drove to the basket and laid the ball against the glass. Lay-ups required discipline—they weren't showy like some fuckin' tomahawk dunk, but they were fundamental in the scheme of things, and whatever your business, you had better know the fundamentals, Jack had insisted. After fifteen minutes, he practiced his jump shot, stopping on a dime right around the top of the key and arching one-handers toward the hoop.

Routines also enabled you to drift a bit, to think about people, as well as problems, and most often the two were entwined. He thought of his father and mother and of the upcoming trip to Ireland. Hopefully the time together would help improve his relationship with Jerry. Funny, he contemplated, I think of Jack, dead and in the grave, more often than Jerry. But the love for his father was there, always on the cusp. It was his focus on the life that brought back memories of Jack so frequently to him.

He started a game of "21" with himself, moving around in a circle to different spots on the asphalt, launching the ball from maybe twenty feet away each time, racing to retrieve the ball for a bunny, keeping score against an imaginary opponent. Two points for a long shot, one point for the layup, provided he made the long shot.

The life. He loved the life, and he would never give it up for any reason. He felt whole involved in the life—in the decision making, the leading of men, the growth of their enterprises, the competition. Like Jack, he came alive with the action.

He moved to the foul line for the first of one hundred shots he intended to take. He thought of Apostoli and their relationship, which was going nowhere. It never would, and he understood why. The Mafioso was a hothead, and to a degree so wasn't he. He needed to work on that. He needed to try harder to control himself when he perceived bad behavior personally directed.

But whatever he did, Apostoli wouldn't be happy until the territories were his again. Someone had to be controlling him, probably Petrelli in Providence, or maybe even Forelli himself in New York. He guessed the former. Petrelli and Apostoli weren't moving against him now because New York wouldn't allow it, so they were waiting, waiting for some serious error on his part. The guy in Providence was probably smarter than Apostoli. Whatever, he was showing results, and they had no cause to move on him. Yet—he reminded himself. He needed to keep his guard up.

Forty out of fifty so far, he mused. Not bad.

It was the other business that worried him more. There was no doubt in his mind that Catherine had passed on reliable information. There was now an infiltrator in their midst. Who? he wondered. Or maybe a turncoat. His intuition told him it was the latter. Someone of his regular group who had been compromised. He thought of the new guy Rafferty that Chris Kiley had introduced—the only new person to join their group in a year. The fuckin' FBI is as crooked as any of us, he thought. In their quest for gang leaders, they were perfectly capable of committing crimes themselves. If Rafferty was FBI, or some other kind of cop, he would stop at murder, wouldn't he? We'll soon find out, Marty thought.

Eighty-one of hundred. Coach Bennett would be proud of his old point guard.

29

Bobby Kelly drove into Beverly Hills with a head full of questions. The offices of the public relations firm of Kramer and Steinberg were located in a nondescript building behind a gift shop on Brighton Way. Parking his '75 Mercedes directly in front of the shop, he considered his watch. 9:00 A.M.

Palm trees swayed in the faint April sunlight, the smog peeling away in the distance. At this early hour, executives hurried along the sidewalk, casting glances at their watches. LA was as uptight a town as New York, Bobby felt, despite the media depictions of California cool.

He walked behind the shop to the six-story art-deco building and entered the lobby. Although he had never been in the building before, he remembered Jason telling him of the firm's third floor location. He pressed the elevator button and the doors opened both for him and for a very attractive young lady. As the doors closed, she looked at him and smiled. When he didn't smile back, she looked straight ahead.

On the third floor, he walked toward a central station where a pretty young starlet-to-be welcomed him with another smile. "Yes, sir, what can I do for you?"

"I'm looking for Jason Ellison," Bobby replied.

"He no longer works here," she announced, flashing her teeth, as if the news was good news.

"He doesn't?" Bobby replied, his eyebrows shooting up.

She met his surprised look, her eyes unblinking. "No."

"Did he leave a forwarding address?"

She gave him a skeptical look. "I don't have that. Could I ask about your business with him?"

Bobby paused, gazing at her, puzzled. "I'm a friend. A close friend. When I got in from New York last night, I called his apartment. The phone was disconnected, and when I went over there, the manager told me he had moved out. Isn't there someone who might be able to put me in touch?"

"Wait a minute," she replied, picking up a phone and dialing a number. "What's your name?"

He told her.

"Mr. Lambert? There's a Sean Kielty here inquiring about Jason. He says he's a close friend." A very long pause followed. "All right," she finally said. "Mr. Lambert will be right with you," she told Bobby.

Within a minute, a handsome man in his early forties appeared from the corridor to the left. "Hello, I'm Steve Lambert, Mr. Kielty. Come with me."

He escorted Bobby to a commodious office, a suite of walnut and leather reminiscent to Bobby of a men's club. He pointed to a leather couch behind a coffee table. "Let's sit over here, Sean Kielty. 'The Big Chill' right?" he asked.

"That's right."

"You were good."

"Thanks, Mr. Lambert..."

"Steve. Please call me Steve." His smile was perfunctory. "So you're trying to locate Jason Ellison." Lambert shifted on the couch. "How well do you know him?" he asked.

Bobby decided to reply honestly. "We lived together for a time," his tone even.

Lambert nodded knowingly and decided to proceed. "All we know is that he moved to San Francisco. About six weeks ago he informed our partners that he wanted to resign and relocate there. I have no forwarding address."

Bobby placed a finger to his lips. "I appreciate the information, Steve," he finally said.

"One other thing," Lambert volunteered.

"Yes?"

Lambert hesitated. "He didn't look well. He started missing a lot of work. Claimed he had a lingering flu bug that he couldn't shake. We were all very concerned," he said, an edge to his voice.

Alarm bells went off in Bobby's head, and he felt himself tense. Standing, he extended his hand to Lambert. "Thanks for your help." He didn't hear the man's reply. He just kept walking away, out the corridor and past the reception area toward the bank of elevators, no longer aware of those around him.

—

If there were a more drug-infested area in New England than the blocks of Mission Main, Terry Cavanaugh didn't know about it. He walked down Horadan Way, in the shadow of the majestic Mission Hill Church and the hospitals of the Longwood Avenue area.

The public housing development had first opened back in the 40's and fallen into great disrepair in the 70's, despite a so-called homestead program which gave people willing to bring their apartment units up to code free rent for a period of one year. Now, in the 80's, the quality of life suffered greatly with the increase in drug trafficking, especially crack, throughout the blocks.

Terry watched three Hispanic gang bangers, maybe eighteen years old, doff their baseball caps as an old woman appeared at the top of the stairs where they squatted. Even in a neighborhood with junkies on every corner, the elderly were shown respect. "Good morning, Mrs. Valdes," he could hear one of them say.

The desolate streets had not long ago been a mainstream Irish middle-class neighborhood, but in the 70's the whites moved out in droves. Now the down-and-out overwhelmed the neighborhood and the entire place had taken on a third world look. "The free rent" program had led to a stacking of families, floor to floor and room to room, with people squatting in every corner. Someday, Terry thought, there might come the huge investment required to rebuild the area, but for now there wasn't much hope for the largely Hispanic and African-American population calling the Main home.

He spotted Elvis Pichardo, street name Chief, on the corner practically across the street from the Tobin School where Maureen taught. He was puffing on a crack pipe. Looking to both his left and right, he passed two small packages to two teens. He did not see Terry approaching from behind.

"What's up, sucker?" Terry said by way of a greeting.

"Hey, Cav, my main man! What brings you to the neighborhood?" Right away, Terry could see that at 1 P.M., he was already high on his own supply. The dealer turned to the two teens. "Now wait until the kids are away from the school. You dig me? Up near the church, a few blocks away, then you sell to them. Not here where the fuckin' cops might show. Now get the fuck out of here. And bring back the money. I got me some business here with my man."

As the sellers moved away, Elvis leaned against the street post. His eyes were glazed, his hair unkempt, the mutton chops so popular five years ago running practically down to his jaw line. He was one-half Hispanic and one-half Black. Terry knew him to be thirty years old, although, with the extra weight, the features bloated from both drugs and booze, he looked ten years older. In prison he had a mustache, but had removed it when some gay boys eye-fucked him in the recreation room one day.

"I need $15,000 worth," Terry said.

"The crack? Sure, man. When you want delivery?" Elvis said, offering Terry a hit of the pipe.

"How about in two days?" Terry replied, waving the pipe away. "I got customers waiting."

Elvis Pichardo savored the jolt. The first was always the best, but the world was always better with each succeeding puff. What was it that Luis Gomez liked to call it—medicinal optimism? "You got it, man," he finally replied.

Terry tried to hold his gaze. "You know, Elvis, you keep usin' right out here on the fuckin' street, you'll be back in Walpole."

Elvis' eyes were bouncing all over the place. "Fuck that. I'm too smart to end up back there."

"I hope so. How's Felipe?" Terry asked.

"Him and Luis is cool, Cav. We all doin' well. The dagos give us our own neighborhood where there's lots of business and then you white folks comes a callin' and then there's the hospitals nearby and all. We doin' good."

He took another hit on the pipe. "Did you want some? Did I ask you..."

He was losing it, Terry thought. He shook his head firmly. It was time to leave. He just needed to be sure the addict remembered what he had requested.

"You whiteys should loosen up. Thinkin' you're better than us. Smarter. Well it ain't so, y'know. Hey, that fuckin' rhymes. It ain't so you know. Ha, ha! We's into new businesses. Did I tell you that, Cav? We's into jewelry."

Terry remembered back to Walpole where Elvis Pichardo could talk the ears off a brass donkey, and the more crack he took, the more he rattled on. Usually, a load of bullshit. But still, his ears perked up.

"Jewelry?" he repeated.

Elvis leaned against the post now, mainly for support. If it weren't there, he might not be standing upright at all.

"You think Felipe smart?" he suddenly asked, smiling through his haze.

"I don't know Felipe the way I know you, Chief," Terry answered softly.

"Well he is, so don't you think you harps is smarter than us. We goin' to have millions soon, Cav. Fuckin' millions. You believe me?" he asked suddenly.

"Take a rest from smokin' that peace pipe, Chief."

"Oh, yeah? Fuck you, Cav. You best be careful with me 'cause, me, Felipe, Luis, might fix your ass like that sand nigger's we cooled up in Marblehead."

Terry stood there, transfixed. Gomez was responsible for the murders and heist up in Marblehead?

Elvis kept up the constant stream of macho bullshit. "That's right. Luis and Felipe go right into white man's land where they think they shit ice cream and now we all millionaires once we cash in the rocks. They depend on me, you know? I wasn't there myself, but who you think is the main planner for Luis? They don't get shit done until I use my brains."

"They're smart to depend on you, Elvis," Terry replied.

"You better believe that, honky. They be in the shithouse without me."

"I got to split, Chief. Can I collect my goods on Friday? Same time, same place?"

Elvis pointed the pipe at him. "When you want it?"

Jaysus, as his Irish aunt used to say. "How about Friday, 6 P.M. on Annunciation Road?"

"Why didn't you say so?"

It was definitely time to leave.

30

"I'm not so bad a guy once you get to know me."

Timmy wasn't so sure but he swallowed his tongue as he had promised his mother he would. They sat together in Fantasia at Fresh Pond Circle in Cambridge, just a block from David Aronson's practice.

"I apologize if I sounded like a know-it-all," Aronson was saying, so Marjorie had gotten to him as well.

The day following the altercation, his mother had sat him down, furious with him. "You know Tim, you and I need this talk. I like this man, and I believe he cares for me. It's been fifteen years since your father and I divorced and, as you know, I've done very little dating since then."

Timmy had sat quietly, showing her respect.

"When I met David at that party in Cambridge, I liked him right away. To me, he was attentive, kind, doting."

That was enough respect. "Well, to me he's an asshole," Timmy had snapped.

Marjorie had held her hand high in the air. "Enough. Enough, young man. To you, no one could ever replace Jack. You won't even give another man a chance." She had twisted the handkerchief in her hands, practically wringing it in frustration.

He had sat in the wing chair, feet apart, sipping the tea, saying as little as possible, trying to calm down.

"Do you love me, Tim?" she had then asked pleadingly.

He had stood and walked to the couch, extending his arm about her shoulders as he bent to kiss her. "Mom, you know I do."

She had then stood, looking him straight in the eye. "Then I want something from you, Tim. I want you to try with David. And I want you to tell Marty to do the same."

He didn't reply right away. "Where's it going, Ma?" he finally said.

She had sat down heavily on the couch. "With him? I'm not sure. There was a strong reason why I waited fifteen years. After Jack, no one measured up, and I didn't even want to try.

"I'm not stupid, Tim. I like his companionship, and I know he likes mine. It's been what? Five months. Who knows where it's going? But I'm happy right now. For the first time in a long time, Tim. And I want you and Marty to respect that."

And he had promised to try. So here they were.

"I just have strong opinions, and don't always know enough to keep some of them to myself," Aronson was saying, toying with his wineglass.

It was time to make the peace. "I'm the one that was out of line, David. Let's just forget about it, okay?" Tim said, offering his hand.

"Agreed," David replied, accepting it.

"So how's your practice going?" Timmy asked, anxious to change the subject.

"A general practitioner sees a little of everything so things are interesting. I love medicine," he replied, smiling.

He was quieter, much more friendly, more accepting of the other person, almost like a new David

Aronson. He was surprising Tim. Maybe there was more to the guy than he first believed.

"Your mother worries about you and Marty and the business you know," he said with concern in his voice. Not trying to be the wise ass.

"She might worry, but she's had a history of it with my father," Timmy replied, holding his gaze, not sure how much he wanted to get into.

"She calls it 'the life'," Aronson offered.

"That's right."

"Any chance you can leave it?"

Timmy glanced at him sharply and then shook his head. "I don't want to," he replied calmly.

"Don't you worry about eventual trouble from the law enforcement agencies?"

"Not really," Timmy replied tersely. "They got nothing on us."

"Marjorie says you have a new girl, a school teacher. What's her name?"

"Maureen," Timmy replied evenly.

"Pretty name."

Timmy glanced at his watch. "I need to get back to Lynn, David."

"And I've got an appointment coming in, in half an hour," David replied warmly. "I've got the tab," he said, reaching for the bill.

"Thanks for meeting with me, David."

Aronson extended his hand again. "Thank you, Tim. I'm glad we talked."

—

"It's called spoons, you know."

"What is?"

"What we're doing right now," Maureen replied, exasperated.

"We're not doing anything right now that I'm aware of. Except lying here," Timmy replied playfully.

"I'm talkin' about exactly that—the way we're lying," she said, poking an elbow into his stomach.

"Jaysus!"

"Stop your whining and hug me."

Timmy lay on his side, his front pressed into her rear, their bodies entwined, his hand stroking her hair. What was the name of the song that Engelbert Humperdinck sang because it fit, right here and right now. "After the Lovin'," that was it. The sex had been wonderful as always, but to be in love after the act was so much better. He could lie here all day with her, with no need to get hard again, with only the desire to be in her presence, to stare at her when she fell into a slight sleep, to study her when she was unaware, to memorize the moment like a photographer snapping a picture.

For a moment, her body tensed as she came awake again. He leaned on an elbow, pushing the black locks away from her eyes. "I need to talk to you about something," she said quietly, its effect enough to break the mood.

When he didn't reply, she rolled over on her other side so as to face him. "I'm worried about Terry."

He nodded, still playing with her hair, waiting for her to take the lead.

"I need to know some things, and I need you and Marty to help him," she said.

"With what?"

"He says the Italians have a grudge against him."

Timmy laughed out loud. "Tell him welcome to the club."

"What are you hearing on the street?"

They seldom talked of Terry, especially after she had told him of her brother's reaction to their involvement. He had long ago decided that the less said, the better.

"He's got big trouble with the Italians, Maureen."

"What?"

"He's been moving into their territories. Not in a big way, mind you, but they're not going to stand for anybody taking those steps. Way I understand it is he's operating—you know, drugs, extortion, some loan sharking—over in Medford, Somerville, Malden."

Burying her face in the pillow, she started to sob softly. "What's going to happen to him, Tim?"

He massaged her neck, his fingers kneading, moving to her shoulder blades, pressing down, trying to drive away her tension and fears.

"My guess is they'll teach him a lesson, Mo. But to them he's small potatoes."

She turned to face him. "I need to tell you something that has to stay between you and me and Marty, and that's it." He ran his index finger below her eye, wiping away the wetness.

"You know the two guys killed over near the community college a week ago? In the restaurant?"

He nodded slowly.

"I was there."

He stopped stroking her face. "What?"

"I was to meet Terry there, and the two guys must have followed me. Terry made me leave before the shooting started. He killed them, Tim. He says it was self-defense, but he killed them." She started to cry again.

He pulled her to his bare chest and let her bury herself there, not saying anything. He thought about what she had said, and its implications.

"I'll talk to Marty, and we'll talk to the Italians," he finally said.

"Please, Timmy, make it right. For me, please."

"We're not exactly best buddies with the dagos ourselves these days, Mo."

"They'll listen to you and Marty," she said, more with hope than conviction.

He wasn't so sure. "I'll talk to Marty when he's back from Ireland."

31

Bobby sat in the kitchen of his apartment on Sepulvada, the photos spread out on the marble counter. Randomly, his mind moved between the pictures at hand and the vision, tangible and stolid, that lay before him in the hand mirror.

When a friend recently remarked that he was losing weight and his face was thinning, he had the photos taken. The scale said he weighted 172, down only about six pounds from his norm. But the photos told another story. He looked worn and pale and tired, and he felt tired, frequently. Then again, on many days he felt as strong as he ever had. He shifted between the photos and the hand mirror on the counter. Any day now he should hear that shooting would be commencing on "Falling In Love" back in New York. Whatever his situation, he had to look his best. He was already a bit young to be playing Meryl Streep's husband, but Hollywood could be forgiving if the camera didn't betray you. Tyrone Power had been just twenty-two when in 1936 he starred with Loretta Young, and Lauren Bacall was just nineteen when she played opposite Bogart in "To Have and Have Not." Make-up could hide the pale look, but he couldn't afford to lose much more weight, particularly around the face.

He walked to the slider and pushed it open. Out on the balcony he looked down on the stalled line of traffic, not really observing the confusion, his mind instead traveling around the same series of questions with which he had been coping for days now.

He was HIV positive, very alone, and very afraid. What could he do? He would go back to New York in two days, stay close to Dr. Devlin, continue with the medicine, closely monitor his situation. What else could he do? He felt more in the closet now than ever before. Here in Los Angeles he'd been half in and half out, nobody in the entertainment industry much caring. But still, the fewer who knew of his sexual orientation the better. If it became generally known that he was HIV positive, then his career would be in jeopardy. People would avoid him as if he carried the plague.

He thought of Jason—crazy, confused thoughts of love, of rejection, of anger. Was Jase really in San Francisco? Probably. Their city, which Jase could now be sharing with someone else. Was he ill? He needed to see him, to let Jase know of his own illness, to learn more about what had gone wrong. Right now he was in desperate need to reconnect with Jase, to confront him, to vent, to let him know of the harm he had caused. And then there was another reason. He still cared about him, and in this most lonely of times, he just wanted to see him.

The one place he wasn't going was home. There would be no solace there, no forgiveness. They must never know of his orientation or his sickness.

He closed the slider and sat on the bed. Just four hours before his night flight to San Francisco. Maybe he could rest for a couple of hours, stop thinking so much and just sleep.

—

"You know what the spics call him?" Chris Kiley asked.

"Fuckin' quitter is what I call him," Gil Rafferty replied, fidgeting with his cup.

"Hands of Stone," is what. What the hell you talkin' about? Roberto Duran's won 70 of 71 fights, the greatest lightweight of all time," Chris said, practically shrieking right there in the booth, the mid-morning customers at Bickford's on Route 1 in Saugus looking askance at them.

"Quiet down," Ray Horan ordered gruffly.

Gil Rafferty stirred his coffee while he munched on the blueberry muffin. "He quit in New Orleans last year against Leonard, didn't he? Hands of Stone, and heart of shit. He's all done. He's yesterday's fighter."

"I got $3,000 says he beats Davey Moore," Chris replied. "You give me the 5-2 odds against him and you're on."

Gil Rafferty put forth his hand. "It's a bet. Moore's a middleweight, and a real champion."

Ray Horan decided it was time to go. "I need Gil with me on an errand, Chris. Okay with you?"

Chris shrugged his shoulders. "I got to get back to the port anyway."

Outside, Ray pointed toward the Hilltop Steak House in the distance. "Let's take a walk, Gil. The wife wants me to bring home some nice rump steaks." They headed north along the sidewalk, the southbound cars streaming by them as if they gave prizes to whoever got to Boston first.

He knew enough to convey the order out in the open, as Marty always did. "I need you to take care of some action for us," Ray said evenly as they climbed the hill, no one within a hundred yards of them.

Rafferty didn't hesitate for a moment. "Sure, Ray."

"There's a guy over on Dudley Street in Roxbury, name of Dana Carter, an ex-con drug dealer. Marty wants him taken out, Gil."

Gil Rafferty stopped in his tracks and stared at Ray. "You want me to ice a guy?" he asked, incredulous.

Ray looked him in the eye. Rafferty was stocky and balding with a beak of a nose and an energetic manner. He almost always appeared to be in constant motion.

Would he respond as Marty had predicted? "We all gotta make our bones at one time or another," Ray said, "and it's your time."

Gil shook his head vigorously. "Ray, no offense, but if Marty wants me to off some guy, he should tell me himself when he gets back from Ireland."

Ray smiled to himself. Marty had been dead on.

—

"I understand you're looking for me," Terry Cavanaugh said, with the mocking lilt in his voice, the phone propped against his ear.

"Who the fuck is this?" Rocco Apostoli replied, as if it couldn't possibly be.

"Like I told the goon who answered the phone—I'm Terry Cavanaugh."

He had simply called the social club on Prince Street in the North End and asked for Apostoli. With the security these guys practiced, it was no wonder the Feebs were routing them across the nation, Cav thought to himself.

"You got the balls to call me?" Apostoli ranted. "When I get my hands on you, you fuckin' Irish piece of shit..."

"I hope your phones are secure, Rocco, otherwise the FBI will be reporting your filthy mouth to your parish priest."

"What do you want, turnip?"

"You know what, Rocco? I think I'm making the most important phone call you've received in years. Do you want to know who whacked your niece and her husband, or don't you?" He paused for effect. "And who has the $4 million in ice?" He paused again. "If so, then I want something in return, cabeesh?"

Rocco decided to proceed cautiously. What was it Gino had recommended? An anger-management course? Maybe he could calm down for a few minutes—rip the Irisher's head off later.

"What would you know about it, Cavanaugh?" he finally said, his voice under reasonable control.

"If you're willing to meet with me, you'll find out. If it turns out you don't like my information, you're no worse off than you were five minutes ago. Right?"

He was right, Rocco thought. "Let's meet," he replied softly.

"You know Salem?"

"The witch place? Not really."

"Go up Route 128 to 114 and follow it east until you hit downtown Salem. I'll see you on the front steps of the superior court, right across the street from the district court. Lots of blue uniforms walking back and forth there."

"You're shittin' me," Rocco said.

"9:00 a.m. tomorrow. And come alone. Walk up Bridge Street toward the court. I'll be watching you all the way. Who knows? If things go well, we can grab a hot dog over at Salem Willows for lunch. Maybe even become best buddies someday. See ya."

And then he hung up.

32

There, rising out of the sea, the Irish landfall appeared. As the Air Lingus flight descended, Marty watched the white spray of surging waves smashing against steep walls topped by a green flatness that extended as far as the eye could see. He squeezed Judith's hand tightly and tapped his father on the shoulder. "Have you ever seen such a sight as that, Dad?"

Sheila leaned into Jerry, straining to capture the scene from her aisle seat.

Five days away, Marty reflected. Five days to put problems aside and reconnect with his heritage. It was his first international trip, and so he and Judith would be depending on his parents' knowledge of the country to make the most of each day.

After passing through customs, they drove south toward Dublin, fascinated by the changes that came upon them in stages. First small farms dotting the main highway approach, their slate roofs cluttering the landscape, with rocks and heather everywhere. And then, quite suddenly, rural turned to urban. The city came into focus quickly, almost too quickly, with no suburban sprawl to announce the variance, the way it does close to almost any huge American city.

Excitedly, they pointed out different sites to one another as they passed into the commercial sector: the maze of docks; square buildings huddled close to one another; breweries running together, one after the other; trolleys dividing the centers of streets. In the working class section, houses ran low and slanting, and in front of many of them little children played Annie—over.

They headed down Grafton Street, the approach to Jury's, their hotel. Along the way shoppers carried mesh bags filled with goods and above them, close to the hotel, a banner announced that the Rolling Stones would appear tonight at the football stadium just down the road.

After check-in, Marty and Judith felt the need to stretch, to shake the tiredness. They strolled behind Jury's, past skinny kids with scabbed knees kicking a soccer ball along the curving street leading downhill to the stadium. Two gray-haired men, probably pensioners, ambled toward them, exchanging the day's gossip with one another. As they passed, Marty heard one say, "Baile Athe Cliath."

"That's Dublin in the Gaelic," he whispered to Judith.

"Is it now?" she said, a phony lilt in her voice. "How's a Jewish girl to know? By the way, when do we get to visit Israel?"

He loved her intelligence, her quick repartee, her wit. She was like no one he had ever known—bright, cool, confident in the sense that she knew herself and was clearly comfortable with that person. She had introduced him to her interests but it never appeared that important to her that he accept them—art, especially the works of the Impressionists; English mysteries, with emphasis on Agatha Christie and P.D. James; antique shopping.

As her lips brushed his cheek, he thought of their relationship. Would it sustain itself? Probably not, he reflected. He was an Irish romantic, head over heels in love, and she a Jewish pragmatist, to whom, he guessed, relationships were fleeting. He sensed a certain selfishness within her, a lack of real commitment so typical of their generation. In matters of the heart she was temporary and he was permanent, and that didn't bode well for their future.

Nor, of course, did his work. In the end what he really loved was the life, and the life was in reality his mistress. Eventually, it would separate them, just as it had brought them together. He had no right to expect that it wouldn't. Even if he were misreading her, even if she loved him more than he realized, the day would come when she would ask him to give it up. And he could never do that.

As they neared the huge concrete stadium, a fleet of uniformed Dublin cops piled out of a police wagon, dressed in black wool jackets and trousers, holstered .38s and visored caps. Security for the concert.

"A penny for your thoughts," Judith said coyly.

"Actually I was thinking of you."

"A wonderful subject if I do say so myself. And what exactly were you thinking?" she teased.

He stopped under a chestnut tree right before the entrance to the stadium. "About how much I love you."

She moved into him, kissing him on the lips.

"Hey! Enough of that now!" one of the policemen standing near the ticket booth yelled out, a huge grin spreading across a face which contained the map of Ireland itself.

—

The second day they strolled about Trinity College on an April day when sunlight dappled yellow through new leaves on old trees. Professors armed with pigskin briefcases hurried toward ancient stone walls connected one with the other by bricked archways, and bright-eyed students pedaled bicycles across timeworn paths.

In the afternoon they visited the mall on Grafton, friendly merchants greeting them with a "top o' day." Tired, they later sat on a blanket on St. Stephen Green as ducks paraded by them on the embankment. Two teens sauntered toward the water, the boy's hand settled on the girl's rear, he obviously unconcerned with what others thought.

Jerry pointed them out and wrapped his arm around Sheila's neck. "What was that line from the Sinatra song? Now I remember. 'Love, like youth, is wasted on the young'!"

Sheila laughed her old laugh. Lately she had been drinking much less, relaxing more, and, in turn, Jerry seemed more accepting, more friendly. Studying them, Marty thought that time, indeed, was the best healer. The horrific events of five months ago—for his father the loss of two brothers, for his mother the overwhelming intrusion of evil into her quiet life—were still there but receding, and they both were adjusting.

"Tomorrow we'll take the rental over to Dun Laoghaire," his father was saying. "I want you young people to see the Baroque homes overlooking Dublin Bay, and the ships, heading out to the Irish Sea. Then we'll visit Cork."

"Long as we don't have to visit downtown Tel Aviv," Marty teased with a straight face.

"Huh?" Jerry said.

"He's just being a wise ass," Judith said, rolling her eyes.

Marty bent to kiss her upturned face. Sheila smiled at Jerry and winked. "Then again, maybe love is not wasted on the young," she said.

—

On that very same day, Terry Cavanaugh stared intensely at the thin man crossing Bridge Street from the parking garage. Apostoli was alone, but in the event that he were not, Terry had positioned Mick Riley on the park bench just outside the newsstand kiosk at the top of the street.

Terry blew into the paper cup and sipped the coffee, watching Apostoli move toward him through a horde of prospective jurors on their way to the building. Standing halfway up the steps of the superior court, he felt safe. The soon-to-be jurors were all focused on how they might avoid service, and the large number of policemen in the area were busy shuttling both people and messages between the superior and the district courts.

He waved to Apostoli as the Mafia chieftain approached the steps and then descended to meet him on the sidewalk itself. He extended a hand, which Apostoli ignored. Sheepishly, Terry grinned at him.

"It's too crowded around here if we're going to talk," Apostoli grumbled.

"We can take a walk down Bridge Street. There's plenty of park benches down at the other end. First though, I need to know whether you're carrying." He pointed up the stairs to the main entrance where a short line formed within the doors to pass through security. "After you."

"I'm not carryin'," Rocco replied angrily.

"Prove it. You know, so we can start off our new relationship the right way," Terry smiled.

"You'll soon be a dead funny man, Cavanaugh," Rocco muttered close to Terry's ear.

"If I am, then you won't know who murdered your niece or ever recover the jewels, will you, Mr. Apostoli? Are you coming, or am I leaving?" He flashed the devilish grin once again.

Apostoli studied him, hard faced, and then bounded up the stairs, and through the doors. Placing his keys in a tray, he proceeded through the detectors and cleared. Turning, he watched Terry follow the same procedure.

Once inside, they simply turned around and headed out. Nobody was concerned with anyone who was leaving.

They walked south on Bridge Street without speaking for a time, each considering the surroundings. Terry knew Mick Riley would trail them at a reasonable distance. The question was, did Apostoli have someone doing the same? They passed the many quaint shops that together make Salem a traveler's delight—charming bookstores; old-fashioned banks with benches, not ATM's out front; small scale eateries; ethnic neighborhood bars.

"So what do you have?" Apostoli finally asked.

"Like I said on the phone, the names of the people who ripped off and murdered your niece and her husband."

"Where are the jewels?"

"I don't know where the jewels are, Mr. Apostoli, but with your powers of persuasion I'm sure you'll find out. I do know they haven't been fenced yet, at least not as of two days ago."

"And what do you want?" Apostoli asked, irritated.

Terry pointed to a park bench at the end of the street. "Let's sit over here for a bit. What I want is a clean slate with you, Mr. Apostoli. We start clean with my keeping the piece I've been working..."

Apostoli raised a hand in protest. "You mean the piece you stole from us. I don't think so. Maybe we let you keep your life, and that's the best deal you're gonna get."

Terry spread his arms expansively. "I would like to keep my life for sure," he said, smiling the soft charming smile, the disarming one. Then he hardened, the lips thinned, the rose flush came into his cheeks. "And I will if you keep sending those boy scouts to do me in. You want war with me? Then let's have one. Only thing is, I don't play by any rules. You, your fuckin' brother Victor, your family, his family, are all on the table. Eventually, you'll get me, but not before I get a few close to you. You see I don't give a shit, Mr. Apostoli, and when a boyo doesn't give a shit, he's doubly dangerous."

Apostoli sat half facing him. He would take care of this crazy bastard later. What he needed now was information, but not at the price of backing down.

"You're forgetting who started this trouble. You moved in on me. Nobody does that, cabeesh?"

"So where are we?" Terry asked briskly, looking about, spotting nothing of concern.

"You tell me what I need to know, and the slate's wiped clean. We recover the jewels and you get a finder's fee of $50,000. Then you go off on your own and bother somebody else. That's the best I can do. It works out I get the guys responsible, the jewels, maybe just maybe, I throw you a little work subcontracting for me. Maybe."

Terry picked up a pebble and threw it into the air. "How do I know you'll hold to it?"

Apostoli held his gaze. "No one ever accused Rocco Apostoli of welshing on a deal." He offered his hand.

This time Terry left his hanging. "One more thing. No one except you ever hears where this information comes from," he said.

Apostoli nodded. "Agreed."

Terry eyed Apostoli closely, the same Cheshire cat grin playing around the corners of his mouth. "Let me have that hand again, Mr. Apostoli."

He looked about one more time. "You want Louis Gomez and Felipe Pichardo. Do you know them?"

Suddenly Apostoli stood. "Let's start walkin' back. Yeah, I know them."

"It was Luis's people who were providing drugs to the Taliks. Luis learned of the safe and the jewels the same way I did—from his crackhead cousin Elvis."

Apostoli said nothing more most of the way back to the superior court. He seemed to be lost in his own thoughts. When they arrived, he turned to Terry. "If your information checks out, and I get the jewels back, I'll be sending you the cash. You'll have a week to clear out of our territory after that. How can I reach you?"

"I'll call you in a week. How's that?" Terry replied.

"Good," Apostoli said, spinning away quickly and heading off in the direction of the garage.

33

The Mission District is one of San Francisco's oldest neighborhoods. Its main artery is Misson Street itself, home to a variety of restaurants, hotels, businesses, and gay bars. It was at one of the gay bars on Mission that Bobby learned Jason Ellison was very ill with AIDS and confined to a bed at San Franciso General Hospital. In late afternoon, he arrived at the huge brick complex on Potero Avenue, not far from the 101 Freeway. The facility is a small city unto itself, handling everything from gunshot wounds to mosquito bites. It contains one of the largest AIDS wards in America.

As he walked through the double doors on the third floor, he tried to gather his thoughts and organize his intended comments. He stopped at the half-open door to which the receptionist had directed him, steeled himself, and entered slowly.

What was lying in the bed between two other patients was not Jason Ellison. It just could not be, Bobby thought. The emaciated skeleton stared straight ahead, perspiration soaking his jaundiced, tight skin, a blanket pulled up close to his shoulders, the thin body shivering. A nurse's aide sat in a straight back chair wiping away the wetness from what appeared to be an infectious mouth.

The aide, an Hispanic woman in her forties, smiled at Bobby. "Can I help you?" she asked.

"I'm his friend," Bobby replied, the words coming forth naturally, surprising him.

The skeleton emitted a dry cough, and then another, which led to a spasm that lasted for seconds that seemed like minutes. When it receded, Jason looked at Bobby for the first time and a slight smile crossed his lips. "Hey, Sean," he whispered hoarsely.

Aside of him, another patient gasped for breath and the aide moved to attend him. "Can you stay with him for a just few minutes?" she asked Bobby.

He nodded and sat in the chair, not really wanting to hold Jase's stare. "So how are you doing?" he finally said, regretting the stupid comment as soon as he had uttered it.

Jason strained to speak. "Sean, I'm sorry. Truly sorry," his voice barely audible.

"Sorry about what?" Bobby said, placing the damp cloth against his cheeks.

"I should have stayed with you. You were the only one who cared..." His voice trailed off.

"Shhh," Bobby whispered. "Try not to speak. Let me..."

He was interrupted by a rattling sound followed by a convulsive spasm, Jason fighting for air now. Then just as suddenly he was quiet again. Bobby touched his face and wiped off a bead of perspiration with his finger, the skin feeling both cold and hot simultaneously.

"I'm alone, Sean," Jason whispered. "Will you stay with me?"

"I'll be here," Bobby replied gently.

A strange look appeared in Jason's eyes, and he smiled to himself. "I depend lately on the kindness of strangers," he finally said, looking to the aide. "What movie is that line from?"

Bobby took his hand and grinned.. 'A Streetcar Named Desire,' he replied. "Haven't your parents been here?" Bobby asked.

Jason shook his head ever so slightly. "They wouldn't come," he whispered. "And Brian..." he muttered just before the dry cough overtook him again.

Bobby gathered Brian Whoever had left him as soon as AIDS had been diagnosed.

Jason wiggled his index finger at Bobby, beckoning him to come close to his face. "Did I get you sick?" he asked, struggling with the question. Before Bobby could answer, the cough started once again.

The aide came to his assistance, an sponge in hand, squeezing cold water into hot pores, stroking his head gently as the cough slowly subsided.

—

Bobby stayed the three days it took Jason to die. On that last day, holding Jason's hand as he fought for air, his eyes protruding, his skin taut and yellow, Bobby made the decision. He would inform his family of his own condition. There was no fate worse than being alone at the time of death. While he still had his health, he needed them to understand that he, like Jason, was a human being full of love, a human being very much afraid of the future, a human being who did not want to depend on the kindness of strangers at the hour of his death.

—

"The guy's a real batsmith. He hit .349 last year, and he'll do it again in '83," Gil Rafferty was saying.

"Boggs? He's a singles and doubles hitter, that's all. We ain't goin' nowhere with him. We need more than one power hitter like Jim Rice to have a good year. Those fuckin' Orioles play for three-run innings all the time. Put two guys on and the next guy clocks a home run. We need power in Fenway Park, especially with that pile of shit we call pitchers," Stevie Guptill replied.

"We got Oil Can," Chris Kiley said.

"Shit can is what I call him," Stevie answered. "And Tudor throws up marshmallows and Hurst loses as many as he wins."

"This is probably Yaz's last year," Ray Horan said.

They stood at the rail waiting for the mechanical rabbit to begin its run from the backside of the oval at Wonderland Park in Revere to their position near the starting blocks.

"I got $100 says that the #2 dog takes it," Gil Rafferty said.

"I want that bet too," Ray replied. "Paulie, here's a hundred. We got four minutes to post time. Get Gil's dough and lay the bets down. He's going to go off at least 7 to 1."

"What am I, a fuckin' gofer?" Paulie Cronin replied, a hurt look on his face.

"Hurry up! It's almost post time!" Chris screamed.

Ray touched Gil Rafferty on the arm. "Let's take a walk."

They strolled along the rail in front of the grandstand. On the dirt track itself, young men dressed in short white shirts and creased pants attended the dogs, each leading one pup toward the starting blocks. Along the path, a mix of discerning die-hard gamblers looked for any sign that might favor one dog over another. The #2 dog, adorned in a white blanket, looked alert, bouncing on his toes like a fighter before the bell rings. Following behind him, the #4 dog dragged his head, his eyes glassy, ready for a nap. The #8 dog, saliva streaming from his mouth, looked like he had already run the race.

"I think you and I got the winning entry, Gil. Look at that #2 dog perk up."

"You can't tell nothin' by that Ray. One night I was here, you know, and I bet the #1 dog, the one named after that fuckin' crook James Michael Curley? Looks like he's ready to lap the whole field. I mean, he's out front by six lengths with me having laid down a C-note to win. The little bastard's draped in the red blanket lookin' like a fuckin' comet circlin' the track. Then you know what happened? A quarter-mile from home, with my C-note about to become $600, he decides to stop and take a shit right in the middle of the track. If I had my Glock, I would have shot the peckerhead right there."

"Speaking of which, you and the Glock, I mean, Marty's back from Ireland. You remember that little matter we discussed—the guy over in Roxbury?"

"Of course I remember," Gil replied.

"And they're off!" the announcer screamed as Swifty, the mechanical rabbit, rolled along the inside rail increasing in speed every second as the dogs catapulted out of the starting boxes.

"You know Red Rock Park across from where Marty lives on Lynn Shore Drive?"

"Yeah, I do," Gil responded evenly.

"Meet Marty there tomorrow night at eight."

"You mean about the assignment?"

"What the hell else? For a walk in the park?"

Halfway around the oval, the #2 dog separated from the pack, his stride lengthening, his colors showing clearly against the inside rail. "He's saving ground on the inside!" Gil yelled.

Turning for home, the #2 dog maintained his lead. The mechanical rabbit zoomed ahead as the dogs bounded after him in their incessant and always frustrating pursuit.

"He won! He fuckin' won!" Gil screamed. To Ray, he didn't appear nervous, he didn't appear overly anxious in discussing the meeting. Maybe Marty was wrong. Rafferty had handled every assignment well to date, and he checked out. The guy was efficient and cool, but then again, maybe he was a hell of an actor. Whatever, they would find out tomorrow night.

"$700. Not bad," Gil said.

Paulie walked down the pitched asphalt slope from the grandstand to the rail.

"You got our winnings?" Gil asked excitedly.

Paulie shook his head. "I didn't get the bet down."

"You what?" Gil stared at him, incredulous.

"I gets in the line which is takin' some time, y'know? Like I'm standin' there eatin' my ice cream..."

"What ice cream?" Gil asked.

Paulie looked frustrated. "The one I went to buy before I stood in line to bet."

"With four minutes before post time, you went and bought fuckin' ice cream before you got to the line?" Gil asked.

Paulie shrugged his shoulders. A light came on in his eyes. "When I saw the line was long, I moved to the other line. I gets to the front fast, y'know? Then the fucker with the eyeshade tells me they don't take $100 bills at his window. I started arguin' with him, and he slams the window shut, says the race is on. What am I supposed to do?"

"Want me to tell you, you dummy?" Chris says.

"It wasn't your money," Paulie replied defensively.

"Can you believe this dummy?" Chris said, circling his fingers in the air and pointing to his temple.

"Okay, cool it. That's enough," Ray said. "It was my money, and I'm forgetting it. Leave Paulie alone."

For some reason he thought of Jack, who always protected the least gifted of their crew whenever someone got on Paulie too much. "Paulie's a good soldier," Ray said, wrapping a burly arm around his shoulders. "Right, Paulie?"

34

"So they have the right then to just come in here and walk away with the company books?" Marty asked calmly.

"They do, Marty. Since the RICO laws went into effect. The FBI has jurisdiction that transcends that of the Boston or Lynn Police. They have almost Gestapo-like powers now."

John Carmody was an Irish lawyer who handled mostly Irish clients, particularly Irishmen whose businesses frequently found them interfacing with the law. He was a man of carefully calibrated reactions. His deep voice was typically emotionless, his broad face had an almost indecipherable hardness to it. For decades he had kept Jack Kelly out of trouble and now he was trying to do the same for the nephew.

Marty drummed him fingers on the desk as he considered the situation. "What will they find?" Carmody asked.

Marty gazed at his hands, now locked together. "Nothing. They turned the place upside down and left with the one set of books we have. Their accountants will report a perfectly kept record of assets and liabilities.

"The damage comes with them waltzing in here in front of ten or twenty customers. That's really great for business. You couldn't have gotten an injunction?" he asked, without an edge in his voice.

Carmody shook his head. "The RICO laws give them broad, sweeping powers allowing them to act against what they term as "strongly suspected" criminal interests. I'm going to meet with them in their Boston office and if I can't get them to back off on the basis of you and Timmy never having been charged or convicted of any felony, then I'll work the Department of Justice in Washington on the same theme. What about income tax returns?" he suddenly asked.

"We're clean," Marty replied evenly. "Tim and I report all the income from this auto business. We've been audited twice without a problem."

Carmody studied his client carefully. He couldn't help being impressed with the equanimity Marty displayed. Just two years ago the young nephew he had met through Jack Kelly had come across as hotheaded and impetuous. Today, he might as well be dealing with Jack himself, because the nephew had grown in the position.

Carmody really had no interest in knowing the reality concerning the income from the crime enterprises. What a lawyer did not know could not hurt him, and like any good lawyer he didn't wish to ask a question that would compromise him or his client. He guessed that Jack's close association with the Italians had led the Kellys to launder money in the same fashion as Petrelli in Providence or Apostoli in Boston—cash handled by their own accounting team forwarded by trusted couriers to another state, probably New York, and converted to clean money reinvested in legitimate operations and/or protected accounts in other countries. In all probability the Mafia handled all of this for Marty, what with their networks being so well established.

"What else might they look into?" Marty was asking.

Carmody shifted in his chair, trying to relieve the tightness in his lower back. "If everything on the surface is legitimate—the business, your taxes, etc.—then they need to unearth something else, something that will implicate you directly."

"Or someone," Marty replied.

"Or someone," Carmody agreed.

—

Marty slipped on the leather jacket and shut down the lights. He walked down his front path to a calm April night, the pleasing breeze a promise of the good days to come now that winter had almost spent itself. Crossing the street to the walkway above Kings Beach, he strolled directly to the rail and looked down. At high tide white caps smashed against the wall, forcing him to move on.

He followed the circular path into Red Rock Park. On his right, green grass was beginning to show beneath the vapor lights, and on the horizon Boston appeared, its huge structures outlined clearly on this moonlit night. He stayed away from the rail as he walked deeper into the area. At the end, a distance of perhaps one hundred yards from his starting point, he stopped where the walkway turned toward Boston and circled back to Lynn Shore Drive.

Looking over the rail at the craggy rocks below, he reminisced for a moment of the many times he and Timmy had descended the stairwell at low tide to those rocky cliffs, and then moved from their flatness at the base of the steps to a high point some fifty yards out. Once there, they had dived into the cold waters of the Atlantic, as cold in July as in December, he remembered—or they would search for crabs or preen for the teen-age girls sitting on blankets along the red rocks themselves.

But tonight he was here for another purpose—conceivably to commit murder. He felt for the Glock nine along his spine, and glanced at his watch. Rafferty should be here almost any minute. If Rafferty was a problem, it was he who had authorized Chris Kiley to invite him to membership. And if Rafferty were indeed an informer, then he, as the leader, should be responsible for fixing the situation, both for what it is and as an object lesson to anyone else who might also want to imitate Victor MacLaglen.

He had told Ray to tell Rafferty "not to dress," code words meaning to come unarmed. Rafferty would understand that an assignment given tonight would not be carried out that same evening.

And there he was, following the same path Marty had trod, and coming directly toward him. Dressed in a black tee shirt and jeans, Rafferty puffed on a cigarette and then flicked it over the rail into the sea.

Marty considered the setting if it came to murder. Do the unexpected, Jack had always counseled. So he had chosen a location directly across the street from his own home. There would be no FBI surveillance in this area of flat parkland and ocean, and he could see anyone coming for a hundred yards.

"What do you say, Marty?" Rafferty said effusively. "What's up?"

"Let's sit over here," Marty responded, pointing to the bench ten yards back from the rail.

"You know Roxbury?" he began.

"A little."

"Dudley Street's a main thoroughfare. You know where it is?"

"Sure."

Get right to it, Marty told himself. If Rafferty were an informer, a turncoat, maybe even an FBI agent, then he would be wired tonight, his final night on earth.

"There's a real estate office at 500 Dudley owned by a drug dealer named Dana Carter."

"Yeah?" Rafferty nodded, arching an eyebrow.

"I want you to ice him, you follow?"

Rafferty gave him another nod. "What did he do?"

Marty locked eyes, trying to read the older man. He suspected this would be the first of many questions.

"He had an old friend of mine killed. This is payback."

"When did this happen?"

"A year ago."

"You want me to kill him?"

"That's what I said."

The repetition didn't surprise Marty. In fact, it was exactly what he had expected.

"When you want this done?"

"Within the week."

"Not much time," Rafferty muttered.

"It's time for you to make your bones, Gil. You up to this?"

Rafferty pulled the pack of cigarettes out of the tee shirt pocket. He appeared anxious. His hand shook slightly as he lit the cigarette.

"Of course. I just—you know—never iced anyone before, but I'll get it done. Who was your friend?" he asked nervously.

"What difference does that make?"

"None." Rafferty shrugged his shoulders. "Just wonderin' is all."

From across the lawn, Timmy approached from out of the darkness. Dressed in black trousers and a black turtle mock, he closed quickly and pressed the .38 behind Rafferty's ear. At that same moment Marty stood, the Glock suddenly appearing in his right hand.

"What the hell..." Gil started to rise.

"Stay put, Gil," Timmy ordered.

"Take off the tee shirt!" Marty demanded.

"What the hell's happening here?" Rafferty screamed.

"Take the fuckin' shirt off," Timmy said, pushing the .38 tighter against the base of his skull.

Gil pulled the tee shirt up over his head. Nothing. No wire.

"Stand up," Marty directed. "Lower your pants."

"Hey!" Gil protested. "What are you guys, homos or somethin'? What the fuck's wrong?" he pleaded.

"Do what you're told!" Timmy yelled.

Gil unbuckled his jeans. "What! You think I'm wired. You think I'm some kind of canary?" Marty reached into the band of his shorts. Again, nothing.

"Get dressed," Timmy said, still standing behind Rafferty.

"Wait a minute. Take off the sneakers," Marty said.

Again, nothing.

"You think I'm a songbird? Is that it?" Rafferty asked belligerently.

Marty pondered the situation. If Gil Rafferty were the informer, there was absolutely no way he would be at this place, at this meeting without a wire. He knew the topic in advance and he knew with whom he'd be meeting.

Gil Rafferty was not the informant.

"I ain't no squealer, Marty, believe me," Gil was saying, the fear continuing to build in his throat.

Then who was, Marty began to wonder.

"Then why all the questions, Gil?" Timmy asked.

"I just want to make sure I understand the situation is all."

"Why didn't you follow through when Ray told you what I wanted done?" Marty asked.

Rafferty spoke rapidly. "I never killed anyone before, Marty. I wasn't goin' start just on Ray's say so. I wanna get close to you. Be sure I make a connection with you, y'know? And I heard that's the way it's done. You give the order. What did I do wrong?"

Marty stared across at Timmy. "Nothing. We're just being cautious, Gil. With the FBI on our case..."

He stopped in mid-sentence. He had made a huge mistake. There was no greater way to sow discord among the crew than to falsely accuse one of its members of disloyalty.

35

Elvis Pichardo never saw the Buick until it was too late. He was walking down Prentiss Street on the Main heading toward Huntington Avenue and the AA meeting over at St. Ann's, enjoying the night air, smoking his reefer. He couldn't and wouldn't give up the reefers or the crack, but he was proud of his progress with the hard stuff.

He now attended the meetings at St. Ann's twice a week. Perhaps in time he could cut back, he thought, but for now, he needed the support. After all, the program was supposedly a bridge back to life. So far he didn't have to get up and announce to the whole group what an asshole he was like some of the destitutes who sat in the rows of chairs with him. At the midnight meeting, you got all sorts of people and even a little show, like last week when the guy with the tattoos started throwing chairs and had to be restrained. Too bad I didn't have my blade with me that night, Elvis thought. That would have restrained the drunk permanently.

Before he reached Huntington, the light blue Buick cruised to a halt and the window on the passenger's side lowered. "Excuse me, sir. Can you direct us to Zachary's Restaurant?" a small, pale man asked.

As Elvis started toward the curb, the impact of the .22-caliber automatic knocked him backwards, the bullets caroming around inside his skull as he fell.

—

Luis Gomez strolled with Delores on his arm through the lobby of the Sheraton Boston Hotel to the elevator, which led to the Prudential Center underground garages. She snuggled against his shoulder while they waited to board, murmuring something in his ear, the words causing him to smile broadly.

The dinner at Legal Sea Foods had been excellent, and the fish the best Boston, and therefore, the world had to offer. And Delores had been good company, although a bit unsophisticated. But she was only fifteen, so he had told her to stand erect, let her boobs rise high, give an impression that she was older, use the fuckin' napkin.

"You wait here while I get the car," he directed as the elevator opened to the garage level. He left her in the lobby with four or five other women whose men were also trying to remember where in this expanse of at least five football fields their car might be. He had marked the location down somewhere, but after five or six Dewar's and water, he wasn't sure exactly where.

He headed north because that looked the most familiar. Thank God the parked vehicles had thinned out considerably. He spotted the green Impala back where the overhead pipes were hissing, looking as if they would be sprouting a torrent of water any second now. His car was sandwiched between two other vehicles, the one on the left with its hood up as one man yelled to another man behind the wheel to try the ignition once again.

He paid them scant attention, not wanting to get into a "help thy neighbor" situation at 1:00 A.M., not with Delores waiting for him and he, with great expectations. So he turned toward his own vehicle, fished for the key and never gave another thought to his surroundings, at least not until he felt the cold barrel against his head.

—

Felipe Pichardo preferred the 70's disco music to the new wave reggae stuff, so he sat in his pad at Annunciation Road, watching "Saturday Night Fever" on the VCR. John Travolta was dancing up a storm, squiring different ladies around the ballroom floor, looking sharp, demanding all your attention, a real star. What the hell had happened to him? Felipe wondered. The last few years he had faded, grown fat, even dropped out of sight.

From the hallway, someone slammed a door and someone else screamed shrilly. A moment later, three or four teens rushed noisily down the corridor, the hour being 2 A.M. not of any consequence to them.

He reached for his .38 thinking maybe of going out there telling them what for, when the phone rang.

"Hello," he responded listlessly on the second ring.

"Felipe, this is Luis." The voice was softer than usual, the breathing uneven.

"Yes, Luis?" he replied, puzzled.

"I need you to get the jewels and bring them to me."

"At two o'fuckin' o'clock in the morning?"

Luis's voice shot up an octave. "Felipe, are you listenin' to me? Bring the jewels. I've found a fence. Come alone to 400 Atlantic Avenue. You with me?"

"I'll be there in fifteen minutes, Luis."

—

"Meet him downstairs and relieve him of the merchandise," Rocco Apostoli instructed Dominic Saladna and the small, pale man. "Then put him in the freezer for now. If he doesn't have the jewels, bring him here."

Luis Gomez slumped on a red painted ladderback chair in the tiled kitchen tucked away in the corner of the basement area. Across from him, Rocco Apostoli sat in a second chair, a pine table separating them.

"What made you think you could get away with it, Luis? That's what I would like to know," Rocco was saying.

Blood trickled from Luis's nose, and he had great trouble breathing through the pain. His cheekbone was discolored, the huge purple lump spreading by the minute. His hands and legs were tied to the ladderback. He didn't respond, his total energy now devoted to inhaling and exhaling.

"Huh?" Rocco bellowed. Outside, the hum of the rows of freezers permeated the corridor, and in the corner of the kitchen, the radio blared loudly, making conversation difficult.

"I didn't know it was your niece, Rocco. Not until later," Luis responded slowly, his head sagging.

Dominic reappeared at the door carrying a duffel bag. "He's here, and with the merchandise," he said.

"Leave it over there," Rocco answered, pointing toward a long counter running down the side of the kitchen.

"You won't hurt our families?" Luis asked, his tone frantic.

"Did I say that Luis? Did I? I think I said your wives would be safe as long as I felt you were telling me the whole truth."

Luis sighed audibly. "I've told you who was involved—me, Felipe, and Elvis."

"No one else?"

Luis shook his head. "I asked the Irish—the Kellys-in, but they said no after thinkin' it over for a while."

"Marty Kelly?"

"And Timmy."

"They knew about the hit?" Rocco asked, trying to hide his astonishment.

Luis nodded. "They knew."

"You have anything else to tell me, Luis?"

Gomez coughed and wheezed. "We wouldn't have hit the Arab if we knew he was married to your niece. Believe me, Rocco."

Luis Gomez knew he was a dead man as soon as he saw Rocco Apostoli when his blindfold had first been removed. He could only hope the Mafia chief would not seek vengeance against his family.

Dominic Saladna stood in the corner with his arms folded. The pale man edged into the room and stood alongside him.

"Your families will be safe, Luis," Rocco finally said. "I believe you have been honest."

He turned to Saladna. "Take him to the freezer and hang him on the meat hooks with the other guy. Then drop the temperature down to—50 degrees."

After Saladna and the pale man first untied and then dragged Luis from the room, Rocco sat there for the longest time. The Irish Corsicans had known. Son of a bitch.

36

"There's a lot of rumors out there about Luis Gomez and the Pichardos," Chris Kiley was reporting. "Street says they made Apostoli's meat delivery run for Easter. Might be sittin' on someone's table out in Hopkinton right now, part of the ham dinner."

Marty found himself drifting, still thinking of the informer within his midst. Every time one of the men spoke he couldn't help concentrating on that person and weighing the possibility. He scanned the warehouse floor from left to right as the men took turns theorizing about the fate of the Hispanics.

On his extreme left, sitting on a crate, Chris Kiley read from the Globe story describing their disappearance. The most intelligent of the crew, the most athletic, the team leader on the waterfront, he had roots straight back to Jack. Smart and knowledgeable, could he have cut himself a deal with the Feebs?

To Chris's left sat Gil Rafferty, complete with sullen look nearly every time he looked Marty's way. Just last week he had taken care of Dana Carter, putting two Black Talons—real heavy bullets that explode on impact—in the back of his head as he walked to his car over at the train station in Newton. Shortly thereafter, Marty's mother had received a phone call from Ginger Dalton. She had been clever not to call him directly, and she had left a simple message. "Tell him thank you regarding Carter. He'll understand." In his mind Rafferty could now be eliminated as a suspect, but with the accusation he may actually have lost the man. Right now, Rafferty looked like he didn't want to be here.

To Rafferty's left, Ray Horan sat sipping his coffee. Marty would stake his life on Ray's loyalty. He didn't give Ray a second thought.

Then came Paulie Cronin, fidgeting with his Pepsi can, slow-witted, solid as an enforcer so long as someone carefully laid out the directions and did the thinking. He wasn't smart enough to conspire.

"The whores are tellin' us that they whacked the Arab up in Marblehead, not knowing the wife was Apostoli's niece," Stevie Guptill was saying.

Marty wondered about Stevie. Not because of any personal characteristics or any missteps on his part, but because of what he represented. He controlled their small stable of pimps and prostitutes so he consistently met all sorts out on the streets. But he was another with ties back to Jack and the early days. It just didn't figure.

Completing the circle, Joey Dunn and Freddie Quinlan sat side by side. Baby-faced Joey, the numbers chief, had a brother George who was a state legislator, and another brother who was a state cop. With the transition from Jack, could he have sold out? And Freddie, a loyalist of long standing, his leg-breaker along with Paulie, smarter than Paulie, could he have been turned?

Marty caught himself. Relax a bit, he cautioned himself. Having made one mistake with Rafferty, he did not need to make another. There was even a chance Catherine had been wrong. He would simply keep his guard up, set small little traps with useless information and see what came back to him. He could not let himself become paranoid.

—

"You handled the situation perfectly, Rocco. You have my admiration," Gino Petrelli said, extending his hand across the checkered tablecloth at Mother Anna's in the North End.

Outside, the mix of noontime foot traffic hurried through the light rain: young mothers juggling mesh bags full of cheeses and fresh fruit, pasta and wine and holding the hands of their little ones; tourists pointing out the qualities of an old world neighborhood to one another; young executives rushing to meet favorite people at favorite restaurants.

Sitting erect, Petrelli ate his fettucine Alfredo as if he were back in Rome with the patricians, but at least this time he had agreed to their meeting in Rocco's backyard.

"And you recovered all the jewels?" Petrelli was more affirming than he was asking.

"Except for a few trinkets," Rocco replied proudly.

"And the Irish knew all along," Gino said, pontificating, looking off into space. "Interesting."

"They could have warned me and they didn't." The more Rocco thought about it, the more angry he became.

"What do you do about it?" Gino didn't ask the question as if it were a question. It was rather to test his response, Rocco felt. Like the teacher giving a test.

"What can I do about it with you and Forelli protectin' the bastards?" Rocco fumed, downing his Dewar's a little too fast, while Petrelli toyed with his wine glass stem, acting like an older version of Robert Young in "Father Knows Best," about to deliver the object lesson.

"You're not thinking, Rocco," Petrelli said condescendingly. "The real issue is how we convince New York—Forelli—to let us move against the Irishers, without our being labeled the instigators of violating the truce. Cabeesh? And I have a great idea."

"What?" Rocco said, leaning into the table.

"This Cavanaugh did you a big favor."

"To save his own ass."

Petrelli shook his head. "He did you a big favor, and he should be rewarded."

"He's got his life, and I'm giving him a piece of the price on the jewels," Rocco replied defensively.

"What do the Kellys have now? 12-1/2 % of the entire area. Right?"

Rocco nodded slowly. Where was this going?

"Give this Cavanaugh a piece of their 12-1/2%. We tell Forelli—I tell Forelli—that we're simply replacing one Irisher with another. We're showin' gratitude to an Irisher who saved us millions and helped us identify the people who killed your niece. And we're not violating the truce. The Irish still have 12-1/2%, except that 3% of that is going to your new friend Cavanaugh."

Rocco swallowed more than sipped some of the Dewar's. "Forelli would buy that?"

Petrelli didn't answer right away. "Why not?" he finally said. "Isn't Tim Kelly seeing Cavanaugh's sister?"

"How'd you know that?"

"Well, isn't he?"

"Yeah."

"Well, think my friend. We're on the side of the angels. We tell Forelli there's a tightness between this guy Cavanaugh and the Kellys."

Rocco began to smile for the first time. "Marty wants to see me soon. He knows I was out to ice Cavanaugh and asked if I'd hold off until we met." He paused for a moment and then a frown appeared on his forehead. "But there's no way he'll share his territory with anyone, Irisher or not."

Petrelli poured himself three inches more of vodka right from the bottle. "He'll have no choice, Rocco. If we convince Forelli of Cavanaugh's good deeds, the closeness between the sister and Timmy, the fact the territory is still all-Irish, what have we done wrong? And in the process, we might cause a rift between the so-called Irish Corsicans and Cavanaugh over either the territory or the sister or both."

He smiled to himself in admiration of his own perceived cleverness. "We'll have created an old-fashioned Irish stew. Let the boyos, as they call themselves, either share the territory, or become embroiled with one another. If they share the territory, we've lost nothing but you've subtracted plenty from the Kellys. If they end up fighting one another, to the disadvantage of profits for us all, we tell Forelli they're out of control. We might even "arrange" three or four episodes—incursions into our territory—which prove that point."

Rocco ran a piece of the warm Italian bread into the gravy on his side dish. Maybe he hadn't fully appreciated his superior, he began thinking. "It could work," he said.

Petrelli smiled the condescending smile once again. "Oh it will, my friend. And then we'll be rid of the Kellys once and for all."

37

"What the virus does is infect certain types of white blood cells, principally those CD 4 cells I told you about last time."

Behind Dr. Devlin Central Park was preening in full bloom now, the bluish May sky umbrellaing the trees. Through the window Bobby could see that all six softball diamonds were occupied. Somewhere down there the cast of 'La Cage aux Folles' was engaged in a game that he was missing.

"These CD 4 cells are also called 'helper' cells. They have important functions to perform with the immune system."

Bobby had asked the question, but really wasn't listening for the answer, his mind instead on the question he really wanted to ask.

"Often the virus damages the lining of the intestine which contributes to the weight loss you're experiencing," Dr. Devlin was saying.

"Which, in turn, leads to lost opportunities," Bobby interjected.

"What do you mean?"

Bobby shifted in the easy chair and crossed his legs. "I heard from my agent this morning. I lost the part in the DeNiro movie."

"I thought that was pretty well set, and there was just a delay in the start?"

"It's about the weight loss. They thought I looked too thin in the new tests. Too thin to play Streep's husband. They told my agent they want a more healthy looking guy. They picked David Clennon."

Devlin tented his fingers under his chin. "I'm sorry to hear that, Sean..."

Later, he would wonder why he interrupted and asked what he asked next. Maybe because with all the medical mumbo-jumbo, he just needed to know. Maybe because of having been with Jason at the end. Or just maybe because he was psychologically depressed, the weight of the whole overwhelming him.

"Am I going to die, Doctor?" he blurted out.

The doctor dropped his hands on the desk and interlaced his fingers. "I can't answer that, Sean. Not easily." He stood and walked to the window, probably just to have something to do, Bobby considered. Devlin straightened the curtain and then sat back down.

"Let me give you some good news first. We're learning more about the HIV virus and about AIDS every day, but it's still very early in the war, Sean. In 1979 only eleven Americans had AIDS. Today, four years later, it's like an epidemic. Yes, a strong percentage of HIV positive patients develop AIDS each year and die, but not everyone. You know, I'm part of a research group that's sharing information—information about the virus, its treatment, why many develop AIDS but not all..."

"I saw my friend die, Doctor. Jason? The one I told you about?"

Devlin stared at him. "I'm sorry, Sean."

"It was horrible."

Devlin let a moment pass before continuing. "Not everybody dies, Sean. Are you hearing me? And we're beginning to make some progress. Someday, this will be a controllable disease, like diabetes—a serious, lifelong, but manageable disease. There's a lot of hope, Sean."

"You'd make a good thespian, Doc," Bobby said, breaking into a small smile.

"I'm not acting," Devlin said, returning the smile. "You're young, your immune system's holding up well so far, your CD 4 count is low but not low enough to cause severe illness. There are lots of positive signs."

"What do I do next?"

"We'll continue to monitor your immune system at least four times a year and continue with the AZT. Will you be staying in New York?"

"I'm going home—to Boston—for just a while, but, yeah, I'll be here."

"I want you to get into a support group."

"Like AA?"

"That's right. An HIV support group. We think it's important that you have the opportunity to talk with others similarly infected. As with any disease, it's important you stay positive, Sean. Are you back in the cast of 'La Cage aux Folles?"

"I'm going back next week."

"One other thing." Devlin hesitated for a beat. "Have you told your family yet?"

"I'll be in Boston next weekend. I'll tell them then." I'll need a support group for sure after that, he thought to himself.

—

They lay stretched out on the couch in the dark, the only light permeating her living room coming forth from the small Zenith, the announcer running through a montage of Henry Fonda movies on the occasion of the legend's death.

"He could play anything—drama, comedy, westerns..." the announcer was saying.

"We meet with Apostoli tomorrow," Timmy suddenly stated, letting the words hang there for a moment. "We'll try to resolve things for Terry."

She moved closer to him, positioning her lips under his ear. "Thank you," she whispered.

"Don't thank me until after the meeting. Marty and I don't rate too high with Rocco."

"Terry tells me things are better lately," she replied.

"In what way?"

"I don't know. That's all he said on the phone. He said he may be around again soon. Maybe it was just bullshit."

"How about we go out—see a movie?" she suddenly asked, changing direction.

He shook his head. "There's something I want to ask you. Mind if we just stay here tonight?"

She pushed into him with her breasts touching his chest. "What? You want to play?"

"I had something more serious in mind," he said, standing and moving to the closet for his sportscoat. He brought out a small gift wrapped box and held it in the palm of his hand as he walked to her.

"What the hell is this?" she asked.

"Anyone ever tell you, you have no sense of romance? The man you love presents you with a small box. You remember my retarded friend Paulie Cronin? Paulie could tell what it is. Use your imagination."

"It's a ring!" she blurted out, grabbing for the box.

"Now you're a clairvoyant! Why not just open it?" he grinned.

Unwrapping the box, Maureen opened its cover. She lifted out the pear-shaped, white gold ring and held it between them.

"Tim, it's beautiful!" she exclaimed.

He slipped from the couch to the floor, kneeling on one leg—but only for a moment.

"Get up! I am not going to be proposed to the old-fashioned way. God knows you're too old-fashioned as it is."

"What do you want—to be playing spoons while I propose?"

She stood and beckoned him to join her. "No, silly. What I want is to look one another in the eye, toe to toe, two equals who respect one another, who want to be together always..."

"Are you proposing, or am I?" Timmy teased.

"Yes."

"Yes what?"

"Yes to whatever you are going to say. I accept."

"What about the life? My being in it, around it..."

She stood on her toes and slipped her arms around his neck. "I love you, Tim. I'll always love you, and I want to spend the rest of my life with you. Yes, I'll marry you, but I don't want to go through life like this—worrying about you, worrying about Terry."

"Maureen, listen..."

"No. Hear me out. I'll marry you, but I'm not going to bring children into a world of evil and greed and death. I don't want our sons or daughters around it. So I'm asking you ..."

Timmy placed his hand over her mouth. He answered her with quiet composure. "I've been thinking about it, Mo. I have." He drew her into an embrace, resting her head on his chest. "I can leave it—I just need a little more time to work it out."

"How much time?"

"Before we get married, I'll be out."

"I got a feeling this will be the longest engagement on record," she giggled.

He pulled her even tighter to his body. "No, it won't. I can promise you that."

38

The Red Coach Grill on Stanhope Street was the perfect place for such a meeting. It sat in the shadow of the Hancock Tower on a small side street between Stuart Street and Columbus Avenue and was frequented largely by office workers from the surrounding buildings ending their day with a cocktail. Oblivious to others, the young executives, both male and female, were focused on detailing the vagaries of marriages gone wrong, and their need for extra marital activity, or on describing to a subservient, dominated colleague, their business triumph of the day.

Marty and Timmy arrived early, first of all to position themselves as they wished, at the rear of the restaurant facing the entrance, and secondly to scan the crowd in advance, assuring themselves that neither Apostoli nor the FBI had already planted an observer.

"Here they come," Timmy announced.

"Hey, Rocco, thanks for coming," Marty said, standing with his hand extended. "Good to see you, Dominic," he said, nodding to Saladna.

"Sit here. What'll you have?" Timmy said.

Briskly, Apostoli surveyed the room. "What's this? The poontang club?"

Marty summoned a huge smile. "It's a good place for us. They'll pay no attention and it's noisy as well."

"Self-absorbed assholes," Rocco sniffed piously.

"What'll it be gentlemen?" asked a petite redhead whose hair clashed with her red uniform.

"Dewar's and water," Apostoli replied.

"The same," Saladna, another dominated subservient, added.

"So how have you been, Marty? Tim?" Rocco asked sincerely, a faint smile near the corners of his mouth.

Apostoli was too warm, too friendly, Marty observed right away.

"First of all, thanks for holding off on moving against Terry Cavanaugh. We appreciate that," Timmy began.

"Call it professional courtesy. I expect you'd do the same for me," Rocco answered, sweetness cloying in his tone.

"I asked Marty if he could ask you to wait so we could discuss whether there's any other options here," Timmy began.

"He moved into my territory. Started operating right out of my back pocket," Rocco replied calmly. Why wasn't he exploding out of his seat, screaming about intrusions? Marty wondered.

"He also killed two of my men," Rocco added.

"According to his sister..."

"The one you've been dating, Tim?" The smirky smile again.

Timmy gave him a look, trying to gauge meaning. "That's right," he finally said. "According to her, your two guys followed her, planning to kill him. Cav thinks he was defending himself."

When Saladna snorted in contempt, Rocco glanced at him sharply.

"Look," Rocco said, addressing Timmy calmly. "What would you have me do?"

Marty shot him a skeptical glance. The only way Rocco Apostoli should be reacting is to stay on the course that any intrusion into Mafia territory had to be paid for. The question should have been "what would you have done?" And they all knew the answer to that. So where was Apostoli going?

"If you could make the peace with the guy, give him one more chance..." Tim was pleading, when Apostoli suddenly interrupted.

"You're awfully quiet," he said, directing himself to Marty.

"I'm with Timmy, Rocco. We would both appreciate your help."

Apostoli's shoulders twitched for just a brief moment. "Then we'll forget about it, how's that?"

Marty's gaze became a stare.

Timmy beamed and extended his hand toward the Mafia chief. "Rocco, thanks so much, I..."

Apostoli left it hanging in space. "I met this Cavanaugh, you know."

Here it comes, Marty sensed.

Apostoli sipped from his glass, taking his time, relishing the moment.

"Is that right?" Marty said.

"You remember me askin' you about my niece's murder over in Marblehead?"

Marty nodded.

"I found out Luis Gomez took that action along with the Pichardos."

Marty met his stare, unblinking.

"Yeah, I had Luis and his pals in for a little talk. Before we hung them on a meat hook and cut them up, they gave me the story. The whole story."

"What concern is that of ours?" Marty asked quietly.

"It should have been, Marty. It should have been your concern. Gomez told me he approached you on the hit. You knew all along who killed my niece and robbed the jewels." He'd never seen Apostoli so measured, so controlled. The accusation hung there in the air, making it seem even more sinister.

"I'm not a songbird, Rocco," Marty replied evenly.

"I guess not," Apostoli said. He waved to the redhead who was over in the corner making time with three sexed-up male executives who obviously had had too much to drink.

"Another round here," Apostoli yelled, pleased to be in charge of the table now, although it was not his meeting.

Saladna, who hadn't said a word, piped in. "Could have saved us a lot of aggravation."

"Well, yeah, but it turned out all right, y'know? It was Cavanaugh who tipped me off," Apostoli said. "He didn't consider it informing, he did the right thing."

"You're full of shit," Timmy said, his voice rising.

Rocco considered him. "I don't think so, Tim. Now me and Cav are pals, almost like best pals—y'know?—and as a reward for his service, I'm not only canceling the hit on him, but he's going to get a piece of the pie. Not my pie, mind you, your pie."

So that was it, Marty thought. And for some reason, he drifted back to a summer day on Glendon Beach in Dennisport. He had been swimming in the waters between the jetties. At the time, he must have been around fourteen or fifteen, unconscious of any lurking dangers. Proud of his abilities as a swimmer, he had stroked confidently toward the south, the sun beating its warmth into his cool skin, providing that exhilarating feeling that only the swimmer knows. Suddenly, he was caught in a riptide and, in an effort to free himself, turned away from his course parallel to the beach and tried to head for shore—unsuccessfully. The harder he swam, the more he seemed to be pushed outward to the sea.

From out of nowhere Jack had appeared, lifting him from under his armpits and then slowly stroking sidewards until they were free of the current. Back on shore, his uncle sat him on the sand and explained the importance of remaining calm in such a situation. Whatever the problem, there is always an out, he had explained, provided you don't panic. Think, he had emphasized. And above all, don't show your fear. Concentrate on how you can free yourself. And they had gone right back into the ocean, Jack insisting they move into the riptide, watching Marty from a distance as he once again encountered the pull. Once entangled, he had continued parallel to the beach and, in just seconds, passed through the swirling waters.

Jack had swum toward him, embracing him, congratulating him. "People are like the water, Marty," he had said. "They'll fool you, catch you up in difficult situations, overwhelm you if your fears show, but if you can remain calm, think, hide your concerns, then you'll win out."

"From now on, Cavanaugh runs 3% of your 12-1/2%," Apostoli was saying, alternatingly moving his eyes from Marty to Timmy. "It's up to you guys which

3% of the territories he gets, but we need to know soon."

"Who's we?" Marty asked softly.

Apostoli no longer was the relaxed Apostoli. His words were now laced with hatred, his manner acerbic. He leaned forward as he spoke. "We, is Gino Petrelli, Dominic here, and myself. And, oh yes, Michael Forelli, you remember Michael Forelli?"

Marty felt his lips thinning, a flush coming to his cheeks, but he said nothing.

"What the fuck makes you..." Timmy began. Marty placed a hand on his forearm.

"Anything else you want to tell us, Rocco?" he asked quietly.

Apostoli was enjoying the moment. He looked to Tim. "Only that you all understand the piece about Cavanaugh informing me needs to be kept confidential. I would hate to see that pretty girl friend of yours minus a brother should the spics find out who squealed on them."

"Hey, look at it this way," he smiled broadly. "The territory remains all Irish and Cav's practically a member of the family anyway, right?"

Marty placed his index finger on one eyebrow and ran it the length. Their personal signal that he was sure Tim would not miss. There was nothing more to be said here, not on this night.

Marty stood and picked up the tab. "Enjoy the rest of the evening," he said, as he signaled the redhead.

"Oh we will. Be sure of that, boyos" Apostoli replied derisively.

—

The next day—a beautiful, early May day—Marty and Judith walked from the cottage at Dennisport down Glendon Road to the beach itself, the stroll a welcome respite from the heavy physical labor of opening the cottage for the season.

He hadn't felt like talking much on the drive over the Cape Cod Canal and, perhaps sensing his mood, she had concentrated on the radio, on the generational songs that he could do without but she loved—"Eye of the Tiger," "Jump," "Always on My Mind." When they arrived, he had busied himself with raking the huge piles of leaves, remnants of last fall, and repairing the broken fence, while she vacuumed the interior of the tri-level cottage.

And he really didn't have much to say once they spread the blanket on the sand. They were practically alone, except for an aging swimmer who, coated with grease, swam fifty yards off shore, the stroke smooth and rhythmic despite the fact the water temperature had to be no higher than 50 degrees. Along the shore, a lone woman walked her golden retriever, the dog yelping in his fruitless chase to catch the low flying gulls coasting around him.

"You're awfully quiet today," Judith said, rubbing the lotion into her forearms.

"I've got a lot on my mind."

"Well, I'm all ears," she offered.

He didn't reply.

She stared at him for a moment and lay back, her eyes squinting as the sun won its battle with the only large cloud in the sky.

"Bobby's going to be in Swampscott his weekend," he finally said, just for the sake of saying something.

"Is something about that bothering you?" she asked, the reporter in her surfacing.

"No, it's not that. It's the life. Lots of things are going wrong lately."

"Such as?"

He picked up a pebble and scaled it toward the water. "Just some things," he said.

"Well, that answers a lot," she said sarcastically.

"I need to think them through myself," he replied softly.

"Right. You do that," she said, the anger rising in her voice.

"You don't understand. I can't share these things with you."

"You'd be a big hit in the newsroom, Marty. I mean with the specificity of your language and all—"things," "them," "the life." I have to be a fuckin' foreign interpreter to know what you're talking about."

"I don't want you to know what I'm talking about," he replied firmly.

She turned on her side, away from him and the sun. "If I have a problem, I need to be able to discuss it with you, and I think, in general, I do. And I feel better for your help. But a relationship cuts two ways. When you can't talk to me, then what you're saying is my advice, my input, is not important."

He reached for the portable radio in the beach bag. "I'm not saying that at all." But his flick of the switch effectively cut off the conversation.

The sportscaster was speaking of the upcoming June celebration in honor of Tony Conigliaro at Fenway Park. His thoughts drifted to days when he and Timmy would marvel at the fact that a St. Mary's of

Lynn graduate was a member of the Red Sox. Not only a member, but a productive home-run hitting contributor. Their Italian friends, in particular, would rave and rant with pride in his success. "That's the Conig!" they would scream from the bleachers, as the lanky young stallion raced around the bases. On June 6, the Red Sox would both honor and try to raise money for their ill-fated teammate, now recovering from a near-fatal heart attack. He would buy some tickets, take Timmy and Ray. It would be good to see a ball game in person and also see the '67 Red Sox back together again.

He looked to Judith who was either sleeping or feigning sleep out of irritation. He turned off the radio, stood, and walked to the shore.

He studied the old swimmer for a full minute, wondering what he was thinking all alone out there in the ocean. Whatever, he envied him. Right now all he wanted was to be alone with his own thoughts, to think his way through the riptide that was threatening to overwhelm him.

39

Telling his mother would be the most difficult. Later, he would inform his brother and his cousin, and that would be easier, largely because he could anticipate their highly prejudicial reactions. But Marjorie was the person who had brought him into this world, the mother who had nurtured him through the trying days of his youth, helping him cope with the realization that his father was the leader of the Irish Mafia. And then, when he had embraced the arts, how proud she had been of his having attended Emerson, never once missing his student performances. He often felt the arts were her protection, her defense mechanism as well as his, against the evil permeating their lives.

In his early days as a professional, she had faithfully followed the soap opera on television, ventured to New York countless times to see him perform on Broadway, and then shared his delight with his first appearances in film. She was both his mother and his biggest fan. And now he would be shattering her illusions.

They walked in the early Friday twilight near Fisherman's Beach, Humphrey Street abuzz with the homeward bound, long lines of cars stretching for miles back toward Lynn. When they reached the beach, they sat on a bench above it, facing across the street to the layers of homes rising on the Swampscott hills like a child's gingerbread cake.

"I'm terribly sorry you didn't get the part in that DeNiro movie," she said mordantly.

"They'll be other parts, Mom," he replied, more optimistically than he actually felt.

"But 'La Cage' looks like it'll run forever, doesn't it? Any other film possibilities right now?"

"I'm sure something will happen soon, Mom. My agent feels the success of 'The Big Chill' is bound to trigger some opportunities."

"You look a little thin, Bobby. And pale as well. I hope you're taking care of yourself." She patted his hand.

"How are things between you and David?" he asked, at once regretting not picking up on the natural lead-in she had provided.

"Fine. He and Timmy are getting along much better. David will be coming over tonight," she added. "And Tim wants to take you to breakfast tomorrow. He and Maureen have some event in Boston tonight."

There was an awkward moment when he realized that she has stopped talking, that there was an expectant quality to the silence. Had he been asked a question?

"What did you say, Mom?"

"I was saying that you'll see Marty tomorrow as well. He'll be coming by after noon."

He placed her hand in his. "Mom, there's something I need to tell you."

She beamed him her best smile. "You found a girl."

He shook his head vigorously. "No, Mom, it's not that. It's..." He paused for a beat. "Mom, I need you to listen to me, to hear me out. I've got a problem and..."

She squeezed his hand firmly. "Whatever it is, we'll solve it."

He looked straight ahead, across to the hills, and picked out a light in a kitchen window halfway up, determined to fixate on it until he had finished.

"Mom, there is someone or was someone for the last two years. He's gone now, he passed away, but I loved him as much as any man could love a woman. We were soul mates, if you can understand that. No woman ever made me feel as loved as Jason did. What I'm trying to say is that I'm gay, Mom. I've been gay for some years now, back to when I first went to New York, and, by inclination, long before that."

When he finally looked to her, she was reacting very differently from what he had expected. She was nodding to herself, absorbing and inculcating the news, trying to come to grips with it, but she was not overwhelmed by it. He should have known better. A woman who had to deal with crime on her doorstep for the better part of her adult life was used to surprises, to difficult news. If nothing else, she was resilient.

He had decided to tell her everything at once. But now he was hesitating, torn between wanting his loved ones to share his pain and his anxiety about the future and his desire to spare them, to hide his sickness from them for fear of overwhelming them with too much hurt at one time.

"There's something else, isn't there?" she finally asked quietly.

He looked across the street once more, choosing that same light on that same hill. "I'm sick, Mom. I'm HIV positive."

The silence that followed was deafening. She sat there quietly for the longest moment, saying nothing but reeling within, he knew, from the blows he had delivered.

"I'm feeling a bit cold, Bobby. Could we start back now?" she asked, standing before he could respond. Taking his arm hesitatingly, she asked a mother's question. "Are you seeing a doctor?"

He tried to answer optimistically. "A very good one, Mom, Dr. Paul Devlin in Manhattan. He's on the cutting edge of research on the virus..."

"I've read about the virus and the AIDS epidemic coming to the USA..." she interrupted, stopping in mid-sentence, trying to control her emotions.

"Not everyone who's HIV positive develops AIDS, Mom," Bobby said gently.

She didn't seem to hear his answer. "We need to have you see other doctors. Maybe..."

"Mom, I have one of the best now. I'm on a new experimental drug mainly because this Dr. Devlin's in the forefront..."

"We'll talk to David about it," she interjected.

Her crutch. David. Now was not the time to dissuade her. "We can tell him tonight if you like, Mom."

She nodded vigorously. "Yes, I would like that. He can possibly help."

He stopped in his tracks and turned to face her. "I'm sorry, Mom. Sorry to cause you this pain..."

She placed her hand over his lips. "Bobby Kelly, you've never done anything but bring your mother joy," she said as she moved to embrace him.

—

Later, they sat with David Aronson in the living room, the three of them discussing his plight. Bobby might as well have been talking Chinese based on David's limited knowledge of the topic. "I'm just a general practitioner, Bob, so I don't know how much help I can provide. This Dr. Devlin sounds very knowledgeable, and I've never even heard of the drug AZT."

No surprise to Bobby, but the comfort of David's involvement was a salve to his mother so he played along. "Have you any HIV positive patients?" Bobby asked.

"No, but if you'd like, I can put you in touch with some specialists in Boston..."

Bobby waved him off. "Thanks, David. But I feel I'm in good hands with Dr. Devlin."

"I believe you are, Bob."

"Do you want David or I present when you tell Timmy?" Marjorie asked.

"I'll do it myself, Mom, tomorrow."

—

On Saturday morning, Vinnin Square hummed with traffic at that point where Swampscott, Salem and Marblehead intersect. Outside the bagel shop, pedestrians hurried through the early morning sun shower on their way to the multitude of shops ringing the strip mall.

"So how's Maureen?" Bobby was asking, awkwardly, searching to find the right moment. Timmy seemed absorbed somewhere else.

"So when are you planning to tell me?" he finally said, averting Bobby's glance. He didn't wait for an answer. "You broke our mother's heart, you know that?" He looked around at the other circular wooden tables as if defying anyone to accuse him of talking too loudly.

"She told you?"

"You know what she said to me?" he asked, his face red with flush. "She wanted to tell me before you did, to spare you the difficult..." He stopped in mid-sentence.

"I also have to hear it from that asshole doctor, him, right in the middle of our family business. When I came home last night, they were still up—wanting to spare you the pain. How the fuck did you get into this situation?"

Bobby studied his hands as he rubbed the back of his right with his left index finger. "I'm gay, Timmy. That's how."

"My brother's a queer. I can't believe it," Timmy replied, stirring his coffee in a frantic swirl. "A handsome guy like you's got to lie down with a fuckin' man?"

"I prefer to lie down with a man," Bobby countered.

"It did you a lotta' fuckin' good, didn't it? Now you're walking around with AIDS..."

"Get the story right, will you Tim? I'm HIV positive.."

"What's the difference? A queer's disease is what it is. Wouldn't Dad be proud of you? A fuckin' son of Jack Kelly's is a fag. Unfuckinbelievable. Wait till Marty hears this."

"He's not my overseer, Tim. And neither are you."

Timmy didn't answer right away, instead choosing to blow hard into his hot coffee and ball his bagel wrapper, trying to control himself and failing.

"Where's the fairy that got you infected?" he asked. "Or was there more than one and you lied to Mom."

Bobby stared him down. "What are you gonna do, Timmy? Shoot him? He's already dead, and he was my friend. And I didn't lie. There was just one partner the last two years."

"Jaysus," Timmy said. "And what about before that?"

"What are you taking a survey for the Kinsey people, Tim?"

Timmy threw the bagel wrapper into the barrel near their table and stood. "Fuck you, Bobby." he said bitterly as he stormed out.

—

When you want to get drunk, go to a place that serves a really strong drink, Timmy had always felt. So they sat over at Romey's in Danvers near Liberty Tree Mall, the circular bar teeming with patrons who knew a good deal when they saw one. In the large dining room off the bar, people partook of the mediocre food while singing waiters paused between courses and took turns breaking out in Broadway songs.

"Give me another double scotch, Wayne," Timmy said to his favorite bartender.

"CC and ginger," Marty said, holding his empty up.

"Damn pervert," Timmy mumbled.

"How did your mother take the news?" Marty asked sympathetically.

"Better than I did, I can tell you that. She says David helps her, but he doesn't know shit from shinola if you ask me."

"About?"

"About AIDS. Can you imagine my brother's gay? Can you Marty?"

"He must be tapping drugs out there in LA, running with the crazies," Marty replied softly.

"When did he tell you?"

"He stopped by the dealership just before noon."

"He tell you his fuckin' partner's dead?"

"The guy who infected him? Yes."

"Good thing the fucker's dead because if he were still alive, I'd air condition the dirt bag," Timmy said, his voice rising even above the din. "I'm ashamed, Marty," he said in a more quiet tone. "I'm ashamed, I'm angry, I'm hurt. And I'm scared. I'm scared for him where he's probably too far gone in the head to be scared for himself."

"I read him as being plenty frightened," Marty said.

Timmy signaled Wayne for another round. "I can't talk to him anymore. I don't want to see him. What'd you say to him?"

"Mostly I listened. I asked him how he could do this to his family that loves him. And then I told him to go before I took a swing at him. I kept thinking of how Jack would feel."

Timmy stared into his drink. "I don't ever want anyone else to find out about this. Bad enough that asshole Aronson knows."

Timmy breathed in sharply, filling his lungs with the stale barroom air. Just about everything was going wrong lately—the Italians linking up with Cav, his brother infected with the HIV virus, the FBI leaning on them, and most importantly, his own increasing desire to leave the life, to settle down with Maureen.

When was there a right time to tell Marty? Certainly not now, not with the problems they were encountering. And maybe never. Maybe he could never gather the necessary courage to explain his feelings to Marty. He was not afraid of Marty, that wasn't the issue. He wasn't afraid of any man. What he was fearful of was disappointing his best friend, of letting his spiritual half down.

Suddenly Timmy felt a hand on his shoulder. "Timmy, Marty. Aren't you even going to say hello to your old pal?"

Terry Cavanaugh was dressed in a white turtleneck and blue slacks and had obviously been drinking heavily. On his other arm was a pretty black-haired young girl who looked like she was strung out.

"I just stopped by to thank you—y' know—for your part in gettin' me a piece of the territory." His voice was heavy with drink and dripped with sarcasm. "Y'know..."

"Fuck off, Cav," Timmy interrupted, standing.

Suddenly the pretty girl laughed. She was attractive, but her laugh was all little girl.

"Hey, I'm tryin' to be friendly here."

Marty turned so as to face him directly. "Be friendly somewhere else, Cav. And like I've told you once before, stay out of our way."

The smile faded from Cav's face. "I was hoping we could all be friends, my being the future brother-in-law and all..."

Cav never saw the elbow coming. As Timmy turned toward him, he dug it straight and true, on a flat trajectory into Cav's stomach. The air went out of him, and he grappled for Marty's arm to right himself.

Marty stepped in between them as, recovering, Cav reacted by reaching out to grab at Tim's shirt. Quickly, two muscle-bound bouncers arrived on the scene. "Hey, let's all settle down here!" the biggest one exclaimed.

Cav raised his hands in mock surrender. "No problem here. Just a small disagreement. Me and my girl was just leavin'."

Marty watched his hands back into his side, assuring himself first and foremost that Cav was not reaching for a weapon.

"This here's my future brother-in-law," Cav continued, not knowing enough to leave it. "We were just arguin' over who would be best man at the wedding—my friend Rocco or my friend Dominic."

Timmy stood there staring, the look on his face indicating, bouncers or no bouncers, he was ready to pounce again.

"Is he leaving, or isn't he?" Marty asked the bouncers.

Cav smiled his fuck-you smile and turned to the girl. "Let's go, Penny."

As they strolled to the exit, Marty followed them with his eyes. At the door, Cav turned and pointed his index finger and thumb back at Marty, the smile hanging there all the while.

40

"The sixth of June is D-Day in more ways than one," Stevie Guptill was saying between gulps of his coffee.

"Marty and I were there last night and you wouldn't believe the scene," Timmy replied. "Here we are—35,000 of us—there to honor Conig and Buddy Le Roux announces he's taking control of the Red Sox from the other two owners."

"No wonder the team's messed up," Gil Rafferty said.

They stood around the coffee urn on the warehouse floor as Marty stood off to the side conversing with Ray.

"This will push Yaz into retirement for sure. We're coming unglued," Chris said.

"Let's gather," Marty suddenly directed, moving to his seat at the top of the row of crates.

What was there about group behavior that made people sit where they always sat—the parishioners in church, senior citizens, kids in the first grade, the crew members here today—all like dogs protecting their space. That's what it was—a territorial inclination. And a discussion of territory was exactly why he had called them together today. He would begin by letting them vent.

"So what's up out there?" Throw it out, open-ended.

Sitting in a semicircle, they looked one to the other, waiting to see who would begin.

"We're getting our asses kicked, that's what's up, Marty," Chris said angrily.

"What the hell's that mean?" Timmy replied.

"It means the Italians are back kicking our asses like they were before Jack straightened them out," Chris said. "It means they're laughin' at us. It means they plant that asshole Cavanaugh right into our territory, him looking like he won the Irish Derby, thumbin' his nose at us."

"Why we lettin' this happen, Marty?" Paulie Cronin, in his innocence, asked.

"I've told you all before, Cav's getting a piece comes right from New York and Forelli, and from Providence and Petrelli. He did them a big favor, and they rewarded him."

"They're jerkin' us around is what," Chris insisted. "And we're sittin' here while they screw us over."

Marty decided to listen some more. How widespread was the discord? Was one of the dissidents—such as Chris right now—the informer in their midst as well?

"Cav's not settling for what you had to agree to, Marty," Stevie Guptill said. "He's pushing into Somerville and Cambridge beyond the agreement. The pimps report they're being challenged in a few of our locations like over in North Cambridge and near Dilboy Field in Somerville."

"The books are being pushed for a percentage in some areas where he doesn't belong," Joey Dunn said. "And the small-time crack dealers as well."

"Yeah, and on the waterfront the dagos are backin' him when he wants to put more than his share of guys on through the shape-up," Chris added. "Like I said, we're gettin' our asses kicked."

"What else?" Marty asked.

"What else?" Chris fumed. "You know Marty, Jack wouldn't have stood for this shit. He would have..."

Marty raised a hand to stop him. "Jack's dead, Chris."

Chris snorted. "Yeah, so I noticed. And we're dead, too. Getting kicked in the balls while Tim here's gonna marry the broad that's sister to the guy helpin' to lift our asses into space."

From his seat alongside Kiely, Ray Horan placed his hand on Chris's forearm. "Chris, that's enough," he ordered.

Kiely brushed off the hand, stood and angrily trod toward the coffee urn, Timmy following him with his eyes, glaring.

"See what's happening to us? Do you?" Marty barked. Standing, he walked toward them, tossing his empty paper cup to the floor. "This is exactly what Apostoli wants! Think! Why do you think they gave a piece to Cavanaugh? They did it knowing that it could create problems for us."

"Well, it friggin' well has," Chris muttered as he crossed the floor.

Marty let it go and waited until Chris sat down. "Let's go through this step by step. Number one, Apostoli and Petrelli boxed us in through Forelli. So for right now, we can't do much until Cav screws up. And he will or they will. They're gambling we will, but we won't. Not unless you play into their hands. Number two, they would love to see us involved in open warfare with Cav so they can report we're both out of control."

"What do they give a shit we're out of control?" Joey Dunn asked.

"So they can take it all back," Timmy answered.

"Exactly," Marty added.

"So what do we do? Just stand still?" Chris asked, his voice rising.

"That's just what we're going to do," Marty said firmly. "We'll move when it's time, and right now it's not the time. Not with the FBI watching us so carefully. Now with Cav, cut him off where you can without causing a major showdown. Otherwise, let him play his games. It's a pisshole in the snow is all. And stay together out there."

"If Cav gets any tighter with the Italians, we're going to have major league problems," Chris Kiely said, his tone quieter now.

"He's Irish. From their viewpoint, we're all assholes. It won't happen," Marty replied. "Just buy us a little time. I have a plan of my own, but we're just not ready yet."

If Chris Kiely asked what the plan was, Marty was ready to move him to the front of the line of those he suspected as the planted informer, but he didn't. Instead, he surprised him.

"Now you're sounding like Jack. You make us whole again, Marty," he said encouragingly.

41

John Carmody stood tall in the lobby at One Center Plaza as Marty and Tim came through the revolving doors. Briskly, he moved to greet them.

"Remember now we've volunteered to cooperate with the FBI, but whatever they ask either of you first pause before you answer. That will give me the chance to interject myself if need be. They've agreed this is an informal meeting, no recorders, no depositions. You're just two good citizens doing their duty. Okay?"

"Good morning, John," Marty smiled.

Carmody arched his eyebrows and smiled back. "I'm sorry. I'm probably more nervous than you guys, not knowing what's on their minds and all."

He pointed to the bank of elevators off the lobby. "Let's go up. They're on the sixth floor."

Once there, they were greeted by a middle-aged receptionist with pouty lips who coldly pointed them toward a long conference room in the corner. As they entered, a tall man in a gray suit stood to greet them. His tie was pulled tight, and the top button on his starkly white shirt was open. There was a subtle hint of casualness in an otherwise professional demeanor. "I'm Agent Chad Pearson," he announced in a southern twang. "Thank you for coming by. This is Agent Lisa Kennedy, my deputy," introducing a diminutive brunette with a pixie hair-do. "Please have a seat."

"No attorney?" Carmody asked right away.

"We're both attorneys," Pearson replied, his eyes smiling. "Coffee's right over there in the corner. Help yourselves."

"I want to reiterate that my clients are appearing voluntarily," Carmody started again, too anxiously, Marty felt.

"That's understood, counselor," Pearson replied softly. "We're off the record here."

"Well, then, what's this about?" Carmody asked.

Pearson smiled again. "I'd like to address some questions to Martin and Timothy."

"Go ahead," Carmody said.

"Martin," he began, the tone soothing, "do you know an individual by the name of Dana Carter?"

"No," Marty replied tersely.

"You sure?"

"I know a lot of people, Mr. Pearson, but I don't believe I know a Dana Carter."

"Never met him?"

"Didn't he just answer that?" Carmody interjected.

"Mr. Carter's no longer with us," Pearson said, fingering the open button on his neck. "He met his demise a few months ago. He took a few bullets through the head out in Newton at the train station on his way home."

"I'm sorry to hear that," Marty responded evenly.

"Dana Carter was a drug dealer over in Roxbury. He ran a real estate business on Dudley Street. That is he did until..."

"I said I don't know Dana Carter, and I have no knowledge of Dana Carter," Marty repeated forcefully.

"We have someone who says you do," Palmer said, letting it hang there in space like wet wool.

When no one responded, Pearson pressed on.

"And how about a George Doucette? Did you know a George Doucette, Martin?"

"I knew him," Marty nodded.

"How did you know him?"

"If he's the person I'm thinking of, I met him over in Southie at a social club."

"He didn't work for you?"

"At the dealership? No."

"Don't confine yourself to the dealership. Did he ever work for you?"

"No," Marty shook his head.

"How about you, Tim? You know either Dana Carter or George Doucette?"

"Just Doucette. I've met him around. I knew him casually is all."

Pearson studied his notes. "Terry Cavanaugh. Either of you know him?"

"Yes, I do," Marty responded.

"I know him," Tim nodded.

"He's a convicted felon, and you've both been seen with him," the deputy said, speaking for the first time.

"I'm engaged to marry his sister as I'm sure you know," Timmy offered. "I wasn't planning to marry him."

A loopy smile creased Pearson's face. "We understand that, Tim, but we're just curious about how well you know him."

"Not very well. He just happens to be the brother of my girl. That's it."

Pearson smiled the silly, relaxed smile once again. He looked at Marty. "Do you know Rocco Apostoli?"

"I know him," Marty volunteered.

"How do you know him?" Lisa Kennedy asked.

"I met him through a mutual friend at a party."

"You know him well?" she persisted.

"We're not bosom buddies."

"Do you know..."

"Excuse me, Agent Pearson. Are we to go through the entire list of every businessman in Boston here?" Carmody interrupted. "Through their legitimate business enterprises, my clients meet a number of people. If some of them have a criminal record, that's hardly..."

Pearson raised his hand in protest. "I just have one other comment."

Marty braced himself as Pearson's eyes narrowed. He was friendly and casual, but also smart, Marty reasoned. Keep the guard up. The Feeb would be going back to Carter, the only real surprise in the line of questioning. Something had gone wrong with Carter.

Pearson addressed himself to Marty, his tone soft and friendly. "I'd like you to think a bit more about Dana Carter. A lot more, in fact. Not right now, mind you, but over the next few days. Maybe you've just forgotten. Whatever.

"You see Marty if you can recall, then we wouldn't have to bring our witness forward to the grand jury. And if you could provide us with helpful information regarding Rocco Apostoli and his activities, we can cut a deal on the Carter matter, and make sure you receive a better deal than you're otherwise going to receive," he concluded, the voice now edgier, harder.

Marty leaned forward and placed his elbow on his knee and his hand under his chin. "You're bluffing, Mr. Pearson. If you had any witness that tied me to your Mr. Carter, we wouldn't be having this pleasant conversation. You'd be lugging me before the grand jury directly."

Pearson played with the open shirt collar and nodded. "We have that in mind, Martin. But with a little cooperation, it can be avoided. Do me a favor and think about what I've said."

"There's nothing to think about. Are we done here?"

Pearson smiled. "We're done for right now."

—

Afterward, in the lobby, standing together in a corner, they reviewed the meeting.

"What's he got?" Timmy asked.

John Carmody lit up his Newport and blew out some smoke. "He's got something."

"He wants both us and the Italians," Marty said. "We need to find out who this witness is and fast."

42

"The spot of tea will do you good." Catherine Slattery set the pot on the counter and then placed the Dunkin' Donuts alongside.

"But the donuts won't," he countered.

"And how's things with Judith?" she asked.

He shrugged his shoulders and dipped the plain donut into the tea, the Irish way. "When I'm preoccupied, I'm not good company, Catherine."

"And just who might that remind me of?" she teased.

"Am I like him?" he asked the only person in the world that he would ever ask.

She shook her head. "Oh, yes. The spitting image, as the old folks used to say. And you're a brooder like him, too." She reflected, caught in her memories. "Jack used to say it comes with leadership—the loneliness, the heavy burden, but I think it's also the Irish way. If we're not sad or brooding, we're not happy."

He smiled broadly, relaxing for the first time in days. "What's causing the troubles?" she asked.

"Mainly this informer thing. It's got me a bit unnerved, Catherine. I'm seeing too much in the shadows, but I'm not seeing things clearly. Any news from Danny?" He caught himself. A month ago he wouldn't have asked her the direct question.

"I would have been in touch if I heard anything. Are they building any stronger a case?"

He nodded his head. "The FBI says they have a witness against me. It would have to be someone within the crew, one of the direct reports..."

She mulled it over for a moment. "I know most of them from back to Leo's day, and it's hard to imagine any one of them turning."

"Unless the Feebs have one of them by the short hairs," he said.

"What are you going to do about Cavanaugh?" she asked suddenly.

"Nothing for now. The dagos gave him the 3% with Michael Forelli's blessing. So he's protected. I'll wait and see what goes down."

"More tea?" she asked.

"I have a business appointment back in Lynn, Catherine." He stood and bent to kiss her.

"It'll come to you, Marty. Give it time."

When he left, he looked around for any surveillance. Nothing.

—

Michael Forelli sat very erect, his hawkish face studying the first edition in front of him with great care. His hair was longish and steel grey, his dress impeccable, the grey pinstripe a perfect fit. He found the rare book beautiful and crisp, a wonderful addition to his collection.

He flipped the pages of W.C. Heinz's The Professional—in Hemingway's opinion, the best novel about boxing ever written—lovingly. Standing, he walked around the perimeter of his library, the shelves four stories high, ringing the ornate room. He climbed the ladder on the east side of the room and selected a space for the Heinz book between Hemingway's A

Farewell to Arms, signed by the master himself, and Melville's Moby Dick.

It was time to devote some thinking to other matters, to the business itself. Descending the ladder, he sat behind the desk and selected a Havana cigar, ran it under his nose to absorb its richness, and then lit it with the box of wooden matches. Puffing vociferously, he got it going and then ran it under his nose again. He sat back, inhaling its fragrance and then he began to smoke it slowly, enjoying it thoroughly.

Eventually, of course, good books and good cigars must give way to the dealings of the life, and so he thought first of New York. Here in East Islip, on his vast estate, 1983 went on without missing a beat. With Reagan restoring public confidence in the presidency, the suburbanites were thriving, playing the market, becoming paper millionaires. Half of them belonged in jail more so than he or any of his associates, he felt. And now that that idiot, Carter, had been ousted, inflation was in reasonable check. His profits were reasonably well protected. No, things were fine in the suburbs, whether one was talking New York, Philadelphia or Boston.

It was in the cities where chaos reigned. Take New York City itself. Maverick gangs were forming everywhere, cutting into the profits—inhumane groups like the Jamaicans who would cut your balls off as soon as they would look at you; the Westies, crazy Irishmen who if they had enough to drink, would place your head right there on the bar after they decapitated you; the Black crack dealers out of control, illiterates who had no regard for human life.

The Mafia was decidedly different, he had long ago surmised. There was a structure to their activities, rules, codes of honor such as Omerta, a businesslike approach to matters of life and death. For centuries they had greased the palms of the authorities—the courts, the police, the politicians, the influential—in order to attain their goals. They honored their business, and they protected their women and children from the ugliness of the profession.

Today these vigilante groups would just as soon kill your family as look at them. Crime was rampant now in the city, causing law enforcement officials to crack down on all of them out of fear of those who operated without a social structure and values. The only good to come of it all was that the police were easing up on the Mafia what with the necessity to devote resources to the crazies.

He stood and walked to the enlarged map of the eastern United States pinned to the corkboard behind his desk. Thanks to his leadership, New York had held together in these difficult days. And through his political influence, the FBI and the U.S. Attorney's office in Lower Manhattan were beginning to charge the Irish maniacs in Hell's Kitchen with violations of the Racketeer Influenced and Corrupt Practices (RICO) Act. Pretty soon Jimmy Coonan and his group of nut cases would be gone from the scene. In Philadelphia, Carlo Giambra was in firm control, the Italian presence solid throughout the City of Brotherly Love.

And then there was Boston. He worried about Apostoli, an Italian not of the old school. What was his business? Meatpacking. Forelli sniffed the air at the thought. He liked Petrelli, a gentleman with some taste, some values, some culture, and he depended on Petrelli to keep Apostoli under control and so far it was working. Profits were a bit off, but not by much.

He thought of the reports he was receiving from Boston regarding the Irish, surprising reports of their beginning to battle one another and of their causing problems. He smiled when he thought back to his meeting with Jack Kelly. He had liked the man right away. Unlike Jimmy Coonan and the other Westies, Kelly had brought a social order, a structure, to Irish crime in Boston. Granted, there were other Irish groups—Winter Hill, Bulger—but Kelly had prevailed and had ruled as he, Forelli, had—with efficiency, effectiveness and compassion.

He had met the nephew but once, on the ferry to Staten Island, when he had struck an agreement with Jack Kelly, shortly before his heart attack. And he had been impressed with his maturity, and his bearing, as well as his startling resemblance to his uncle. So he was both surprised and displeased by these recent developments—profits reportedly slipping a bit in the Irish—controlled territories; the FBI beginning to roust them, calling too much attention to them all. He had agreed to Petrelli's strong suggestion that they reward the new Irisher. What was his name? He couldn't remember. He had done them a favor and his sister was due to marry one of the Corsicans anyway.

He expected Petrelli and Apostoli to honor the agreements made. After all, if they could not, then they were no better than the new groups he detested. On the other hand, if the Irish fell apart under the nephew, then steps would have to be taken. Business was business.

43

"Let me relax you," she whispered as she came up behind him. Placing her hands firmly into the crevices of his neck, Judith kneaded the muscles. He sighed audibly as she silently went about the work.

Far below them, the city had come alive for the perfect June night, its citizenry bustling about, rushing toward the mall at Copley Place or the restaurants surrounding Copley Square itself. From the balcony, they could hear horns blaring constantly, piercing the night air. In the distance the sky swelled with the slow-deepening purple of early evening.

"You need to talk about it," she breathed into his ear.

He did not respond. He often wondered why it was that everyone expected a reply to his or her comment. Sometimes, as the nuns had emphasized in his youth, silence is golden. Other times there was just nothing to be said in response. Still other times you just hoped the speaker would not notice or just go on to another topic.

"Hello? Earth to Marty. Are you there?"

He laughed and pulled her around to his front and sat her on his lap. He placed his hand beneath her chin and kissed her long and hard. "I love you," he said, nibbling on her ear.

"Sometimes I wonder," she replied, more coldly than playful.

"I do need you."

"Do you, Marty? Do you really need anyone?"

"I do. I need you. I need this relationship."

She stood and walked to the railing, her back to him, the breeze pulling the negligee tight to her firm body. "A relationship involves sharing, a commitment, a willingness to give something of yourself to the other person."

He decided to let her vent.

"You're not letting me into your life, Marty. You need to make a decision. Either share with me the problems you're facing or get out of the life, or give me up. We can't go on like this."

He moved to her and placed his arm around her waist. "I'm protecting you, Judith."

"You're shutting me out."

That's not my intent."

"But it is the result."

"I don't want you involved in this dirty business. I don't want you worrying..."

"I worry now," she interrupted.

She turned and walked back through the open slider. He watched her move to the bar and ease herself behind it. She didn't look back toward him. He measured the distance between them, not the actual distance, but that ever-widening psychological gulf when people find good reason to embrace physical separation. She was here now but she wasn't and the chasm was deep and becoming deeper. How to stop its movement?

He studied her as she poured herself the Jack on the rocks. Three months ago, one month ago, she would have asked him if he wanted something. Now she didn't even look up as she poured the amber.

He was losing her.

She crossed the room with that sway that had first attracted him back at the dealership. At first she didn't say a word as she leaned forward, peering down at the street, her elbows on top of the wall. "You need to make a decision, Marty. I love you, but you need to make a decision," she said, her voice firm and cold.

"I know," he replied softly.

—

"How are you finding the support group?" Dr. Devlin asked, tenting his fingers against his lips.

Bobby laughed out loud. "We were discussing doctors last night."

"Really? In what connotation?"

"The way most doctors are treating potential carriers of the HIV virus these days. We all have friends who are gay or drug users who are profiled together as members of high-risk populations. Did you know doctors are avoiding them, afraid of physical contact with them?"

"Doctors are people, too, Sean. Some of them are afraid, and there are powerful forces out there in the medical profession who want to generate new guidelines to segregate people who are potential carriers. Thank God most of us don't feel that way."

Bobby drank a little of his ice water. "Those of us already infected are treated even worse. Some of my group have friends who are segregated in hospitals, in rooms recognizably marked. They say the staff hides behind masks, avoiding contact in spite of all the protective layers. Others report doctors don't spend much time with them at all."

Dr. Devlin sipped his water. "Whenever there's a major problem in this country—the Japanese internment, McCarthyism, this new AIDS epidemic—there are those who respond poorly. Give us time, Sean. We'll get it right."

"I know <u>you</u> will, Doctor. I bragged about you."

"I'm not among the barbarians?"

"Decidedly not."

Devlin picked up the file folder and studied his notes. "Your CD 4 count is low but still holding. A healthy person should show 1,000 cells per cubic millimeter. Illnesses develop with a count below 200. You're at 400. How are you feeling?"

"Still tired occasionally," Bobby replied.

"It's been almost three months since we diagnosed you with the virus. It's a good sign. A number of people develop AIDS quite rapidly."

Devlin closed the file folder. "How was the trip home?"

Bobby stared into the water glass. "Not very good."

"Reactions?"

"My mother's stoic but in her own way, more accepting, but there's no way my brother and my cousin can accept my being gay. That's even worse than my being HIV positive in their world."

"The support group help you to understand their reactions?"

"To a degree. Most of us are experiencing similar problems." He raised a hand to his eye and brushed away a small tear. "It's difficult when those you love fall out of love with you."

Devlin stood and walked around his desk. He sat down in the straight back next to Bobby and held his hand. Bobby sobbed softly, trying to regain control.

44

"Yes, Gino?" Rocco Apostoli replied. He propped the phone against his car as he cut into his huge steak.

"This line is safe?" Petrelli asked.

"Absolutely."

"How are things with your Irish friend?"

"Cavanaugh's doin' all right. Just as we asked. A little push, just enough to irritate."

"Good. Good. And the profits? Are they holding?"

"Wait a minute, Gino." He placed his hand over the phone and yelled to his wife in the kitchen. "Maria! This steak's not hot enough! Will you cook the God damn thing so that I'm not eatin' the cow itself!"

A petite woman stormed into the kitchen and scooped up the plate without so much as a look at Rocco.

"Fuckin' hurt feelings," he muttered to Petrelli. "I might as well eat one of the sides of beef right out of my meat locker."

"Can we get back to the issue?"

"What issue?"

"The profits, Rocco."

"Off a little, like you said to be sure they were. Cavanaugh's a street guy, not a leader. He doesn't have enough systems in place to be sure his own guys aren't robbin' him."

"What reactions from the Corsicans?"

"Basically they're sittin' still, almost as if they know what we're up to."

Petrelli considered the comment for a beat. "Marty's smart. He'll be slow to take the bait, but eventually he can't let Cav push him too far. He has to react. That's what we want—him reacting, causing trouble."

"You want anythin' else done?"

"Tell Cavanaugh to slap one or two of Kelly's key people around a bit. See where that leads."

"He doesn't consider that he's workin' for us, you know."

"Indirectly they're all working for us. What do you mean?"

"I mean Cavanaugh takes orders from no one. He's a complete loner. He scratched our backs, he feels, and now we're scratchin' his."

"Let him think whatever he wants to think. Just plant the idea we wouldn't be adverse to his expanding a bit more if he wants—if he can pull it off."

"I got ya."

"And Rocco..."

"Yeah?"

"Treat the wife a little better. I heard your comments. Develop some class."

Rocco didn't bother answering. Imagine that pansy criticizing him. Some day soon maybe he'd have the bastard on a meat hook and then carve him up, just like the spics.

—

Terry Cavanaugh sat at a rear table at the Powerhouse Tavern at Sumner and East 1st in Southie, like a king being attended to, the hangers-on forming an entourage around him. Playfully, he arm-wrestled with different challengers, winning more than 80% of the tussles.

In front of him, the bar ran the full length of the room to the right of the entrance. The American and the Irish flags adorned the wall behind the bar with pictures of prominent Irishers aside of them—Jack Kennedy, Michael Collins, James Michael Curley. Next to Cav's table stood an old-fashioned jukebox and a cigarette machine. In the far corner, opposite him and close to the bar, was a unisex room fronted by swinging doors.

On a Friday evening the smoke-filled tavern was crowded with a cross-section of Boston's Irish: the union types from the waterfront, tired and weary after a long week, hoisting longnecks noisily along the bar; old men, lonely for company, sitting peering into their boilermakers, looking for someone to listen to their stories of long ago; and the young men, pushing and shoving for attention, yearning to be a part of the entourage around any recognizable player.

Mick Riley stood at the bar downing the Bud as fast as it could be served. He looked to the entrance for a moment and that's when he saw Ray Horan and Chris Kiely. Pointing in Terry's direction, he made sure that Cav also noticed who had just strolled in. Cavanaugh nodded in acknowledgment and focused on the wrestling, his pile of greenbacks building as he asked for another challenger.

At the end of the bar, Ray and Chris spoke with a number of the union workers, talking the ritual macho talk, upstaging one another with stories potentially to be bettered by the next teller.

Cav pushed the young ironworker's arm down to the table and then stood with his whiskey glass in hand. "That's it for tonight, guys," he said, scooping the dollars into his pants pocket. He walked to the bar and stood next to Riley.

"Let's go see what trouble we can cause," he said.

They moved toward the entrance and the head of the bar. Pushing his way into the circle around Ray, Cav signaled the barkeep. "What do you say, Ray? How about a drink?"

Ray heard him, but didn't answer. He continued with his story until the end, until the punch line led to a roar from the small group.

"A drink for my friend," Cav said to the bartender.

"No thanks," Ray replied.

"Hey! I'm just tryin' to be sociable here is all," Cav said, holding his drink high.

Ray stared at him as the noise subsided, the crowd now sensing trouble developing.

"Be sociable with your own then," Ray said. "I don't drink with any Irisher who's in bed with the guineas."

"Fuck you, old man," Cav replied, as he threw the remnants of his whiskey glass into Ray's face.

Instinctively, Ray grabbed him by the throat.

"Okay! That's it! Take it outside to the alley, but not in here!" the bartender yelled, hoisting a baseball bat in the air.

"You game, old man?" Cav taunted.

"Let's get to it," Ray replied through clenched teeth.

They filed out to the alley, Cav's entourage urging him on against a man twenty-five years older, the union workers gathering in support of Ray.

In the alley, the men formed a circle except for two or three posted on the sidewalk to warn of any approach by the police.

"Ray, walk away, please," Chris pleaded in a low voice. "We don't need this."

"Nobody throws liquor in my face, Chris," Ray replied angrily, shedding his jacket.

He moved to the center of the circle in full recognition that there would be no Marquis of Queensbury rules applied here. Immediately trying to gain the upper hand, Cav bull rushed him. Ray kicked him in the kneecap with his raised foot and as Cav stopped in place, threw a short, right hand to his nose. As Cav bent to address the pain in his knee, Ray drove his knee straight into the younger man's groin.

From the circle, Cav's supporters pushed forward, ready to assist until they saw the .38 in Chris's hand. "Let them be!" he yelled.

Cav threw a wild roundhouse right and fell to the pavement as the sound of sirens grew more distinct.

"Let's split!" someone screamed from the back of the crowd.

Someone hoisted Cav to this feet as Ray and Chris ambled toward their car parked along Sumner Street.

45

"Thank you for coming."

Marjorie Kelly fidgeted with her coffee cup in the study of her Puritan Road home. Across from her, Marty and Timmy sat in rapt attention, like Irish boys everywhere, paying traditional respect to the older parent, particularly to the older woman.

"I want you to hear me, not just listen, but really hear me," she said firmly.

Marty eased back on the couch while Timmy toyed with his coffee.

"When Bobby first told me he was gay, I was devastated," she began," as I'm sure you both were. But I've been thinking, and I want you to think along with me. I've come to grips with Bobby's being gay, even though at first I wasn't entirely sure I could. You know what I decided? I decided my son is a well-adjusted, bright, talented, artistic, kind human being. So why shouldn't I accept him?

"At first I felt ashamed. What do I tell members of the family? Our friends? I worried about what they might think. But what's changed? He hasn't really changed. He's still my Bobby, my son. He still loves me, and you Tim, and you Marty. He still thinks of us as his family, as the people on whom he depends.

"He may have changed his sexual preference somewhere along the line, and it's made you angry and ashamed and feeling as though everyone will look at you and wonder...why? He really hasn't changed his appearance, his warmth as a human being, his charm, his loving ways. He is the same lovable young man you loved just days ago. I'm not asking you to accept his gayness. What I am asking is that you accept your brother, Tim. And you, Marty, your cousin who adores you. No matter what his sexual preference, he is your blood. My blood. Help him through this difficult time. Help me if you love me. Don't turn your back on him because of some macho Irish Catholic bullshit. He needs you, he needs your acceptance, your love, because..."

Her lips began to quiver. "Because he may die. Love him, not his preferences, his make-up. Love Bobby the person, the human being."

She lowered her head in search of a tissue. "If you love me, make peace with my son. I want you both to make peace with my son."

Jack might as well have been talking, Marty thought. No wonder he had married the woman. And although he had his prejudices, Jack has possessed the universality of view to rise above them.

Marty did not respond, showing deference to his cousin. But he knew what would follow because his twin in spirit thought as he did and acted as he did. Timmy looked across at him, both seeking concurrence and sensing affirmation. He stood and leaned over his mother. "We'll take care of it, Ma. We'll make things right."

—

As she walked along, it passed through Maureen's mind that it frequently takes until late June before the really hot summer makes its appearance in Boston. The wrestling contest for domination of the atmosphere between late winter (forget spring) and early summer, plays itself out until close to the Fourth of July.

But this summer, the summer of 1983, every day was perfect, because every day was one day closer to August 6. She glanced at her watch as they strolled past the Park Street Station, heading across the Common toward the long aisle of benches.

"You've got only one more month of freedom, bub," she teased, placing her hand in his.

"When you're married, maybe you'll begin to practice love, honor, and obedience," Timmy teased. "Take the vows and learn to respect your new husband."

She smirked and pulled back her hand. "They don't do that vow shit anymore," she responded haughtily.

"I don't plan on marrying a heathen who won't obey her Irish husband."

"Too late, pal. You're caught," she laughed. "Where are you taking me on our honeymoon, by the way? Stop keepin' it as a surprise."

"Charlestown. It'll be an upgrade from Southie for you."

"Ha, Ha. Funnyman. Where, wise guy?"

"Ireland. You know Marty and Judith were there in the spring. I thought you might..."

"I'll love it! Ireland. Oh, Tim, I can't wait." She threw both arms around his neck and pulled his head to her lips.

"Everything's going to be so perfect like this very day," she murmured into his ear.

—

"What's wrong with you two fuckin' guys! Getting into a fight in public with Cavanaugh! First Timmy takes a pop at him and now this! How many times have I told you? What would you guess, Ray? Nine? Ten? I feel like I'm dealing with fuckin' morons!"

Marty stood at the big bow window that fronted the beach. Across the street teenage boys and girls climbed atop the sea wall and timed their jumps into the breakers below. He started to pace as he thought about the situation.

"You should have seen Ray clean his clock," Chris Kiely bragged, breaking the silence.

Marty stopped dead in his tracks and gave off an icy stare. "That's just what Apostoli wants. Open fights between Irish gangs. Something more to report to Petrelli and probably to Forelli as well."

"It was my fault, Marty," Ray volunteered.

"I know it was. You'll get no argument from me."

"What were we supposed to do? Lie down for the guy? He threw a drink in Ray's face," Chris yelled in frustration.

"You two get the fuck out of here before I lose my temper," Marty replied softly, as he walked into the kitchen.

46

They met at a West Lynn institution, the Lido Cafe, right around the corner from Waterhill Street where Harry Agganis had spent his boyhood years. The Lido was one of those neighborhood cafes where the food surpassed the pricier restaurants by a long shot or otherwise they wouldn't have stayed in business for over fifty years.

"You're not drinking?" Marty asked.

"You go ahead. Like I said on the phone, there's something important I need to say," Timmy said apprehensively.

Marty took a bite of the cheese pizza and chased it with some of the beer. He studied Timmy carefully but really didn't have to ask what the topic might concern. Not when you've been at one with somebody for better than thirty years. Not when you've been inseparable since pre-adolescence. For some reason he thought back to the time when he had played quarterback for English against one of Stan Bondelevitch's great Swampscott teams led by Timmy, a punishing runner and simply the best linebacker the Big Blue ever had, according to Bondelevitch himself. It had been painful seeing Timmy on the other side, crouching there over center, ready to break up their plays. There had been no trash talking among teens, just a straight-out business approach to the competition. Whatever he attempted as quarterback, Timmy anticipated the play. And when Swampscott was on the offensive, he just knew where to hunt down Timmy from his position at safety. They looked alike and they thought alike, as

Jack had so often pointed out. They had reminded Jack of the Corsican Brothers from the old Douglas Fairbanks, Jr., movie. Twins with one soul.

Later, when Jack had taken them into the life, they had made the same mistakes together. Wild, impetuous actions, like the time they had robbed the Mystic River Bridge payroll without Jack's permission. But then they had matured together, rising in the crime family, earning the respect of the others until the night when Jack had chosen him as the heir opponent over Timmy, his own son.

"You want to get out," Marty said it softly, understanding in his voice.

"How did you..." He stopped himself. Of course Marty would sense it just as he could sense the way Marty would react. "I'll be married in just a few weeks, Marty, and here we are fuckin' fighting with my future brother-in-law. I promised Maureen I'd get out before we start a family and live like normal people, her not having to worry about me ending up in prison or on a slab somewhere.

"She's willing to wait a while if I want to stay in it, but the sooner I get out the better. I know there's never a good time to leave, and I know now's a particularly bad time..."

You can say that again, Marty thought, as Tim continued with the explanation. If there ever was a good time for an exit, this wasn't it. The string of concerns was with him perennially these days: the loss of the territories to Cav and the Italians; his own declining relationship with Judith, due to his inability to open his heart fully to her; his cousin diagnosed as HIV positive; the FBI closing in, buoyed by an informant somewhere in his midst; and now this news, not unexpected by nonetheless devastating in its own right.

"I'd like to close things down soon, y' know? Right after the wedding if we can. It would be sort of like a wedding gift to Maureen, and I'd devote full time to the dealership then. What do you think?"

Marty balled his right fist and stuck out a playful short jab to Tim's chin from across the table. He answered as Tim knew he would. "You do it if that's what you want."

47

"The grand jury is the only secret proceeding in American jurisprudence," John Carmody was saying over a cup of tea in his ostentatious conference room. "Its workings are generally not known by the average citizen."

Marty listened attentively as his lawyer continued.

"First of all, it's a reasonable cause hearing. Is there reasonable cause to believe you committed a crime? If the grand jury believes so, they go for an indictment and then later you have your day in court. Unlike a trial or a regular court proceeding, grand jurists can even put questions directly to witnesses. And you as the defendant have no right to an attorney being present, not unless you're testifying yourself.

"Then, whenever any witness testifies, that witness receives what is called transactional immunity, which means the witness cannot thereafter be prosecuted for any crime related to any transaction he or she testifies about. Any crime at all, except, of course, perjury committed during the testimony itself. This brand of immunity is to encourage witnesses to make full and complete disclosure to the grand jury—to help the prosecution catch bigger fry."

"When would the grand jury be called?" Marty asked.

"Like I said, it's a secret proceeding. At any time. They'll want to be sure the witness or witnesses are solid. My guess is probably in August, two, maybe three or four weeks from now. It's close."

"And this witness? Do we find out who it is?" Marty asked.

"There's no word at all on who it is, and they don't have to tell us. They do face a greater standard of proof in the courts, though, than they do before the grand jury. Whatever, the rumors are out there, but they're not moving yet. We haven't received a subpoena." He paused for a beat. "There's some good news here," he added, half-smiling.

"If there is, I'm not seeing it," Marty said.

"The Racketeer Influenced and Corrupt Practices Act—RICO. In order to charge you and Tim with that, they would need to go above and beyond an individual case and establish a pattern of racketeering. It doesn't appear they're going in that direction. They can't make a case."

"So everything's coming down to the witness?"

"And therefore a specific charge," Carmody said. "And if the witness isn't already in a witness protection program, he or she will be between the grand jury indictment, if there is one, and the trial itself."

Marty sipped his plain tea and stared out the window over Carmody's shoulder. He was running out of time.

48

Runners on second and third with one out in the last of the sixth. Bobby stood on deck as the batter laced a hard line drive straight into the third baseman's mitt. Two out. Bobby strolled to home plate swinging two bats. It was when he threw one to the side that he spotted his brother standing near the edge of the screen behind home plate.

In his surprise, he didn't acknowledge Timmy's presence and then, with the roar of the "La Cage" cast overwhelming him, he attended to the business at hand. In the distance, three other softball diamonds practically blended into theirs, outfielders from one game virtually shaking hands with fielders from another contest. But there was nothing like playing softball in Central Park, all of them low in a bowl shaped by the surrounding trees and the skyscrapers on Fifth Avenue and Central Park South and West.

Stepping into the batter's box, he adjusted his cap and tapped the bat against his cleats. Positioning himself comfortably, he watched the first pitch sail high and away. On the second pitch, he extended his arms and drove the ball on a straight line to the gap in left center, scoring both runners. He romped into second base, his wheels tired from the effort.

From the bag he looked for Tim, who was nodding in slow approval. Why was he here? Bobby wondered. With the pitch, the next batter slashed a single to left, and Bobby raced around third heading for the plate. Halfway there, he simply ran out of gas and slid too soon, making himself an easy out at home. Still, they had taken the lead.

After a 1-2-3 top of the seventh, his teammates, fellow actors all, gathered in the bleacher near third base shouting "I told you so's" to the cast of "My One and Only" on the other foul line. Spectators began to mix in with team members as the players collected their gear.

"How did you get here?" Bobby asked irritably, as Tim approached him from around the screen.

Timmy decided to answer the question in the narrow sense. "I stopped by the theater looking for your new address, and the stage manager told me the cast was here."

"That's not what I meant," Bobby responded coolly. "What brings you to New York?"

"I need a reason to visit my brother?"

Bobby hoisted his gear over his shoulder without saying anything.

"Ma thought I should talk with you." As soon as he said it, Timmy regretted it.

"Ma said you should talk with me? Is that what you said?" Bobby asked, facing him directly.

Timmy sighed and tried again. "Can we take a walk? You got the time? There's some things I need to say."

Bobby wouldn't let it lie. "Things from you or Ma?" Then he remembered something the leader of the support group had stressed at their last meeting. Don't wallow in self-pity when it came to family. Accept their difficulties with the situation and provide them with the same support you expected.

"Let's walk over to Sixth Avenue. We can get a drink at O'Neal's."

"Sounds good."

They climbed the embankment to the loop utilized by joggers and bicyclists and dog lovers and virtually anyone else enthralled with the idea that right here in the middle of the greatest metropolis in the world sat the greatest park in the world. They followed the circle until Central Park South crossed into Sixth Avenue.

"You were hitting the ball pretty good back there," Timmy offered.

"Slow pitch."

"Still, you drove it. How are you feelin'?"

"About the same."

"Isn't that a good sign?"

"Maybe and maybe not. Some of the early research shows the virus can lie dormant for years and then progress rapidly. It's always there, a worry, you never know."

They walked into one of Jack's favorite New York spots—O'Neal's at West 57th. As Tim entered, he quickly noticed that all the wait staff was young, energetic and obviously involved in the acting world.

"Hey, Patrick!" Bobby greeted the Irisher serving behind the bar. Along the elongated bar itself, the crowd stood three deep at four o'clock.

"What can I get you?" Patrick asked.

"Club soda for me. I've got the play tonight," Bobby replied.

"Straight whiskey," Timmy said.

"Hey! A real man's man!" Patrick replied.

"He is that," Bobby smiled.

When they had the drinks, Bobby pointed to the rear of the restaurant. "We can get a seat back there."

They sat alone at the very last table. Timmy surveyed the crowd and when he looked at Bobby caught the bemused look on his face.

"No!" Bobby said emphatically.

"No, what?" Timmy asked awkwardly.

"No, it's not a gay bar."

"You could have fooled me."

"So what did you want to talk to me about?"

Timmy downed the whisky in one swallow and signaled to a wholesome blonde that he needed another. "You know I could never accept this fuckin' lifestyle..."

"What lifestyle?" Bobby interjected.

"What lifestyle? Do I have to tell you? Guys goin' down on each other, fairies flutterin' their wings..."

Bobby let out a loud sigh. "An awful lot of macho men are gay—boxers, weightlifters..."

"Yeah, whatever." Timmy waved his hand dismissively. "I was taught differently, and I thought you were, too."

"So you came all the way to New York to lecture me about lifestyle?"

The blonde reminded Timmy of a young Marilyn Monroe with her pouty face, reddish lips and headlights up to high beam. She deposited the drink and wheeled away.

"I came to tell you something and to ask you something else."

"I'm all ears. Whatever it is, it looks like you need a few snifties before getting into it," Bobby said, pointing to the whisky glass.

Timmy stared at him. "I can get to it. Don't worry about that."

"So?"

A pained look crossed Tim's face. "So I want you to know that I care about you, Bobby. Like I said, I can't approve of this bullshit—he waved his glass in front of his face—but you're my brother and you matter to me. You always have, and you always will. I just want you to know that if ever you need me for anything, if you get sick, have some kind of setback, well then, whatever..."

Bobby raised his palm to interrupt, in an attempt to alleviate Tim's obvious difficulty. "Tim, you..."

"Shut the fuck up and listen," Timmy replied. "I just wanted you to know I'll be there, is all. And one other thing."

"Yeah?"

"I want you to be my best man at the wedding in three weeks. I want you there, and I want you to be my best man."

"I didn't get an invitation to the wedding," Bobby teased.

"You just did, asshole."

Bobby placed his hand on top of Timmy's. "Of course I'll be your best man. And Tim, thanks so much. I know how hard..."

Timmy looked askance at the hand on top of his. "Hey! I don't want people thinking I'm gay."

Bobby laughed. "I know. God forbid. Better for them to know you're a fuckin' racketeer."

Timmy smiled broadly and winked at him. "Not for much longer. After the wedding I'm leaving the life."

Bobby grabbed his hand and pumped it vigorously. "Tim, that's just great!" he enthused.

Timmy scanned the big room. "Easy on that happy shit," he said, scowling, withdrawing his hand.

"Don't worry," Bobby laughed. "It won't rub off on you."

49

"So Timmy's gone to New York to see Bobby. I'm pleased to hear that."

Sheila Kelly handed her son the Canadian Club and ginger ale as they sat beside the swimming pool in her backyard.

"Where's Dad?"

"He'll be here in an hour or so. Why don't you take a swim before then?"

"I think I will." He sipped some of the CC and moved toward the diving platform. He walked to the very end and prepared to jump.

"Oh! I forgot to tell you. Ginger Dalton called you here yesterday."

He paused just before leaping. "Oh yeah? Again? What did she say?"

"She said she didn't want to call you at your house or at work because she was afraid people might overhear her. She said to tell you thanks on the Carter matter, and she wants you to call her so you can get together for a drink so she can thank you personally. I always liked that girl," she continued. "Wasn't she your very first serious girl friend? Who's this Carter she's talking about?"

He made believe he hadn't heard the question and dove deep into the pool. Thinking . Why would Ginger want to meet with him again?

Surfacing, he swam freestyle down the length of the pool. When he reached the end, he flipped against the wall and began breast stroking. Ginger Dalton had called again. Why?

The FBI was now talking confidently about an impending charge to the grand jury. They had asked about Carter. Only three other people knew of his order to eliminate Carter—Timmy, Ray, and Rafferty. Even with Ginger, he had been careful, never answering her request directly. Either one of his most trusted aides had informed on him, or Ginger had been co-opted.

He stopped at the end and rested an arm on the pool wall. He was missing something. He could feel it, could almost put a finger on it. And then it came to him. All along he had been focusing on the idea of an informant, one informant. What if the FBI, as Catherine Slattery had told him, had an informant and, in addition, a witness. Two people, not one. What if the stool pigeon had led the FBI to a potential witness. And now Ginger had been asked to implicate him further.

He started to swim again and suddenly stopped halfway down the pool. He crossed sideways toward his mother's lounge chair. "Mom, have you ever mentioned the two phone calls from Ginger Dalton to anyone?"

She thought for a moment and picked up her glass of iced tea. "No, certainly not. That's your business. No, wait a minute. When she called yesterday, I was alone. I haven't mentioned it to anybody but you today. When she called that first time, weeks ago, I was with Marjorie and David. I did mention it to them. They couldn't help overhearing me repeating the names—Ginger Dalton calling about a Dana Carter. David even asked me something about it."

—

In the summer twilight, only a few others were playing hoops at the Meadow. At the opposite end, four Blacks were wrapped in their own game of two on two and paid him scant attention, which was exactly what he needed right now. Dressed in tan shorts and a white tee shirt, Marty played a version of twenty-one: score seven points from the right base line, seven from the left and seven from the foul line—but all in a row. No misses, or go back to zero and start again.

Across the Meadow, as far as the eye could follow, groups of young boys chased baseballs down, attempting a few more pitches, a few more at-bats before the setting sun called a halt to their activity. Beyond the baseball diamonds, older men with potbellies and coolers relived their youth by playing softball, while young women pushed baby carriages along extended foul lines.

David Aronson. Marjorie's guy. What was he? Marty wondered. A copper? A fuckin' Feeb? He had to be the informant. Marty cursed himself as the ball bounced off the hoop at six points. He was cursing his stupidity, not a bouncing ball. How had he missed it? Missed it? He hadn't even considered it, focusing instead on his own crew, not on his own family, suspecting Rafferty and Chris and Stevie and practically everyone else.

He thought back to that meeting with the FBI guy—Pearson—at One Center Plaza. It all made sense now. They had mentioned Dana Carter as part of a fishing expedition to panic him and gain his cooperation. And they had hinted at a mysterious witness against him. No name, no push then, because they probably didn't have Ginger Dalton convinced to testify at that point. But this recent call asking him to meet with her indicated they now did. When he had originally met with Ginger at his home, he was sure he did not indicate he would kill or have Carter killed. He guessed they had now promised her what Carmody had called transitional immunity if she were to help them nail him—catch him actually admitting to her that he had ordered the killing.

At the right base line, he threw in the one-hander that brought him to fourteen points. Moving to the foul line, he thought about the importance of maintaining his rhythm. He dribbled the ball three times and let it go. Swish. He ran in for the rebound and laid the bunny against the backboard. At seventeen. Four to go. Back at the foul line, he bounced the roundball three more times and, studying the front rim for a second, let it fly. Perfect. He ran under the basket and laid the bunny against the backboard. One long shot to go.

He would have Stevie Guptill check out Aronson quietly and carefully. But if he were right, the doctor bullshit was strictly a front. The sons of bitches had moved Aronson right into his family. Right into his aunt's home! None of them had been dumb enough to discuss the life with the asshole, but he had to assume a woman in love had told her lover something of his and Timmy's involvement in the life. She didn't know much, but she knew enough to provide background and new information to him.

And Ginger Dalton. When he had tried to contact her, just this afternoon after leaving his mother's, he had reached her roommate instead. She was traveling, but she would be in touch. Translation: the FBI was hiding her, protecting her, that is, until they were ready to place her in direct contact with him. Direct entrapment, he corrected himself.

He rolled the ball with is thumbs and fingers and lifted his last shot just over the rim. Perfect. Twenty-one. Recovering the ball, he sat on it, using the chain link fence for support. They thought they had Marty Kelly. Well, they didn't, not yet. Not quite yet.

50

Terry Cavanaugh didn't really know Lynn that well. He had come in from Route One near Lynnfield and driven across the city. At 7:00 a.m., what with all the traffic, that was no easy feat. He calculated it had taken him almost one half hour to reach Gardiner Street, just off Boston Street in West Lynn.

Just as he drove down the roadway, the skies opened up, spreading the darkness low on the horizon as the rain pushed in to create a dismal mid-July morning. He coasted along, seeking out the creme-colored three-decker that Mick Riley had described. Unlike Quincy and with that scum Victor Rodriquez, he had decided not to reconnoiter the area ahead of time himself. He had sent Riley instead.

If Riley was correct, then Ray Horan was another creature of habit, like Rodriquez. Mick had observed Horan from a distance on the long, flat street and noted that he left the apartment every morning at exactly 7:15, walked up to Boston Street to the Little River Inn for a cup of coffee which he then carried back to his car before heading off to the dealership.

Terry cruised past the Lincoln School in the stolen car, heading east on Gardiner. He eased into an empty spot about fifty yards up from the triple-decker at number 22.

Fuckin' Horan had surprised him, beaten him to the punch and embarrassed him. An old man like him. The prick had almost broken his kneecap with his first move or otherwise he would have had him. But no man embarrassed Terry Cavanaugh and lived to tell about it.

While waiting, he checked the area one last time. Occasionally a car would come out of a driveway on the residential street. To that person or anyone else, Terry would look like just another guy waiting to pick up a friend on their way to work. Reaching into the glove compartment, he pulled out the .38. He chambered a round and then placed it next to him on the seat.

He kept the windshield wipers working, pleased with himself that he had deliberately waited for a rainy day, recognizing that everything would go much more smoothly with the poor conditions. Traffic should be a bit lighter, neighbors less observant, and the gunfire less noticed.

Later, when it was all over, maybe the Kellys would figure him as the perpetrator, but he would vehemently deny his involvement. Three weeks before his sister's wedding would he be involved in the assassination of one of his future brother-in-law's best friends? Of course not. It was not his style. He had been sure to plant word around the bars that he had been blindsided and sought a fistic rematch sometime in the future. They would probably believe him, and if not, he would plead his case to Mo, have her settle that asshole she was going to marry down. Besides, the Italians would love to see the Kellys causing more trouble. They might even turn to him to run things if the bastards lost complete control.

Suddenly the rain lessened in intensity, and at that very moment, Ray Horan appeared on the front steps in a olive belted raincoat. He bent to pick up a newspaper, scanned the headlines, and then folded it and placed it inside his long coat.

Descending the steps, he turned east for the one-hundred-yard walk to the coffee shop. He walked briskly through the light rain looking straight ahead all the time. And so the car was on him much too fast for any reaction.

Starting up, Terry drove slowly to a point twenty yards behind Ray. He then lowered the passenger side window and cruised toward the curb. There were no cars behind him. When he pulled alongside Ray, he yelled "Ray!" and as Horan turned to the voice, he lifted the .38 and shot him twice in the head.

Quickly he sped from the curb, turned right onto Boston Street and climbed Tower Hill, watching the rearview mirror for any signs of activity. At the bottom of the hill, he cruised into the White Hen convenience store lot at Austin Square, parked the car and, without hesitation, stepped into the waiting vehicle driven by Mick Riley.

—

Paulie Cronin drove the Impala through the gates of St. Joseph's Cemetery in Lynn and headed toward the bank of newly dug graves on the east side. Turning cautiously, he navigated the narrow roadway searching for the spot. He came to a complete stop fifty yards down from Ray Horan's unmarked resting place.

"You wait here, Paulie," Marty directed, as he and Timmy opened the back doors and stepped out.

The sun beat down on them, warming the mid-July day even as early as nine o'clock in the morning. They walked across new mown grass past row after row of carefully groomed gravesites, most marked with either an Irish or an Italian surname.

At Ray's grave, they both kneeled, made the Sign of the Cross, and prayed silently, each to himself. Around them the world stood completely still, as if everyone had stopped whatever they were doing to pay their respects.

Standing, Marty made the Sign of the Cross once more. "We'll make sure his wife and kids are taken care of," he said mordantly.

"He was a good man," Timmy said, standing.

"The best."

Marty looked straight ahead, his hands in his jacket. "Cav called me last night," he said, disdain in his voice. "He wanted us to know he had nothing to do with it. He knew we would think first of him after the fight with Ray and all, but he wouldn't be so stupid as to call attention to himself, not with the wedding coming up."

"You believe him?"

"No. It was either him or Apostoli and his people. My guess is it was him. But it doesn't really matter because they're both responsible—pushing us, causing us problems."

Timmy walked around the perimeter of the grave. "What are we going to do?"

Marty paused before answering. "You're getting out. It's best you stay out of it." He hesitated again, trying hard to control his anger. "I'll tell you one thing, though. I'm going to take care of all business with Cav. You have any problem with that?"

Timmy didn't respond because he wasn't sure how to respond. He just continued to stare at the grave.

Marty studied the mound of dirt. "You know the last time I saw him I was yelling at him about the fight with Cav. Me yelling at our most loyal guy. He's got to be avenged, Timmy. There's another thing," he said, changing his tone.

"What's that?"

"I asked Stevie Guptill to look into something else."

Timmy looked up and waited.

"Your mother's boy friend—David Aronson—he's the informant. I don't expect you to do anything about it, but you need to know."

"What the hell are you talking about?" Timmy stammered.

"What I'm talking about is that the FBI has planted Aronson right on your mother's doorstep. He's either FBI or some other kind of cop. He overheard a call to my mother's home from Ginger Dalton, a call where she mentioned Dana Carter by name.

"There's two people, Tim. An informant and a witness, not one. The FBI, through Aronson, linked Ginger to me, and my guess is that they've been squeezing her for weeks now, threatening her if she doesn't cooperate. And now she's asking for a meeting with me. She'll come wired from ass to elbow. I had Stevie check Aronson out. There's an office in Cambridge, all right, with a sign on the door and a receptionist if anyone's inquiring, but no real practice, no one coming or going."

"I just can't believe it!" Timmy finally replied.

"Believe it. I'm positive. And you know I'm going to have to hit them."

"What about my mother?"

"When she finds out later that the asshole's a complete fraud, she'll get over it," Marty said.

Timmy struggled with the ambivalent feelings now overwhelming him. His future brother-in-law, his mother's boy friend.

"If I don't take out Aronson, the FBI will parade him before the grand jury and they'll publicly embarrass your mother, even if they can't call her as a witness at the trial itself," Marty said.

"It's still a big gamble hitting a fed and a witness," Timmy replied, his anxiety showing through.

Marty replied evenly. "I have a plan. You just stay out of it."

"When are you moving?"

"Soon. We're running out of time. Within the week."

Timmy nodded in acknowledgment, turned away, and started the walk back to the car. Overhead a large silver bird descended toward Logan with a shattering boom, breaking into the silence of the dead.

51

Timmy sat alone on the deck at 40 Glendon Road in Dennisport. He had assured himself that no other family member would be utilizing the cottage before driving down. In the late afternoon, a fiery sun poured through the pine trees, drawing beads of perspiration from his forehead. The drink sat there as it had for the past half-hour, full and unattended, because he had finally decided he needed a clear head with which to think.

For the last half-hour, he had been dwelling on his father, searching for a possible solution through the past, through history. What would Jack do? He had wondered, but not for long. There was no question as to what he would do. His father had been that curious mix of a ruthless loner and a loving, compassionate family man. But the life always came first, despite popular and traditional clichés about family being paramount in most people's lives. No question Jack would kill both Cav and Aronson. He could almost feel Jack's presence here on the deck asking him what possible reasons could he have for not avenging Ray and for not icing an intruder who had invaded his own fuckin' family home?

And yet he was sure his father had never known anyone in his life like Maureen. Jack had never truly found love with another human being. Could he marry this beautiful person just two weeks from now, live with her, have children with her, knowing that he had been involved in killing her brother whom she doted on and loved? And he had promised Mo he would leave the life long before they would bring children into the world.

And as he considered his own new found love, could he then take away the same from his own mother? He could answer that more easily. Of course he could. Aronson had used his mother and therefore couldn't possibly love her. He could testify personally to the family discussions which would include references to the life, and he could tie him and Marty directly to Ginger Dalton. Eventually the FBI and Aronson might even try to drag both Marjorie and Sheila before the grand jury or the court itself to testify.

Sitting there in his bathing suit, staring straight ahead, his elbows on his knees, he suddenly felt ashamed. He picked up the plastic glass full of whisky and threw it over the rail out onto the grass. Forces were pressing in on them from all directions and here he was sitting on his ass, feeling sorry for himself. There really were no decisions to be made. They had been made a long time ago.

He stood and walked into the living room and searched out the picture of him and Marty on the glass-topped coffee table. He picked it up and studied it, remembering back. They must have been eight years old then, standing side by side on Glendon Beach, each holding a horseshoe crab by the tail. On the mantle above the table, another photo pictured them together as Little Leaguers. In his memory, he saw ten-year-old Marty standing on the mound, shaking off signs, sending Timmy, the catcher, his own kind of telepathy, Marty-thoughts, coming in on their own special frequency. A silent conversation no one else could hear, reading each other's thoughts as the batter stood at home plate. "Let's throw the heater," they would agree, without one spoken word.

A third photo showed Marty in his Lynn English red and gray football uniform and he in the blue and white Swampscott colors, the picture taken in their senior year at Manning Bowl after the game.

The Corsicans. The Irish Corsicans. Inseparable. Suddenly he remembered he was already married—to a life and to a lifetime companion who was more a brother to him than his very own.

He began to consider the steps necessary to closing the cottage. He cut the air conditioning and shut down the television. Then he thought of taking a shower before heading back, but first he needed to place the call.

"Hello," Marty responded from his private line at the dealership.

"About that plan that you were talking about?"

"Hey, cousin. Where are you?"

"You remember that old Duke Ellington song? 'Do nothing till you hear from me'!"

—

He calculated that they hadn't talked for over a month now. Not since that night out on her balcony. They had decided to give each other time and space, and he was sure Judith was testing the distance just as he was. But there was one inevitable consequence—as each day passed by, he could feel the distance widening. She had responded to the wedding invitation by indicating she could not attend. Would not attend was probably a better choice of words.

So it was virtually over. On occasion, during the past few weeks, he had thought of calling her. But to what avail? If love, as she had insisted, meant sharing and communicating, then he was not in love. They were secrets never to be shared with a woman.

He missed her, and her softness, and her wit, and most of all, her presence. He steeled himself as he looked out the bow window to the beach. Under the lampposts at midnight, the world looked purplish and black, full of half shadows.

Ray Horan was dead. His uncle's best friend and his most trusted associate shot down on his own street practically in front of his wife and daughters. Fuck love, fuck sharing and communicating. There was only loyalty that really mattered-loyalty to his crew.

The upcoming wedding would relax all enemies, thus making them particularly vulnerable to his plan. Tomorrow we would set the plan in motion.

52

"How can you be so sure?"

Miguel Torres walked in the sun behind Northeastern University just off Mission Main. Alongside of and behind him, an entourage to put even Sugar Ray Robinson or Muhammad Ali to shame accompanied them. On a mid-week afternoon the traffic formed a long ribbon on Ruggles Street backing all the way to Columbus Avenue.

Despite being the lone white man in the group, Marty felt comfortable. They reminded him of the Irish just decades ago when the Yankee Protestants held them back—that is until the Irish achieved both political and economic power. The Hispanics possessed no political base yet, but among them, smart, young leaders were emerging, and in the Boston gang culture itself, Miguel Torres had quickly shown his prowess, swiftly consolidating Luis Gomez's territories.

"Luis came to me, Miguel," Marty responded. "He asked Tim and me in on the deal. I said no for my own reasons."

Miguel Torres looked like that guy Brawny in the soap ads with his white tee shirt and tan slacks. His muscles had muscles, and his black hair was combed straight back with no part. "And what reasons were they?"

"It wasn't my cup of tea, Miguel. Home invasions. But Luis went ahead against my advice."

"And you're telling me Apostoli told you he killed Luis and my cousins?" He suddenly turned around quickly. "Kill that fuckin' bandbox," he screamed, to a diminutive crew member holding what looked like a suitcase next to his ear as he bounced along to the music of "She Works Hard for the Money."

"He told me he tortured them and hung them on meat hooks in his freezer, then had them cut up and buried somewhere out on the Mass Pike."

Torres weighed the information without expression and then changed the subject. "Why you been giving Luis's widow money?" he suddenly asked, indignantly.

"He was my friend."

Miguel nodded. "Do me a favor, Marty. It is appreciated, but I can take care of my own."

"Whatever you say," Marty replied.

"He said that? He said he froze them like fuckin' steaks and cut them up?"

"He did. You seen him lately, Miguel? He's wearing a ring in the shape of one of those Egyptian pyramids. It's one of the expensive stolen pieces he got back from Luis. If you saw the jewels at all, you'd recognize it."

Miguel chose not to reply right away. When he did, he was more talking to himself than to Marty. "Felipe and Elvis came up with me from Puerto Rico. As teenagers, y'know, with no money in our pockets. My aunt, their mother, took me in, gave me a bed, and then later, Luis took me into his confidence, gave me a job." He stopped for a moment and waved his hand in the direction of Mission Hill. "The three of them helped build all of this."

Again he shifted gears quickly. "Why you tellin' me all this now? You expect me to hit Apostoli?"

"What you do is your business, compadre'. I'm telling you now because the asshole just threw it in my face the other night," Marty replied.

Torres walked along silently until they reached the corner of Huntington Avenue, practically right across the street from the Museum of Art. He extended his hand. "They didn't deserve to die like that," he said. And then came the surprise. "But they caused their own problem. I'm not sure if I'll do anything about it," Miguel said, before turning abruptly back up the hill.

53

When the call came, he was ready. Mentally he went through a checklist. Assume the call was being recorded. Assume Ginger Dalton would never reveal her location. Assume she would at least attempt incriminating him over the telephone. He was right on all three counts.

"Marty? Ginger Dalton. Please thank your secretary for putting me right through."

"Hi, Ginger. I tried to call you back, but your roommate said you've been traveling. Where are you?"

He stood and walked around the desk, the long chord in his hand. He tried for a voice tone that masked his deepening concern. Be cool. Be patient. Be smarter than the Feebs.

"Marty, I just want to thank you in person."

"For what?" he interrupted her.

"You know..." She was edgy, hesitant, and so he took advantage.

"You want to see me, Ginger? There's no need..."

She came back strongly. "Yes, yes there is, Marty. I want to personally..."

Cut her off again, he told himself. Now was the time to be aggressive.

"Sure, Ginger. As you suggested, let's meet for a drink sometime. Tell you what. I'm flying around here today, what with the business and my cousin's wedding coming up soon. Give me a call in a day or two, leave me a message, and I'll meet you wherever you say. I haven't got time to study the calendar right now though. If there's a problem, I'll call you back. Give me your number."

She was slow to respond, evidently deciding that was the best she would get for the moment. "I'll call you tomorrow," she finally said.

Say it one more time. Make her the one pressing for the date, not him. "But there's really no need..."

This time he let her interrupt. "Yes, there is, Marty. I'll call."

"Fine," he replied before cutting the connection.

—

A week before the wedding, the Dubliner prepared to enter the rolling waters of Lynn Beach at that point where the MDC bathhouses announced the end of the Nahant Causeway and the beginnings of the rotary that leads directly into Lynn.

Before him, the endless turquoise sea seemed to stretch into infinity. Pretty sailboats darted beyond the breakers, their multi-colors etched against a flawless blue sky. The wind was up, pushing the boats like trains along the track and the waves ran high, cutting down on the view of the serious swimmers one hundred yards out.

The day was perfect, the pale, lanky man thought. A day to die for. And that was exactly what he intended for David Aronson. According to the Kellys, on those weekends when the boy friend and the mother did not utilize the Cape cottage, the informer invariably chose Lynn Beach for his early morning swim.

The Dubliner placed the diver's gloves on his hands and then jumped into the sea, his hot feet suddenly cooled from the sizzle of the sun. Through the undulating waves, he spotted Aronson swimming along, alternating between a ponderous Australian crawl stroke and an even slower backstroke. From a distance of eighty yards, he started toward the informant, each of them now out a hundred yards from shore, as they swam parallel to the land.

The Dubliner noted that Aronson never really looked about. When he tired, he lay in a dead man's float, letting the sun's rays hit square on him. And after two or three minutes, he would start swimming again.

As the Dubliner moved along, he affirmed that it would be particularly difficult for those on shore to observe his actions. The high waves blocked a real view of activity out beyond the breakers. And there he was, maybe thirty yards away now, backstroking from south to north, probably heading toward fuckin' China, the Dubliner thought. Hopefully, Aronson was as tired as he was.

At twenty yards, being careful to reduce the noise associated with his stroke, he stopped and dived down below the surface as Aronson continued his methodical backstroking. Now six feet under, the Dubliner started his ascent, propelling himself upward, his hands locked together, concentrating, ready to hit directly under the rib cage, in an area that would leave no marks. He would hit, lock in, and then drag the informant under. Surprise and emotion were the two elements that would carry the day. First, he needed to be on him like a tiger, and then he had to overwhelm him quickly, venting his anger on Aronson in a wild and frenzied rage.

Surfacing on the ocean side, he slammed his locked hands directly into Aronson's stomach and without waiting for a reaction, grabbed him by the hair as Aronson thrased about in the sea. The Dubliner held tight to the back of his neck with his forearm, utilizing the strength built up from his years as a stevedore on the waterfront. As he pulled Aronson under, he kept his own legs tight, preventing the victim from kneeing him in the groin. He counted the seconds they were under water, swirling about—one hundred and one, one hundred and two. Suddenly, Aronson's eyes stared back at him unblinking and a small line of bubbles ran from his nose. Pushing down even harder, the Dubliner was careful not to leave any incriminating marks on the neck.

An eternity seemed to pass, but he had long ago learned that time went by much more slowly than the emotionally involved person felt. So he waited longer, and even longer, until the mouth opened and the frame went slack in his hands, and then he let go and swam slowly toward the north, toward Lynn, never once looking back, separating himself like a wide receiver from a defensive back.

—

When the call came, Rosie responded with the truth as she knew it. "Kelly Chevrolet, Martin Kelly's office," she began in a cheery singsong.

"Is he there?" the woman asked.

"I'm sorry. I didn't catch your name?"

"Ginger Dalton. I called the other day?"

"Yes, Ms. Dalton. This is Rosie O'Neil, his secretary. What can I do for you?"

"I need to reach him. I'm a personal friend."

"I'm afraid that may be difficult today. He's not going to be in the office..."

"Rose, may I call you Rose?" she interrupted.

"You certainly may," Rose replied gaily.

"Let him know I need to see him today, and that I'll be on the train platform at the Government Center, north side platform, at 4 P.M. I'll wait for him, and then we can get a drink somewhere..."

"I'm not sure he'll even get the message..."

"Please tell him it's very important I see him later this afternoon, Rose."

Replacing the phone on its cradle, Rose filled out the message form, stood, and placed it with the five or six others on Marty's desk. She doubted seriously that he would be in at all, his having indicated to her he'd be down the Cape most of the day at his next door neighbor's barbecue. No one, absolutely no one, was to disturb him.

An hour later, she directed the pale, lanky young man from the window washing company into Marty's office and left him there to do his work. Occupied with a myriad of tasks, she never saw the Dubliner move around the desk and flick through the half dozen red slips centered on the blotter. Having absorbed the information, he turned his attention to the window overlooking the harbor and slid his wipers into place.

—

Trains careened and screeched through the subway station under Government Center, directly under the very offices of the FBI itself. At 4 P.M. the platform was virtually filled with homeward-bound commuters anxious to return on the Blue Line to Revere and Winthrop and other points north. No one paid particular attention to anyone else except for the weary-looking woman who anxiously stood on her tiptoes looking left and right over the heads of larger men and women. Occasionally she glanced at her wristwatch.

The Dubliner sat on a bench against the wall reading his paper, both studying her and assuring himself that no one else was watching her. Every five minutes or so a tilting car would rumble through, disembarking but a few and taking on hordes of new passengers. And just as quickly as the platform cleared, another one to two hundred people would appear. Jaysus, they didn't work long hours in America for sure, he thought. Since 3 P.M., he had been observing the early exodus from the city. No wonder the American economy was going into the shitter.

Convinced she was alone now, he waited for the right opportunity. The federals must have wired her and figured that was enough. They had left her on her own—a big mistake.

As the minutes passed, she seemed to sag a bit in discouragement, looking at her watch almost frantically now. Suddenly, she made some sort of decision because she moved forward on the platform, ready to be in the first line of boarders when the next northbound rolled in. Behind her, a bulky, awkward guy with a beer barrel stomach hid her from view for a moment.

The Dubliner stood, rolled his paper and pushed his way into the crowd, giving off the prerequisite "excuse me's" as he moved to a position behind the beer belly. From around the bend, a glaring light cut through the darkness, its rays expanding as the sounds of the arriving train reached their ears. People looked up from their papers and pocket books and instinctively creeped forward, pushing and jostling as the big train rumbled into view still a hundred yards away.

The Dubliner made sure he gave an ugly look to the young Black executive behind him who was angling for position. Act exactly like the rest of them, he told himself. He waited until the train was thirty yards away and slowing before he half pushed and half grabbed the beer belly, causing him, in turn, to fall into and shove Ginger Dalton directly onto the tracks.

A horrifying shriek came up from any number of passengers as the train plummeted over her body and took what seemed like forever before coming to a halt. "What happened? What the hell happened?" crowd members asked one another as most moved as far away from the edge of the platform as they could.

The Dubliner joined the chorus of screamers and then slowly separated himself, easing his way back toward the entrance along with a good number of others who sensed that it would now be a long commute home from this particular station.

54

"What the hell happened?" With his southern twang, Chad Pearson drew the question out so that it lingered in the air like wet wool.

Lisa Kennedy and two other agents—a Mutt and a Jeff—looked down at their folders then up at one another, each hoping for the other to take the lead. Beyond the plate glass window, Boston winked back at them, the city not yet ready for sleep although the midnight hour grew near.

As the senior agent, Lisa decided to bite the bullet. "It's possible it's all coincidental," she finally said.

"Bullshit!" Pearson snorted. "An agent and a key witness both go down on the very same day, and your explanation is it's a coincidence? I don't buy it."

"Bear with me a moment, Chad."

"I'm listening," he replied, drumming his fingers on the conference room table.

She scanned her notes. "David was swimming this morning as he does most summer mornings. No one saw anything amiss. No one saw anyone else anywhere near him. When he floated up on the tide, the wits described him as having green water streaming from his hair, his eyes half-open. No marks on the body, according to the Lynn Police. No bullet holes, no stab wounds. And the police played it well. Normally medical examiners don't attend drownings these days, but they called one anyway. It's all preliminary, but they believe he drowned."

Pearson stood up and walked to the window, largely to contain his anger. "On the same day as we lose a wit? You're shittin' me!"

"Can I go on?" Lisa asked, agitation creeping into her voice.

When he didn't reply, she looked again at her notes. "At 6 P.M. tonight the M.E. returned my call. They'll be an autopsy in the morning. She'll be surprised if it's anything but accidental. Chad, there was a rip tide today. Swimmers are known to panic, to tire, and drown. He could have go caught in a rip current. Besides which, there's no way Kelly could have been on to him."

"Why not? Because you say so?" he replied derisively.

"That's my report for now," she replied coolly.

"Not quite. What about Dalton? Let me hear your explanation for that fuckin' fiasco."

The tall agent glanced at the short one as Lisa indicated "That's Frank's."

The short agent reached for his cigarette pack on the table and then thought better of it. "Dalton left the safe house in Winthrop at 3:30 P.M. and took the train to the Government Center, wired just as we planned."

"No escort?" Pearson asked indignantly, his question directed to Kennedy rather than her subordinate.

"I briefed you on that yesterday, Chad. Kelly's too smart for us to have her under surveillance when she's supposed to meet with him. She agreed, and I thought you agreed, that we'd go just with the wire." When something went wrong, you needed your boss to hang in there, but it was obvious Pearson was bailing. "Go ahead, Frank," she directed.

The short man flipped his notepad and began reading from it. "Three or four witnesses say people were shoving and jostling one another to gain position on the platform. Directly behind Dalton was a guy named Jeffrey Sterling, an immigration administrator. A couple of wits identified him as pushing in on her, and he claims someone shoved him from behind. It honest to God looks like an accident, chief. No one saw anything different."

Pearson sat down and folded his hands together. "What about Kelly? Where was he?"

The tall agent, who looked like Billy Joel with the bulging eyes and receding hairline, spoke for the first time. "He was on the Cape all day. Fifteen people, none of them crime connected, say he was at a barbecue all afternoon. The next door neighbors on Glendon Road—a couple from Worcester—verify he had breakfast with them in the early morning. He was nowhere near either scene."

Pearson put on his superior look. "I wouldn't have thought he would be."

Kennedy decided to venture forth. "There's something else makes me believe they're just two coincidental accidents."

Pearson's lips thinned. "I don't want to hear the word 'coincidental' one more time today. You all reading me?"

Mutt and Jeff nodded while Kennedy simply returned his stare. "He never got the message about Ginger Dalton wanting to meet him," she said.

"Now exactly how do you know that?" Pearson asked, toying with his shirt button.

"We know he was at the Cape from at least 7:00 A.M. to this very hour. I've already gotten the cooperation of the telephone company. He didn't place a call, and he never received a call. We know Ginger called the dealership at 9:00 A.M., talked to his secretary who told her he wouldn't be available today. She says she left the message about the meeting on his desk. He never saw it, he never knew about it, according to his secretary."

"And you don't find it odd that she didn't call the Cape to tell him about a proposed meeting?"

"I did," Lisa replied coolly. "But he said he didn't want any interruptions, and he's got an ironclad alibi, and we've got no evidence of foul play."

"Where was Tim Kelly all day?" Pearson asked belligerently.

"With the mother, once he learned David drowned."

"Jesus! You know what? They've outfoxed us. Months of work gone down the drainpipe. We place an agent right next to the mother, and we turn Dalton with the threat she might do time and now we have nothing..." His voice trailed off. "Both of those Irish assholes have alibis for the whole day, and my investigators don't find anything that's not coincidental. Well, I find it really fuckin' coincidental that you idiots haven't figured out yet that someone else, under their direction, carried out these murders."

Kennedy crossed her legs and stared him down. "We have absolutely no evidence of murder, Chad. And if someone else were involved, then he must be the freakin' invisible man—that guy Claude Rains. You remember him, Chad? And another thing—don't desert us on this, act like you're above it because I'm not taking the fall. You approved of today's plan. This is 1983, long past the time when the old dinosaurs in the Department fuck up and the rest of us are supposed to go down with the ship."

Chad Pearson continued to play with his open shirt button. Who the hell ever agreed to take women into the FBI in the first place? he wondered.

—

He tossed the empty peanut shells over the rail, his back to the South Boston tenements rising on the hills. Boston Harbor lay still before him and in the distance two ferryboats chugged toward Thompson's Island, carrying teens from the city to their once-a-year environmental holiday.

"What say you, pal?" Maureen Cavanaugh greeted her brother playfully as she bumped him from behind.

He turned at her voice. "Hey, Mo! Now how's the blushing bride to be?" he asked, embracing her and kissing her nose. "Look at you," he said, separating from her, flashing the charm, putting on the brogue. "They's be no prettier bride this whole summer, I say. Now tell me pray, how come you have time for your brother with the wedding just a few days off?"

She pointed toward the L Street Bathhouse. "Let's walk a while."

He kept up a steady stream of Irish malarkey as they strolled south on Day Boulevard. "Yes, sir, when my beautiful sister wants to see me just days before her wedding, soundin' all alarmed, I have to wonder if she's takin' to smokin' the weed..."

"Terry, I have to ask you something," she interrupted, a hard edge to her voice.

"I'm all ears," he replied, grinning as he placed his thumbs in his ears and wagged.

"This friend of Timmy's—Ray Horan. Did you have anything to do with his death?"

Cav reeled back sharply, as if he'd been slapped in the face. He stopped dead in his tracks and placed a hand over his heart. "Listen to me, Mo. I swear on our mother's grave, I had nothing to do with that. Do you actually believe I'd be involved in the murder of my future brother-in-law's best friend just before your wedding?" he asked indignantly. "Jaysus, have some confidence in me, will ya?" he added, the lilt returning, the charm coursing through.

Maureen would not let it go easily. "People are saying you had a big fight with this Horan over at the Powerhouse."

He nodded vigorously as they continued walking. "I did. Yes, I did, but that doesn't mean I had anything to do with his killing! What? Is that fuckin' Timmy acusin' me to my own sister?"

Maureen fought back her anger. "He hasn't said a word about it to me."

Cav decided to soften his tone. "Mo, you think I would cause trouble and spoil your wedding? Why soon I'll be strollin' down the aisle of St. Joseph's over in Lynn so proud of you and of you askin' me to escort you, give you away and..."

She placed her hand on his arm. “Terry, I want you and Timmy to get along. What would really make my wedding special is for that to happen.”

He slipped his arm inside her elbow and drew her close to his side. “For my part, Mo, I bear him no malice. I’ve got my own small piece of the business now, I’m getting along with the I-talians, and my sister’s the prettiest filly in all of Southie.” He kissed her on the forehead. “But it takes two to tango, Mo. You know that. You need to be sure your guy isn’t unjustly blaming me for Horan’s death.”

Maureen swept the hair away from her face and leaned into him. A wide smile crossed her face. “He’s leaving the life, Terry. For me. It’s his wedding present to me and for the kids we want to have.”

Cav stopped again and stared at her. “You’re kidding!”

“No, I’m not. He’s out of it, or will soon be. So you have nothing to worry about from him.”

Cav grinned broadly. “Well now, that is good news,” he replied enthusiastically.

She squeezed his arm tightly. “I’ve never been happier, Terry.”

“You and me will be dancin’ like Fred Astaire and Ginger Rogers on your wedding day, Sis. And things are going to be fine, you’ll see. And how about you guys takin’ me with you to the old country?”

She poked him in the ribs. “I wasn’t asking for you to get that close. Just get along with him, for me, okay?”

55

"No, absolutely not. You just go ahead with the wedding plans as they are. There's absolutely no reason to change anything," Marjorie Kelly stated adamantly, leaving little room for argument.

In the early afternoon, the sun scoured the day as she sat erect under the huge umbrella shading the round table on the patio. Her sons sat on either side of her with Sheila and Marty opposite.

"I mean it, Ma," Tim responded. "Maureen and I are willing to postpone it if you.."

She waved her hand dismissively. "Tim, I'm hurting, but not for the reasons you think. I was a fool in love who got fooled. That's what hurts, not the loss of David."

Sheila shook her head slowly. "According to the early editions, he was an FBI agent. I just can't believe it."

"What surprised me was that he died in a swimming accident. He was a very strong swimmer," Marjorie suddenly offered, thinking on it.

"The police believe he may have gotten caught in a riptide," Bobby said. "That can be fatal for even the strongest of swimmers."

Marjorie looked off in the distance. "I'm sorry for him, but he deceived me. He wasn't what he represented. Coming right into my home, into my heart, lying, trying to entrap my family..."

Marty studied his aunt closely. She possessed a steely resolve that was now serving her well. Aronson was already drifting toward the recesses of her mind.

"Thank God for my family," she was saying. She placed a hand on Timmy's arm. "You just go ahead. I'm just so sorry this happened so close to your wedding."

"An accident can happen anytime, Mom. We have no control..."

"Exactly right," Sheila interrupted. "Marty's old girl friend was killed in an accident on the same day in Boston."

Marty sipped his tea and from over the rim caught Tim's eye. "A tragedy," he said, placing the right amount of sadness into his tone.

"Wasn't she your very first serious girl friend?" Marjorie asked.

"She was," Marty answered pensively. "She was a lovely girl."

"Well, enough of this morbid talk," Marjorie said. "In a week we'll be celebrating Tim's wedding." She placed her other hand on Bobby's arm. "And my other son's home with good news. Tell them, Bob."

Bobby spoke guardedly but with just a hint of optimism in his voice. "Dr. Devlin says my CD 4 cell count is stronger than it's been in months. It's back up from 400 to 700, still not what it should be, but heading in the right direction. He thinks the experimental medicine is helping. Things could change at any time, but right now..."

"So you see, I have a lot to be grateful for," Marjorie said, fondling his hand. "Let's put this day behind us."

—

A ten-foot chain link fence is difficult enough to overcome, let alone a fast-moving Doberman pinscher once on the other side. But Chris Kiely had a plan. Dressed completely in black, he sat in a catcher's squat in a corner of the old Brinks' garage on Hull Street in the North End. Peering through high-powered binoculars, he focused on the yard of the meat packing plant, sixty yards below him.

Silence. A dead silence. Which is exactly as it should be at 11:00 P.M. he felt. Prancing around the back lot, the Doberman spent most of its effort in sniffing about the perimeter of the fence. High above him, a strong light bathed Rocco Apostoli's office in a pale yellow.

Chris shifted his attention to the powder blue Cadillac and studied it through the night-vision field glasses. Save for the ten or twelve fleet trucks parked side by side near the docks, the Caddy was the only other vehicle in the yard. In one corner of the lot sat a huge dumpster.

For the past three evenings, he had observed the plant, trying to finalize a course of action. Every evening, at some time between 11 P.M. and midnight, Rocco Apostoli would douse the light in his office, and within five to ten minutes, arrive in the yard and enter the Cadillac, the dog paying him scant attention, not even bothering to approach him. From there Apostoli would drive the few blocks to the social club on Prince Street in the North End and remain there practically until dawn.

Chris yanked the Sig Sauer 9-millimeter pistol from behind his back and then sought the silencer from his jacket and attached it to the weapon. He looked into the small duffel bag to assure himself that he had everything: the brand new flag of Puerto Rico, the time bomb itself, and the penlight. Zipping the bag, he looked up at the building. Almost anytime now.

Suddenly the room in the distance darkened. Quickly he scooped up the duffel bag and raced to the fence. Once there, he tossed the bag over. As he began to climb, the Doberman growled from deep in the yard and sprinted toward the barrier. From the top of the fence, Chris balanced himself, his left hand on the fence itself, his right grasping the Sig Sauer. He fired two rounds at the dog and began his descent. Landing, he winced as he observed the line of blood running from his palm. For a moment he stood perfectly still, assuring himself he was alone, and then he dragged the dog behind the dumpster at the very end of the fence.

Running toward the car, he grabbed the duffel bag and rolled under the Cadillac, the Sig still in his right hand. He laid it on the asphalt and opened the bag, pulling out the time bomb with his two hands, the little penlight helping him set it for a time five minutes ahead. He attached the wires to the undercarriage and pushed himself and the bag over to the passenger side. Quickly, he scrambled to a position behind the huge dumpster and lowered his body beside that of the Doberman.

It would have been much simpler to have used the Sig on Apostoli, but that was not what Marty had directed. He wanted Apostoli in pieces just like the Hispanics had been left. He kept the Sig in his right hand in the event Apostoli became inquisitive. If so, he would have no choice but to use it.

—

Rocco Apostoli stepped from the elevator, set the alarm, and walked through the front doors into the warm August night. It would be August 6th in one hour, he thought. August 6—the Irish asshole's wedding day. He laughed to himself. The Irish Corsicans were essentially out of the game as Tim's wedding day dawned. Cav had taken out their number one man, and even though they might suspect his or Cav's involvement, they were showing no inclination to retaliate. They were boxed in, both out of loyalty to the agreement—some fuckin' kind of Irish honor—and to family, in this case, new family in the form of Cav. And if they did act, then Forelli would know them for what they were—crazy bastards. And rumors still persisted that the FBI was about ready to pounce on them as well.

He walked around the corner into the parking lot. Were was that dumb ass Doberman now? Probably asleep on the job, dreaming of his next meal.

—

Two minutes seemed like two hours, but suddenly Chris Kiely could hear footsteps approaching the car. For an instant the patter of shoes stopped. Was Apostoli looking for the hound? Wondering where it was? Probably. Chris stole a look at his watch. In two minutes the bomb would detonate. Suddenly he heard the sound of a key being inserted in a lock. The weightless dark of early evening had given way to the thick and heavy night of the midnight hour. Far above him, crickets chirped and stars dotted the sky. It was, Chris told himself, a nice enough night to die.

Once again Chris looked at his watch. Ten seconds. The motor came to life for just that amount of time before Rocco Apostoli's life ended. The small amount of RDX was deadly in its force, detonating at a rate of 15,000 feet per second, ten times faster than a 9MM leaves a pistol muzzle. Heat flashed outward in a great burst of white light. The shock wave slammed into Rocco's body, crushing his chest, lifting him through the windshield, throwing him ten yards in front of the vehicle. A sonic boom riffled the air and orange and black flashes darkened the sky, leaving the car looking like a shell off the assembly line in Detroit.

Chris stood and reached into the bag. He unfurled the flag of Puerto Rico and laid it beside the smoldering vehicle.

Quickly he flipped the bag over the fence and scrambled upward and over. For a moment, he crouched on the other side, listening for any sign of trouble. In the distance he could hear the clanging of fire engines as he rushed up the hill toward the stolen vehicle.

56

"A toast! A toast to my brother and my beautiful and future sister-in-law on the eve of their wedding day. May God in his goodness bring them wondrous love, happiness, and children," Bobby offered.

"Here! Here!" the small gathering responded, all members of the wedding party applauding simultaneously.

"Hey! Save those great words for tomorrow, for the wedding!" Tommy yelled from his position at the end of the table.

The private function room of the Kernwood in Lynnfield pulsed with good cheer and laughter, the party of eleven all clustered around a long, rectangular table, making enough noise for fifty. Sitting between his mother and father and across from his aunt, Marty was paying much more attention to the grouping at the other end. Timmy and Maureen, she radiant in her summer-length dress, sat opposite one another and occasionally blew kisses across the divide. Bobby was seated beside his brother and next to Cav, who was busying himself by drinking far too much and trying to impress the maid of honor and the bridesmaids opposite him.

Marty stole a glance at his watch. 11:00 P.M. So far the plan was working—Aronson was dead, Ginger Dalton eliminated, and almost any time now, Chris Kiely should be taking care of Apostoli. Just one more matter to attend to.

Suddenly, Maureen rose from her chair and tapped for attention on her glass. "I want to thank you all for being here with Tim and me tonight. We're deeply appreciative for all your help in making our wedding tomorrow the lovely occasion we want it to be. To my lifelong friend Karen, my maid of honor; to Bobby, our best man; to my brother Terry, my escort tomorrow; to Marty and Jerry, our ushers; to my good friends Emma and Peggy, my bridesmaids; to Tim's mother Marjorie and his Aunt Shiela, thanks to all of you."

Caught in the spirit of things, Cav stumbled to his feet, almost knocking the water glass over. "I want to add my congratulations to my sister and to my new brother-in-law. You know with him now leaving the life..." He stopped himself and stood taller. "Excuse me. What I meant was with Tim now devotin' full time to his car business and his family, they are gonna be one happy couple." He grinned across at Marty and raised the Chivas Regal so high it splashed over the rim. "I'm so glad to be here. It's just proper that the Cavanaughs and the Kellys are together tonight." Then he sat down forcefully.

Sheila placed her hand on Marty's arm. "Have you heard from Judith?" she asked.

"We're not seeing much of each other now, Ma. I think she may have found someone else," he replied evenly.

"We liked her very much. Didn't we, Jerry?"

Jerry nodded. "We thought she might have been the one."

"The right one to settle me down you mean," Marty smiled.

"That's on my mind," his father grinned. "Get you out of the life like Timmy's doing."

"Maybe in time, Dad. But not right now." He said it kindly, gently, because they had made considerable progress together over the months. A kind of acceptance now best described his relationship with his parents, buttressed by their hope that soon someone like Judith or Maureen would ultimately lead him to the light at the end of the dark tunnel.

"Want anything else to drink, Ma?" He asked her because she now had the problem under control.

Sheila shook her head. "Marjorie?" he asked.

"Maybe a diet Coke."

"I'll get it," Marty said, pushing back from his chair and standing.

He walked to the small portable bar in the corner and stood next to Bobby. "How you doing, cousin?"

Bobby placed his hands on the bar and braced himself. "I'm doing all right, Marty. There's a new movie part—the second lead—opening up for me next month. The film's being shot in New York. A real good opportunity."

"CC and ginger and a diet Coke," Marty ordered.

Across the room Cav was motioning toward them. "Bobby! Come over here! These girls want to spend some time with Sean Kielty!"

"Excuse me, Marty. My fans are calling."

"Bobby, before you go over there, I'm glad you're okay, y'know?"

Bobby extended his hand. "I know. Thanks, Marty."

Marty brought the drink to his aunt and sat down in the seat beside her. "Hard night for you, Marjorie?" he asked gently.

She sipped on the Coke and smiled at him. "Not at all. David was a fraud, Marty, using me to get at my son and at you. When you know a relationship is built on a pack of lies, then it's difficult to feel pain."

He didn't answer her. Instead, he watched Cav meander to the bar, his step a bit unsteady. He had to have been drinking before he even got here, and then Marty calculated he'd had at least four in the last hour alone. Marty waited until he started swallowing the Chivas before walking toward him.

"Marty!" Cav placed his glass on the bar and moved to embrace him. Marty made no effort to resist. He said nothing while Cav belted him two or three times below his shoulders. He needed to convey a message, but he needed to do it without causing a scene.

When Marty stepped back, Cav almost fell into the bar. "Oops! The fuckin' floor's unsteady. Like the decks of that God damn Titanic," he laughed. "Hey, Marty. I meant what I said, y'know?"

"What you said?"

"Y'know. At the table. I'm happy for Mo and Timmy."

Marty motioned him toward the corner away from the bar. As he did so, on cue, Timmy rose from his seat and started toward them.

"Yeah, Marty?" Cav asked, puzzled, his words slurred.

Marty leaned into his ear. "I don't give a fuck about any wedding, Cav. You killed Ray Horan, and you're going down for it."

He turned quickly and headed back to the table.

"Hey! Who do you think you're..." Cav started to shout after him just as Timmy approached.

"Easy, Cav," Timmy said. "What's the matter?"

"Who the hell does he think he's talking to!" Cav persisted.

Timmy grabbed him by the elbow. "Cav, it's our wedding party! You've been drinking too much. Let's not get into an argument. Here, let me get you a new drink."

That quieted him down for the moment, although he continued to glare across at Marty.

"Give me a double Chivas," Timmy asked the bartender.

Maureen broke away from her conversation with the maid of honor and the bridesmaids and swiftly traversed the room.

"What's going on? Why all the noise?" she asked crossly.

"Nothing, Mo. Everything's under control. Right, Cav? Here! Drink this."

Cav threw half the Chivas down before Maureen could intercede. "You're drinking too much, Terry. And when he does, he becomes ugly. I don't need this shit tonight." She directed the last two comments to Tim.

"I'll drive him home," he said, as Cav began to stagger toward the bridesmaids. Tim drew her close to his chest and kissed her. "We should end the night. We have a very special day tomorrow and Irish folklore says the bride and groom shouldn't be together for long, the night before..."

She playfully pushed him away. "Maybe you should tell Father Flynn tomorrow how many nights..."

"Never you mind, colleen. It's a good thing for you that you're staying at Karen's tonight. Go say goodnight to our guests, and I'll take Terry home. Marty can drive you to Karen's."

"How will you get back from Southie?"

He looked at his watch, searching for an answer. "I'll ask Bobby to follow me," he finally replied.

She tugged at his shirt. "Come here, lover. Give me a kiss to last until tomorrow."

He pulled her toward him while the crowd gave out with a low murmur followed by a rising chorus of applause.

With everyone wishing everyone else a good night, she never noticed that Timmy did not speak to Bobby at all.

"Come on, Cav. I'm driving you. We've all got a big day tomorrow."

Cav was still alert enough to question him. "But how will you get home?" he slurred.

"My brother Bobby will follow."

"Oh, okay. Let's go then. After just one more for the road."

"Now!" Maureen bellowed at him from her position across the room.

—

As Tim drove through the tunnel and onto the Southeast Expressway, Cav kept up the line of constant chatter, switching from one topic to another in the manner of the drunk—cloudy thoughts surfacing and then regressing, with moods similarly rising and falling.

"What's wrong with that fuckin' Marty anyway? What the hell's he talkin' about?" And then when there was no immediate response, "Did you see the big bongos on that maid of honor? If she spends one night with me, she'll light up like an electric scoreboard." And then back again to Marty, as they turned onto Day Boulevard.

"Do you know what he said to me? Do ya?" his dark side showing itself.

"Whatever, he didn't mean it, Cav. We've all had a lot to drink, y'know?"

"Well, fuck him. He wants trouble with me, he'll get it." Then the switch again. "So you gave it all up for my sister, huh? Now I admire that. I really do." He playfully tapped Timmy on the forearm.

"Your brother still trailing us?" he asked out of the blue, although he didn't look back.

"Bobby's right behind us somewhere." Slowing down, Timmy turned up East Broadway and signaled a left turn on to P Street. He searched the night, seeking to read the numbers on the tenement stairs. "What number, Cav?"

His head drooping, Cav came suddenly alert. "We almost there? It's number 300."

"Just about," Timmy replied calmly. "How about I drop you off right here. Let you get out, walk for fifty yards, clear your head."

"Great idea," Cav nodded. "I'll get out and walk a bit is what I'll do," the heavy drinker repeating what was rolling around most recently inside a foggy head.

Timmy pulled to the curb. "I'll leave your car in front of the apartment, okay? It's that three-decker on the other side of the street?"

Cav didn't answer the question. He was off to another planet, his mind racing through different constellations. "Tomorrow is going to be a beautiful day for you and Mo. Such a beautiful day."

He patted Timmy on the shoulder. Then he scowled as Mr. Hyde thoughts invaded his picture of Dr. Jekyll bliss. "You remember what Marty said to me?"

"He thinks you killed Ray Horan. I told him he's way off base," Timmy replied quietly, supportively, trying to relax him.

Cav snickered and began laughing, a sinister laugh that emanated deep down in his stomach, gushed up to his chest, and shook the cavity itself as it surfaced.

"What's so funny?"

"You're out of the life, right?" He didn't wait for the answer. "I can tell you anyhow cause we're family now. Of course I killed that prick Horan. He fuckin' embarrassed, blindsided me. But I took care of his ass, didn't I?" He paused and once again headed off in a new direction, not really registering any of his own comments. "What did you think of that friend of Mo's—Karen? Is that her name? Wouldn't you like to plank her?"

"We're here, Cav. And don't head over to the gin joint," Timmy said, pointing across the street. "I'll park the car in front. Okay?"

Cav looked at him the way the drunk who realizes he's drunk always looks at his companion, wondering what he had said, even a moment ago, wondering whether he had said too much. "What did you say?" he finally asked.

Timmy reached his hand across Cav's body and opened the passenger door. "See you tomorrow, Cav. You get a good night's sleep now."

"What's tomorrow?"

"Mo's wedding day."

"That's right! Hey, Tim," he said, coming alive. "Welcome to the family, y'know? I never had a brother." He paused for a moment, thinking on something. "We'll have some drinks tomorrow, right?"

"For sure."

Cav opened the door and then slammed it too hard as he stepped out. As Timmy drove away slowly, he observed Cav staggering in the drunk's attempt to walk a straight line, his attention focused now completely ahead.

Up a hundred yards, Timmy executed a U-turn and parked the car directly in front of the three-decker. He looked around, but at midnight there was no one on the street, the summer cool allowing for sleep after three nights of truly intense heat. He stared back down the road awaiting the break from the darkness. From behind Cav lights suddenly penetrated the blackness as a car left the curb.

—

In the last few moments of his life, Cav thought of his sister. Tomorrow he would walk her down the aisle serving as usher, stand-in father, and protector. That fuckin' Timmy had better treat her right. He thought back to the time when the nun had clipped Mo across the face when they were at St. Bridget's together. Maybe she was in the fifth grade and he in the sixth. At lunch some kid had told him about it, and he had searched out the nun sitting in a corner of the cafeteria and dumped his carton of milk right on her habit. His first expulsion among many.

When he saw Timmy's lights dim, Paulie Cronin started from the curb. The stolen Lincoln bucked for a moment as he accelerated, his eyes searching for Cav along the darkened sidewalk. Then he spotted him at the edge of the sidewalk preparing to cross the street, his head lowered, his walk uneven.

Paulie hit his brakes, stopping completely as Cav gave him a perfunctory thank you wave, and started across about thirty yards in front of him. Once Cav was halfway there, Paulie shut down his lights, pressed hard on the accelerator, and then plowed into the shadowy figure, catching him full force, lifting him from the asphalt. Cav bounced off the hood, falling to the street near the driver's side. Paulie braked the Lincoln within twenty yards and backed up, running over the body again as he tossed the flag out the open window with one of his gloved hands.

Starting off again, he quickly pulled to a stop for Timmy, who raced to the passenger side door. A quarter mile down, Paulie turned onto O Street and pulled the Town Car to the side of the road. Across from them, Stevie Guptill beckoned from an open window. Running to him, they took seats in the back as Stevie pulled away, heading back toward Day Boulevard.

57

Michael Forelli had always insisted on hearing bad news promptly, but even so he was surprised to hear the phone ring at 5:00 A.M. He was lying in bed in his pajamas and robe, sipping his black coffee, reading the first chapter of A Tale of Two Cities for perhaps the tenth time in his life. He marveled at Dickens' syntax, the juxtapositioning of comparisons and contrasts, commencing even with the very first line of the novel: "It was the best of times; it was the worst of times." Later, after he had heard the news, he had to agree with Charles Dickens.

"Hello, Michael Forelli here," he said irritatingly.

"Michael. Gino Petrelli. I am so sorry to bother you in the early morning hours, but I have bad news." He paused awaiting a response, but Forelli kept his silence.

"Rocco Apostoli is dead."

"The Irish are responsible?"

Knowing the question would be asked, Petrelli was ready with his answer, the truth as he knew it. "No, I don't think so, Michael. I believe it to be the work of the Hispanics. Late last night Rocco's car exploded as he entered it at his place of business. My police sources tell me the flag of Puerto Rico was placed near the vehicle."

Michael Forelli considered the information. "Why a flag?" he asked.

"I believe it was important to them to leave a clear signal."

Impatience crept into Forelli's tone. "And why is that?"

"I believe they were taking revenge for the brutal actions Rocco took against them. And there's more. You remember I told you about the Irisher, Cavanaugh, the one who informed Rocco who had murdered his niece? Cavanaugh was run down in South Boston last night. And another flag was left at that site."

Forelli let such a long beat pass that Gino wondered if he were still connected. "Michael?"

"Let me see if I have this right," Forelli began, his voice icy and sarcastic. "You and Rocco have inflamed the Hispanics and with your choice of this Cavanaugh here also injured our profits. And where are the Kellys in all of this, Gino?"

"Not a factor," Petrelli answered hesitatingly.

"Not a factor," Forelli repeated the words derisively. "Not a factor. Who was responsible for the death of Jack Kelly's man Horan?"

Petrelli decided it was time to separate himself from Rocco once and for all. "I'm not sure, Michael, but my guess is Rocco may have pushed Cavanaugh into it or maybe was foolish enough to have it done himself."

"So we have Rocco carving up the spics, screwing the Irish, murdering the Kellys' key man. You know what I think, Gino?"

"Michael, allow me a moment?"

"Proceed."

"I believe Apostoli deliberately set problems for the Irishers. I tried to intercede, to warn him that he was heading in a wrong direction. He involved this Cavanaugh..."

"And you concurred. You remember that you called me Gino?" Forelli interrupted.

"I concurred only to a degree, Michael. If we could have caused a break between the Irish..."

"Forgive me for interrupting," Forelli replied softly, "but who asked you to create any breach among the Irish? I gave my word to Jack Kelly, before his death, that we would honor all agreements. He would have his territory, and we ours. I was made to believe that Cavanaugh was his friend, his ally, his brother-in-law-to-be, and now are you telling me this was not so?"

"Michael, you must allow me to lay out the facts properly, with all respect."

"I'm still listening, and trying to understand," Forelli replied coldly.

"The Hispanics robbed from us, I mean from Rocco, and murdered his niece."

"I agree. But they needed to be carved up?"

"That was not my decision. It was Rocco's."

"And Cavanaugh, the stool pigeon. How deeply were you involved in that decision, Gino?"

"As I said, to a degree, Michael. I agreed to reward this Cavanaugh for coming forth, for identifying the Hispanics for us. Are you suggesting I was wrong?"

"You lied to me, Gino, and I can only conclude that your intention and that of Apostoli was to deliberately cause a problem with our agreements."

"That was not my intent," Guido replied defensively.

"But it was the outcome, was it not?"

"I cannot read Apostoli's mind, Michael."

"Ah, but I can read yours. You fucked this up, Gino."

"I beg to differ, Michael."

"You can beg to differ all you want, Gino, but from what I'm hearing, the behavior of the Kellys in this matter has been exemplary, and that of the Hispanics and us despicable."

"Perhaps Rocco overstepped his authority. If so, I..."

"You failed me, Gino." With his final comment, he cut the connection.

58

The wedding day dawned hot and humid with a pink sliver rising in the east, giving promise of a beautiful August morning. Facing the elongated mirror, Timmy studied his profile in the glass. The tuxedo felt snug, although the collar of his shirt was a bit too tight. He played with the bow tie, adjusting it more to the center, hoping to position it so that he could leave the top button open. To no avail.

He glanced at his watch. 5:35 A.M. The police would have had great trouble finding Maureen to notify her of Terry's death. If they had called her apartment in Southie, there would be no response. If they had visited the apartment, very few in the area would know of her whereabouts. Eventually, they would locate her at the matron-of-honor's home in Winthrop, and then she would be all over him. But he would be ready.

—

At six o'clock, Marty ate alone on the patio as he did every summer morning. A cup of tea, dry toast, orange juice—something light and something he could prepare himself—lay spread before him.

He sipped his tea and considered the situation. All enemies accounted for, except one. And if he were right, someone else would take care of Gino Petrelli for him. Today would be a day to celebrate for more reasons than one, and today would also be the first day in months that he could begin to unwind.

When the phone rang in the kitchen, he wondered who might be calling at such an ungodly hour. He pushed open the slider and reached for the phone.

"Hello?"

"Good morning, Martin. This is Michael Forelli calling from Long Island."

Marty tried to hide his apprehension. "It is good to hear your voice, Don Forelli."

"Michael. Call me Michael. Is this line secure, Martin?"

"It's checked and the house is swept every day."

"Good. Then we can proceed. I understand this is a special day for you."

By now Forelli would know of the killings, would have received an interpretation of the events, and would have come to some early conclusions of his own. Marty paced around the kitchen, being cautious, straining to listen carefully to every word, to every nuance.

"It was to be, Michael, but there are now complications."

"Yes, so I understand. Will the wedding proceed?"

"At this point I'm not sure. You are aware that Tim is to marry Terry Cavanaugh's sister?"

"Yes."

"I'm sure they're discussing the situation right about now," Marty added nervously.

There was a pause, which Marty interrupted as a natural lead-in to the real reason why Forelli was calling. "Martin, I owe you an apology."

"An apology?"

"Yes. You know I greatly admired your uncle. You remember that time when we were all together on the

Staten Island Ferry? When we made the new arrangements?"

"Yes."

"I bonded with him. I liked him because he ran an organization based on loyalty and trust. Where a man's word meant something. But today..." He caught himself. "Forgive the digressions of an old man, Martin. I owe you an apology because, like your uncle, you are a man of your word. Rocco Apostoli was not, always overreaching. He insulted the honor of the Hispanics and now he's dead, as I'm sure you know. Learn from that, Martin. Never take away a person's honor or dignity."

Keep the replies short and keep alert, Marty told himself. "I agree, Michael."

"Apostoli was told to implement the agreement. My word was given to Jack and therefore to you, and my word was violated. I gather this Cavanaugh was not only an informer, but possibly the cause of your friend's death. He was on the ferry that day, too. Am I right?"

"Ray Horan? Yes, he was."

"Do you believe this Cavanaugh killed your friend?" Forelli asked soothingly, trying to lull him to sleep.

Marty paused before he lied. "It's difficult for me to believe that of Cavanaugh. With all due respect, Michael, what I believe is that Apostoli was responsible. Cavanaugh is no real friend of mine, but Timmy is to marry his sister. He would therefore cause us no harm nor we him."

"So the Hispanics were responsible for Cavanaugh's death as well?"

"I believe so. My guess is that they became aware that Cavanaugh informed on them."

"Yes." Forelli paused for a moment. "You have shown great restraint, Martin," he finally said.

Marty worked to place the right measure of sincerity in his voice. "We have an agreement to keep the peace, which I have tried to honor," he said.

"To your credit, Martin. My apologies for all this inconvenience. We will take care of the Hispanics. You understand that must be done?"

"Of course, Michael."

"You go back about your business. You'll have your territories back intact. Can you bring the profits back to where they were?"

"For sure."

"Petrelli will cause you no more trouble. He will be set aside. I never should have agreed to his elevation or to Apostoli's either. Neither was a man of honor."

Marty knew enough to remain silent. It was not his business.

"And Martin, the next time you're in New York, come visit with me. Call ahead and come out to Long Island."

"I would like that," Marty replied.

"And wish Tim well if the wedding proceeds. Tell him I wish him many male children in the years ahead." And then he hung up abruptly.

—

Bobby slipped on his jacket and peered at Timmy standing by the mirror. "You look like you're going to a funeral instead of a wedding."

Timmy turned from the window and smiled. "We can't all be movie stars, big brother. Where's Ma?"

"Upstairs, getting ready."

He glanced at his watch—6:45 A.M.

When the doorbell rang, he was a bit surprised. Could it be Marty already? He walked into the front hall and opened the door. A sobbing Maureen, dressed in the same clothes she had worn the previous night, almost fell over the threshold into him.

"What the hell's the matter?" he asked.

"Tim, Terry's dead! He's dead!" She moved into the foyer, walking in a semicircle, her eyes flying to different corners, her hands animated.

"What are you talking about?" Timmy asked, as Bobby rushed toward the commotion.

"The police—the Boston police—just called me thirty minutes ago." Even in her anxiety, he felt she was studying him carefully, looking for any telltale sign. "He was run down near his apartment last night, they say. They said..." She suddenly burst into tears.

He tried to pull her to him. "Easy, easy. Mo, tell me, what did they say?"

She pushed him away and wheeled into the kitchen. "My brother's dead! He's dead!"

"Bob, get her some coffee, huh?" Timmy said, trying to calm her.

She stood there in the middle of the room, a deer-in-the-headlights look on her face. He embraced her and rested her head on his shoulder. "Maureen, I'm so sorry."

She erupted in a torrent of tears, her head pressed firmly now into his tuxedo. He ran his hand through her hair, trying to comfort her. "We'll postpone the wedding. I'll..."

"No, no! Please! Let me think! There's too many things happening at once." She broke from him again.

"Maureen, listen to me please. I'll call Father Flynn, and we can start chain calling the guests. There's only a hundred..."

She stood at the table, fingering the coffee cup that Bobby handed her. "No! Let me think. Please!"

"Let me get you some Kleenex," Bobby offered, heading toward the bathroom.

As she sat down, Timmy stood above her, stroking her hair. "I'm so sorry, Mo. I..."

Her body tensed, and she arched her back. "Are you Tim?" she asked hesitatingly.

"What are you talking about?" he replied softly, controlling himself.

She stood to face him. "That's why I wanted to come here, Tim. To talk directly to you. To see your reactions. You took him home last night, and you don't sound too surprised about all this."

He placed his hands on her shoulders and braced himself. Bobby came forward with the Kleenex and passed it to her. "Maureen, I drove him home, that's all. I let him out up the street from the apartment and that was it. I'm as shocked as you are. But it's you I'm worried about."

"You swear to me, Timmy Kelly," she said adamantly.

"I swear to you, Mo. I drove him, parked his car, and left."

She stared at Bobby. "And Bobby drove you right back here?"

He hadn't figured that she would come directly to the house, not on her wedding day, not with Cav dead. And he had never figured that Bobby would be right here in the same room with them, listening to this exchange.

The silence lasted for just seconds, and yet it seemed interminable. The kitchen clock ticked more loudly than normal, and tiny beads of sweat appeared on his upper lip. The three of them stood there anxiously, each waiting for the others to speak, like family members waiting for the doctor to provide the results of the biopsy.

"I did," Bobby finally said. "We came directly back here."

She relaxed appreciably and nodded slowly, her face now showing embarrassment. "Tim, I'm so confused. I'm so mixed up. Here I'm practically accusing..."

He drew her close, embracing her. "Forget it, Mo. Just let me hold you..." He stared over her shoulder and nodded almost imperceptibly to Bobby. "I promised you I was getting out of the life, Maureen," he said.

She threw her arms around his neck and pulled him to her lips. "Thank you, Tim. Thank you. I should have known you wouldn't..." She began to sob again.

"I'll have people call the guests. We'll..."

"No, no," she interrupted. "I want to go ahead with it. I do." She shook her head determinedly. "I want to show you my love and trust."

"Are you sure? With Cav..."

"We'll postpone the trip. I can't leave now with the need for funeral arrangements. Is that all right with you?"

He nodded slowly. "Whatever you want is all right with me."

"Then have someone call the travel agency. We weren't going until Monday anyway. Postpone it for a week."

"I'll take care of it," Bobby volunteered.

"How did you get here?" Timmy asked.

"Karen's car. I need to get back, get ready..."

"Mo, listen to me. We could wait..."

She raised a hand and placed it over his lips. "I want to marry you today, Tim. I need you more today more than I've needed you any day. I need to be one with you today."

He embraced her once again. "And you will be," he said.

She turned to the door, and he followed her. "I'll see you at the church," he whispered gently as he kissed her cheek.

59

A hundred guests looked minuscule in the majestic elegance of the huge church. But St. Joseph's was his church, and Maureen had grown to love it as he did, the few times they had attended Mass there together.

Located in downtown Lynn, the magnificent gothic cathedral was built almost entirely of red brick, its steeple stretching high above surrounding buildings, ensuring that all Catholics across the downtown understood St. Joseph's was the closest approximation to heaven itself. Far up the steps, on the second floor, glass doors topped three distinct stairwells, and led to an interior that was both breathtaking and overwhelming.

Lit brightly by dozens of chandeliers hanging from the sloped ceiling, the luminous windows were crafted from expensive glass. The long center aisle ran close to forty yards toward the massive white marble altar that dominated the upstairs.

Maureen stood in position just inside the heavy glass doors, dressed in a column-like sheath, the strapless white gown creating a long interrupted line about her petite frame. Instead of the glitzy beading so favored by most of her friends, she had embellished the gown with an abundance of flirty, feminine ruffles. She carried a bouquet of yellow and white roses. Aside her, Karen cradled a bouquet as well, while the other attendants displayed flowers on their wrists.

Just outside the altar, Bobby left his brother's side and with Marty's help pulled the tabs on the white paper carpet as they began the slow walk back toward the glass doors.

On Maureen's side of the aisle, friends from the Tobin School as well as her entire third grade class preened for the cameraman and twisted necks to look back for their teacher. On Timmy's side, the Kelly clan beamed as Marty and Bobby unwound the carpet. Passing by the crew, Marty winked at Paulie Cronin, whose grin broadened at the singular recognition.

Turning, Bobby proceeded to the front, back toward the altar, all the time focusing directly on Timmy, .looking for some expression, searching for the answer to his unstated question. Timmy glanced at him, but averted his stare, looking instead to the rear, across that great gulf separating him from Maureen. As he took his place beside his brother, Bobby asked his question. "I need to know, Tim. Were you involved?"

Timmy stared across at him. "Of course not. The Hispanics must have done him. But thank you for reassuring her."

One by one, the bridesmaids marched alone down the long aisle, smiling, each enjoying their moment in the limelight, each effecting a practiced, almost posed walk, one debonair and demure, the other sweetly shy. As Karen commenced her walk, Marty realized he was now alone with Maureen. For a moment, he looked behind him out the monstrous glass doors. Down in the streets, hundreds of spectators, most of them female, waited for a look, a smile, a wave, for almost anything from Sean Kielty.

When he turned toward Maureen, she was staring at him, her mind churning a thousand miles a minute, almost as if she were weighing something, a quizzical look fixed there on her face.

He met her look and smiled warmly. "Are you ready? It's almost our time."

"I need to say something to you," she finally whispered.

He blinked in surprise. "Sure."

"Thank you for stepping in at the last minute like this, substituting for Terry..." She looked down, her voice beginning to quiver.

"Hey! They're getting ready to play your song. No tears."

"I don't know what I'd do without you right now, Marty. I..."

"Maureen," he interrupted. "I'll always be there to protect you and yours. Always. Whenever you need me."

Suddenly the organist began the Wedding March and he placed her arm within his and started down the aisle, looking to his left and his right, smiling. He caught the admiring stares of his crew sitting halfway back in the church and those of his mother and father as well.

Ten yards from the altar, he locked eyes on Timmy who was smiling at his beautiful bride. Turning to Marty, Timmy caught the look that penetrated into his soul. The look that for decades had bonded one Corsican to the other against all others, that I-know-what-you're-thinking look.

Marty thought back over time. Back to the Meadow on a clear summer day just like today. He was in his East Lynn Post 291 American Legion uniform on the mound, smiling at Timmy, who squatted behind the plate. How old were they then? Sixteen, maybe. He had slammed the final strike by the batter and was racing in toward Timmy. "Great game, Tim. That a way to call the pitches."

"You're the one that threw the strikes."

"We're a team. No one, no thing can ever change that," he had replied.

Marty stopped outside the altar rail and turned to Maureen. Gently he pulled her veil over her head and moved closer, kissing her on the cheek. And then he stepped away as Timmy approached.

About The Author

John A. Curry is President Emeritus of Northeastern University. He is a graduate of that university and earned his doctorate from Boston University. From 1989-1996 he served as President of Northeastern University, changing its direction from a large, urban institution toward a "smaller but better" research university.

His first two novels, *Loyalty* and *Two and Out*, also available through 1stBooks, were both well received by critics.

Dr. Curry lives in Saugus, Massachusetts, where he is currently at work on a new novel concerning the sexual abuse scandal in the Catholic Church.

Printed in the United States
828300005B

9 781403 383808